Category: Dedalus Europe
General Editor: Graham Anderson

BLOODLINES

FRANCESCO ALOIA

BLOODLINES

(*Questo sangue masticato*)

translated by
Graham Anderson

Dedalus

This book has been translated with funding from *The Centre for Books and Literature of the Italian Ministry of Culture*.

Supported using public funding by ARTS COUNCIL ENGLAND

CENTRO PER IL LIBRO E LA LETTURA

Published in the UK by Dedalus Limited
24-26, St Judith's Lane, Sawtry, Cambs, PE28 5XE
info@dedalusbooks.com
www.dedalusbooks.com

ISBN printed book 978 1 915568 85 4
ISBN ebook 978 1 915568 96 0

Dedalus is distributed in the USA & Canada by SCB Distributors
15608 South New Century Drive, Gardena, CA 90248
info@scbdistributors.com www.scbdistributors.com

Dedalus is distributed in Australia by Peribo Pty Ltd
58, Beaumont Road, Mount Kuring-gai, N.S.W. 2080
info@peribo.com.au www.peribo.com.au

First published by Dedalus in 2025

Printed and bound in the UK by Clays Elcograf S.p.A.
Typeset by Marie Lane

A C.I.P. listing for this book is available on request.

THE AUTHOR

Francesco Aloia was born in 1999 in Marano, a town on the outskirts of Naples. At eighteen he moved to Turin, studying creative writing at Scuola Holden.

He published his first book, *Questo sangue masticato* (*Bloodines*) in 2024. Part novel, part family documentary, it traces the life and career of his grandfather, a minor player in the underworld of post-war Naples who became notorious for the killing of a well-known camorra boss.

THE TRANSLATOR

Graham Anderson was born in London. After reading French and Italian at Cambridge, he worked on the book pages of *City Limits* and reviewed fiction for *The Independent* and *The Sunday Telegraph*. As a translator, he has developed versions of French plays, both classic and contemporary, for the NT and the Gate Theatre

He has translated seven books from French and six books from Italian, for Dedalus. He is the editor of the Dedalus Europe lists. His own short fiction has won or been shortlisted for three literary prizes.

Graham is married and lives in Oxfordshire.

to my grandmother Ada
who taught me how to chew

Y el que no quiera creer
ni me quiera parar bolas
Que se acerque para acá
que yo le muestro la cola

Whoever does not wish to believe
And whoever thinks it's not true
Let him come closer
And I'll show you his tail

Octavio Mesa, *La Pelea con el Diabolo*
(*The Fight with the Devil*)

A WORD FROM THE AUTHOR

The events recounted in this novel do not make any claim to be the truth and do not try to. In certain cases, the facts have been voluntarily twisted for narrative purposes, whilst in many others they have not. Some surnames have been changed, others omitted altogether. The character of Russo is entirely fictitious and represents various individuals who have been, at different times, close to Tanino 'e Bastimento. In any event, I hope I have not landed anyone in trouble—living or dead.

F.A.

THE ORLANDO FAMILY TREE

Gaetano'o Mastrone

ANGELO (il Mastrone, Mayor of Marano + two of Angelo's siblings, Tanino's uncles, Armando and Antonio

m. 1 ELENA

m. 2 Carmelina

Four younger half-siblings

RAFFAELE — **TANINO (CARLO GAETANO)**
aka **TANINO 'E BASTIMENTO**
m. **ADA**

ANGELO—Giuseppe
('The Twins')
(Angelo is the
Beekeeper)

ANGELO-BRUNO-RAFFAELE-ELENA-VALENCIA-ENZA-ASIA ROSA
m. Carmela ('Lello') m. Daniele ('China')

Adelaide
Arianna
Aurora
RAFFAELE

FRANCESCO

Carlo Gaetano
(& other siblings)

Principal members of the family are in bold.
Uppercase for other prominent members.
Lowercase for members also mentioned.

THE OFFSPRING OF ADA AND TANINO
OR THE PRINCIPAL CHARACTERS IN THIS STORY
IN ORDER OF BIRTH:

Angelo, *a destiny fulfilled*
Bruno, *the love child*
Raffaele (aka Lello), *the braveheart*
Elena, *the solitary one*
Valencia, *the exiled one*
Enza, *the rock*
Asia Rosa, *the Chinese one* (*aka China*)

As with certain animals, we have to follow the smell of our blood to find our way home. Sometimes, however, that fork we are looking for, that fatal crossroads from which branch out the spits of land on which we walk, is only to be found way back in the past and imprinted with the footsteps of someone else, steps with a different rhythm and gait, but whose unpredictable trajectories twist, follow, overlap and intersect, to finish finally at our feet, at the spot where we stand poised, waiting to know the way.

I have never paid much attention to history, still less to that of our own blood. I grew up in a place I never felt was mine, that I have always considered dead and for that reason good only for the dead and departed. And this is because the stories I have heard relate to facts clouded in fog, to places that are different today from what they once were and to persons no longer alive, like you. What does linger from these stories is just this: blood. The blood that is passed down, that runs through the generations and unites them in the most suffocating of backwaters I know: that of the family. And when death looms over families, these stories become the only way of keeping on track, of holding together fragments which would otherwise end up disconnected, dispersed and little more than ashes. But you too, in some way, have outlasted the time allotted to you among the living. More than the blood, more than the ashes, the memory of you lives on among the people who have seen you look on the world from the highest peaks and the lowest depths. The memory of you fills the places where you lived, the blades of grass you trampled underfoot and the tremulous voices of those who pronounce your name, remembering who you were. And it is for you that I have returned to Marano. I cannot meet you, but perhaps there does exist a way of coming face to face with you all the same. I don't know if the infernal regions really exist, but I have always imagined them as being like the summers in these parts. And so if I step into this provincial inferno, if I descend into the maze of this history of ours, maybe I shall succeed in finding you.

The first thing to do is to say your name. I know it because your—*our*—family taught me the importance of names, the evocative power they can assume. It is the name that makes us what we are, binds us to other people, allows us to embed ourselves in solid rock and remain there. This has always been clear to you, Tanino 'e Bastimento, first and last king of Marano, delivered into this world as Carlo Gaetano Orlando. It was always clear, as well, to your father, your wife Ada and your seven children, and it is even more clear to me too, who never knew you, who left Marano as soon as I was eighteen and never probed far into this old story until now. I am aware of being cowardly, because I am alive and you are not, but it is the only means I have. And then your voice still echoes, more powerfully than mine, more powerfully than all the others I have heard. A person who has done everything against a person who has not yet done anything, a living person against a dead person, that seems equal to me.

Returning to the facts, the things I have heard and that people have told me have no claim to absolute truth, because there are few actual dates and I cannot discount the possibility that some of them have been changed. Often the versions I have heard of a particular event do not coincide, because every event is the residue of the faded memories and suggestions of the Orlando family and the people who have agreed to talk to me. There are dates that make no sense, memories made solely of names and little else, and in some cases, obvious untruths. The perimeter I have tried to trace around this story is well delineated, as are also the effects it has had on the present. What lies within, however, remains vague, and the further back I have gone in time, the harder I have found it to gather the information I needed. It must also be said that the majority of the persons whose names will appear in what follows—as already mentioned—are dead, and their truths have died with them. So, amen: *'a verità vera nun esiste*, true truth does not exist.

On the first night of summer, the 21st of June 1930, the young militant communist Angelo Orlando took the arm of his fiancée Elena and helped her carefully into his father's car. On the first night of summer, praying to God that no one saw them, they drove away from Marano. When they arrived at the hospital, the Real Casa Santa dell'Annunziata, which still counted as part of the Pendino district but was not far from Cippo del Forcella, Angelo helped Elena to climb out again, then ran inside to fetch a wheelchair and brought it alongside the vehicle so that Elena wouldn't have to walk and tire herself. The Annunziata complex comprised a hospital and an adjacent orphanage, and the babies that grew up there were called 'children of the Madonna'.

The labour was short and the birth not too difficult, and the sisters and nurses were kind and the baby immediately yelled and bawled with his new lungs. Angelo remained by the window smoking one cigarette after another; with one hand he held his hat firmly on his head, as if it could have flown away at any moment. After the birth, Elena found the strength to carry the child herself to the nursery unit, a few corridors away. She spread a white towel in the wooden cradle and carefully laid on the towel the newborn baby. She brushed her fingers over its forehead and set the cradle rocking. The child was given the name Carlo Fraccari, after the director of the hospital, and so it would remain for three years.

The couple returned to Marano when the sun was high in the sky and summer was officially under way. The district consisted almost exclusively of farmland, worked by peasant farmers, and the economy revolved around agriculture. The Orlando family had a sawmill and had for generations made crates and baskets for fruit, and for this reason had come to be known as Mastroni, 'master craftsmen' or 'master carpenters'. Angelo, however, felt he was born for a life in politics and his goal was to make Marano into a real town, and to do this he was obliged to make frequent trips away from home. He would spend whole days at rallies from Naples to Rome. When necessary he went as far as Florence and Bologna and then returned home. When he and his father Gaetano agreed the time was ripe, he married Elena and together they returned to collect the child, as promised. The child was by now responding to the name Carlo, so Angelo decided to keep the name, adding to it that of his father. Eventually, after three years in limbo, the child was brought back to Marano and Carlo Gaetano Orlando was born for a second time, and so both the stars and the natural law of things came together in forming that young boy's very particular identity.

From Angelo he would inherit the boldness and the desire to establish himself as the leader who would guide Marano. From his mother, on the other hand, Carlo Gaetano would only preserve the name, Elena, which he would give to his own first female child.

The name 'Bastimento' I first heard when I was myself a child. It was my grandmother who used it, a woman almost the same age as Tanino—Gaetano was the name reserved for formal occasions. She had not grown up in Marano, but after her marriage she spent the rest of her life there. It was a new word for me, and as often happens, every time I heard it I wondered about it. Years later, Bruno explained where this *contranome*, this additional name, came from. Bruno is the second son of Tanino and the person who loved him if not most in the world then second most. He told me that Tanino, from when he was a very young boy, used to run loose in Marano 'like a stray dog' and that by the age of eight everyone knew him and that because he was by blood one of the Mastroni everyone expected either great things of him or great 'shit-heaps' of trouble. He did not play with the other children, at most he got them together and persuaded them to roam the streets and cause mayhem or steal cigarettes and loose change from their parents. Then it appears that one Sunday morning a priest who knew him well saw him wandering alone in the countryside, while his family and all the other local kids were milling about outside San Castrese church, following mass. The priest said to him: '*Tanì*, you're just like Bastimento,' and pointed to one of his youngest kid goats. He told him that Bastimento was equally lively and left equal amounts of shit everywhere, didn't eat with the other goats, but scrambled up the steepest hillsides and went to browse the grass wherever it pleased. The name stuck with him ever after. Bruno did not actually say this, but I believe Tanino wanted nothing better than to have a name of his own, which would single him out and no one else. From then on, Tanino was no longer a Mastrone and not even his children would be either.

Anyone who has grown up in these parts knows that the *contranome* is not just a simple nickname: it is the local identifier of a person's character and that whole branch of his family. They call you that once, as a joke, and without your realising, the name is sewn on to you like a label. The more potent the *contranome*, the more it endures through time and the generations. It has always seemed most strange to me, once I learned the mechanics of it, that a child of eight like Tanino could have managed in an instant to remove from his back a *contranome*, Mastrone, as weighty as his father's.

Bruno laughed when he told me that in his opinion the only great passion Tanino had in his life was acting the fool. He says that he chose to be a gangster entirely because of the women. 'I mean,' he said, '*I* like screwing, but Bastimento was altogether impossible.' When the first hairs began to sprout on Bruno's chin, this would be the mid-1980s, Tanino started to take him along when he had an important event or reception.

The ones Bastimento liked best were the beauty contests: Miss Campania, Miss Italy, Miss Venice, The New Look Girl and so on. He didn't miss a single one. They knew this in Naples and the surrounding area, so on occasion they invited him along as a judge or, much more often, as president of the jury. Usually Bruno would be sitting near him, watching the women file past in their swimming costumes and his father applauding enthusiastically each time. Then, after having declared the winner and having personally presented her with a bunch of roses on stage, he would make a signal to Bruno, in the midst of the flashing cameras and handshakes, and follow the girl into the changing rooms. When his son was old enough, Tanino began to introduce the runners-up to him after the presentation of the prizes. *Let's see if you're a man*, he would say. Then he would seek confirmation from the contestants: *is he a man then?*

Next Bruno showed me some photos he had brought. In one there is Tanino, aged around sixty, in the middle of five finalists in Miss Campania. He is wearing a black suit, with a white shirt and a red and gold regimental tie; his sparse hair is brushed back, carefully arranged and still stubbornly dark. Tanino's eyes, as in all the photographs of him from a certain point onwards, cannot be seen but are hidden behind an almost black pair of Carrera sunglasses. The smug smile though, is very visible. His arms are holding the waists of two of the girls, a blonde and a redhead, the hands squeezing the young flesh and it seems this was all he needed. What suddenly struck me, looking at the photo, is that as he stands there in the middle, Tanino is the shortest, and yet I'm certain no one was aware of that at the moment the shutter clicked.

Although he never appears in the photographs of the prize-giving ceremonies, there was another man present on those evenings, along with Tanino and Bruno. He was called Antonio Russo and he was Tanino's confidant and personal chauffeur. They were about the same age but Russo was a much more sober man, the sort that doesn't get noticed. He had a bushy moustache, made few demands and was a reliable type. He sometimes stayed at home with Ada and the children when Tanino had things to do on behalf of Marano, and over the years he taught Bruno and his siblings to drive. It was not an affectation of Tanino 'e Bastimento's to have a chauffeur, nor was it because he couldn't drive; it was because of Article 1. It is an old disciplinary ruling and from what I can make out it was a restriction imposed on some ex-criminals or people who needed to be kept under some sort of control. In practice, with Article 1, you lost, amongst other things, the right to a driving licence. Tanino had this ruling applied to him in 1950, but not, it seems, for any particular misdeed. In the 1970s, as a matter of fact, he spent most of his time creating a family, making children and readjusting his eyes to the light of the sun, which they continued to find troublesome. Then, with age and the wisdom he felt he had acquired, he had convinced himself that if he had had the opportunity he would have done very well in politics. After all, he had it in his blood, even if his ideas were different from those of his father. Unfortunately, the possibility of a career in Parliament had already been irredeemably compromised years before, and besides, another thing one lost with Article 1 was the right to vote. Little harm done. Bruno would be the one to become a Deputy. Having an Orlando in

Rome is a fundamental, he used to say, and his second-born was the one he had singled out. In any case, Tanino still had the pleasure of voting for the most beautiful women in Naples and its surrounding area.

The parish church of San Castrese is the church that presides over the cult of the patron saint of Marano. The church is set high up in the old part of town, and the cross above it is illuminated in blue at night. Besides baptism, all the other important church rites were performed there, and so it was for his children and for me as well. In the shadow of the *campanile*, half hidden, is a steeply rising road which crosses the Marano countryside all the way to the Camaldoni monastery. This narrow rural road is made still narrower by uncontrolled vegetation: sprawling climbers spread tendrils over the tarmac and work their way into cracks in the stonework of old and ruined buildings. Leafy bushes and protruding branches line one's passage and make it difficult for cars trying to make their way through. At the top of the hill, shortly before it emerges on to via del Mare, there is a gate on the right, made of rusty ironwork and sheet metal. On the other side of the gate is the *Terra di Bastimento*, the only property owned by the Orlando family. It is a patch of land covering half a hectare: a small farm-holding comprising a kitchen garden, a disused poultry run and an abandoned building engulfed, perilously, by rampant nature more than fifty years ago. At the centre of this piece of land stands the *casarella*, the miniature dwelling, a white block of cement about six metres by four. Inside are a fireplace and a tiny bathroom, the floor is tiled and one of the tiles has risen and trips up the unwary. The dwelling is furnished with odd pieces of broken kitchen equipment, a wobbly table and a threadbare divan. On the walls, apart from lizards and cobwebs, there are hung photos of Tanino and Bruno and Lello as youngsters with their friends. Lello was the third son of Tanino, a year younger than Bruno. One of the photographs on the wall has a white plastic frame and shows the main square of Marano's Old Town, piazza Trieste e Trento (which we, however, have always called via Nova). It is the 17th of January, and I know that because in the middle of the frame towers the great pile of the bonfire for the festival of Sant'Antonio, half extinguished but still ready to smoulder all night. Standing in front of the bonfire is a line of twenty or so young boys and in the middle of them is Lello, the biggest and tallest of all of them by at least fifteen centimetres; next to him Bruno has his arm round his shoulders and is laughing, his eyes blood-red from the camera flash.

Next to the photo hangs another frame, this one showing a print of the Manhattan skyline with the Twin Towers glittering in bright sunlight. The print is one of Enza's souvenirs, Tanino's sixth child. She is the third girl, born in 1976, four years younger than Bruno. As an eighteenth birthday present her father gave her two plane tickets for New York and a month's reservation in a suite at the Plaza Hotel. Enza is the person who loved Tanino most. She is the one who when I was little explained to me who Tanino 'e Bastimento was and she did so here, on 'the farm'. She pointed out another of the photos on the walls and told me: that is your grandfather, my father, everybody in Marano loved your grandfather, grandfather was a man of honour and friend to everybody, even famous people from TV but no one realises that, because he was in prison for such a long time and the people that didn't know him thought he was a bad man.

The farm is the place where Tanino's children grew up. He had them driven up there in the afternoons, after school, because it was good for them to grow in the open air, they needed to know how to work the land and feed the hens. The boys played football and had pretend gunfights, the girls played hopscotch and pretended to be ladies of the nobility. Meanwhile Tanino kept an eye on China, the name that everyone always called the youngest child, because she was born with the typical almond-shaped eyes of Down's syndrome. She is a year younger than Enza, her baptismal name is Asia Rosa and she has never learned to say it, and in fact has never learned to say any word at all, except 'mamma'. Enza says that China could once say 'papà', but I have never heard her do so. Tanino didn't play with his children, only with her, because she was helpless and he and her brothers had to protect her. He would watch her as she listened to music, holding a colourful Walkman to her ear and rocking backwards and forwards on the divan, with her legs crossed. As she does now, too.

Whenever a friend of Tanino came to see him up at the farm he swapped places with Enza, who went inside to look after China.

As soon as she saw a car come through the gate and drive down the rough track, Elena knew she must stop playing, go inside and prepare coffee for the guest. Elena is the fourth of Tanino's children, the first girl. She is a year younger than Lello and a year older than Enza, has never been to New York, and is my mother.

We only go up to the farm nowadays for the summer, when I too come back to Marano. On Sundays we have lunch with various cousins—the twins usually—and a few friends. Beside the house is a large marble table, four or five metres long, with a corrugated iron canopy over it that Tanino's sons had installed a few years ago, after a whip-round. In the afternoon Enza sees to the plants and flowers she has sown, settles China on the divan and turns on the stereo. For the lunch, everyone brings something, but she is the one who cooks the main course: *ragù*—baked pasta or pasta *alla genovese* are the dishes I like best, and usually she prepares one of these. My portion is the most generous and she always serves me last, because that way I can also scrape up all the remaining sauce in the pan. Beside the disused hen-run Bruno has built a brick barbecue, and on Sundays he takes charge of cooking all the meat. He says it is the man of the house who should be at the grill and since that role in the family is vacant, he feels it is his right, by virtue of seniority. He spends hours getting the fire just right, fanning it with strips of cardboard from the packet of meat he has just unwrapped. He serves up fennel sausages almost carbonised and says 'this is how they're meant to be', even if no one has offered a comment, then turns back to cook the spare ribs and the pork chops. By the time he has finished he stinks of smoke, is all sweaty and his eyes are as red as in the photo on the wall. He pours himself a glass of water and if I look at him while he's doing so he tells me 'this is the only thing I drink, I don't touch alcohol any more 'cos I do stupid things, you enjoy yourself and get pissed'. He hasn't had a drink for ten years, more or less since the time his wife and children left him.

Elena does not usually come to these lunches. She says it's her relatives, she can't stand them and if she comes then she's bound to quarrel with Bruno because he talks too much, or with the twins because they say, every time, she ought to go out and get laid occasionally and start to relax a bit. She stays at home by herself and when we're up at the farm everyone asks me about her, when's your mamma coming, your mamma never comes, what the fuck's she doing all alone in the house in this nice weather. Then they ask how things are going in Milan and I reply I'm studying in Turin, that everything's fine and I go back in September, when lectures start again. They say good for you, don't come back here, there's nothing here in Marano for you, nothing in Naples. Then Enza comes from the little house with the desserts and the liqueurs, pours me a limoncello and I toss it down, while the sun goes down and the air grows cooler. When Bruno hears the mention of Turin he points at me and says my nephew has become a Juventus fan, Juve are good but Napoli used to be better, Platini was no good and Maradona pissed on his head. Then he gets to his feet and mimes a Diego goal, celebrates as if he had just seen him score, says that the swerve he put on the ball could only have been done by him, that even when he didn't score, Diego dominated, that he took a pasting from defenders all match long without reacting, on the contrary instead of complaining he'd go and score. He adds that I'm unlucky because I never saw him play, that he'd give anything to be fifteen again and bring back that Napoli team.

Shortly before it grows dark everyone goes, more or less at the same time, the twins come up to me and slip a bit of dope into my hand, give me a wink and say give a bit to your mamma as well. Enza tells me to make sure I lock everything up when I leave, gets in the car with China and drives off home. After a while my friends arrive, we put the music on and the five or six of us sit round the marble table. We drink whatever drinks and liqueurs are left, we eat the remains of the barbecue and talk about our lives: Biagio and Gennaro have to get to their work early tomorrow, Peppe has to get back to the barracks at Varese and Chiara has commercial law work to hand in.

When it's by now about three in the morning and we realise no one has spoken for the last five minutes, Biagio gets up, waves goodbye and heads off to his car. Before he goes, Gennaro asks me if I want a lift on his scooter, I say no, not tonight, I'm going to walk, the pasta is still heavy on my stomach.

Once I am alone, I take a cloth and wipe the marble top, where there are dried up traces of sauce and sticky rings of Coca Cola. I tip the rubbish into a big transparent plastic sack and double-knot it. I go back inside the little house to sweep up and collect my things before going off. Above the photo of Lello and Bruno and the print of Manhattan, the photo of Tanino 'e Bastimento is still hanging, the one I associate with his name, with him in his sunglasses, hair brushed back and wearing the suit and tie and the already mentioned smile on his lips. I step closer to see better, to see my reflection shine back at me from his nearly-black glasses, but nothing happens. One of those spiders with small bodies and long wavy legs is resting half-concealed on Tanino's darkened eye and I must have breathed on it, because it suddenly skitters away, off the frame and up high, and I can follow it for a second or two, then it disappears into a crevice in the wall just below the ceiling. I clean the glass over the photograph with the sleeve of my sweatshirt and find a faint layer of dust on my arm. Tanino's face is just the same, the same as when Enza pointed him out to explain who my grandfather was. At that time, however, I still did not understand.

I lock the doors as Enza told me to, check them a couple of times, then I put the chain round the gate and snap the padlock shut and begin the descent back to the parish church and home. The road is so steep that it's easier to go up than go down: I have to plant my feet firmly on the ground and every step forward is a little jump into the void. There are no street lamps and I use my phone torch to see my way. On the uneven and pot-holed tarmac are the flattened bodies of several pigeons who, with the roadway being so narrow and hemmed in by its walls, have no means of escape unless they fly straight upwards. When I come out on to the square round the church I stop to let the wind cool my face and light a cigarette. At the other side of the square some cars are parked next to the low wall, and a green Panda with fogged-up windows is rocking delicately to and fro. From here you can see my house as well, the light in the kitchen is still on. Mamma knows I smoke but she doesn't like it if she can smell it on me. In some ways I am glad to be back. Here, things happen in a more straightforward fashion, facts are facts and hardly ever embroidered. Things move more slowly in Marano, and sometimes I feel justified in standing still, avoiding having to press forward with life. But this time there is a shadow hovering over everything around me, a shadow that has maybe been here all along but which I am only now seeing, perhaps because I'm growing up, perhaps because distance has made things clearer. Tanino 'e Bastimento's photograph continues to appear before my eyes, his expression that gives nothing away or seems increasingly to resemble a cynical smile, a smile of challenge. It seems as if he is waiting for me to make a move, inviting me to look more deeply, I feel as if I have a duty to penetrate further into his story, into the deeds he did and the words he spoke, and maybe then I shall be able to see his naked eyes.

Shortly before I finish my cigarette, the green car stops rocking, the driver's window winds down and I see him light up a cigarette too. I stub mine out on the ground and make for home.

On the night of the first of June 1963, feverish and in handcuffs, Carlo Gaetano Orlando was transferred, along with a handful of other detainees, from the prison at Viterbo to Porto Azzurro, on the island of Elba. While the ferry was crossing the placid Tyrrhenian Sea, all Tanino could think about were his wife Ada and his son Angelo, just seven years old—the same number he had spent under lock and key. He had never set eyes on the child outside prison walls and when Ada brought him with her on her visits he sat on his mother's lap, observing Tanino without showing any emotion. In Tanino's eyes, this was welcome behaviour, he hated the children who collapsed into tears and lamentations or hurled themselves to the floor on being confronted with their gaoled fathers. Angelo, in contrast, always seemed perfectly calm, held his head high, and if his father looked directly at him didn't bat an eyelid. In the meantime Ada stroked her son's legs and it seemed to Tanino she did it more to calm herself than the boy. Not that she ever missed a visit, let it be said. Every month she and the child got in the car with Russo to be driven to Poggioreale; then came the years at Palermo and at Viterbo, when they would take the train, or sometimes the plane, and go to where Tanino 'e Bastimento awaited them. Seven long years in total, and for all that time Tanino had had proof of Ada's loyal devotion. On that ferry, however, he couldn't help thinking that getting to Elba was a very different matter. He had never been so far from Naples and Marano, and this sea seemed different to him from his own, he felt that in these waters he could even drown and they would not rescue him and set him again on dry land, they would have left him to his fate.

The ferry arrived at the island in the morning, then he and the other detainees were transferred in an armoured van to the coastal town of Porto Azzurro, on whose outlying rocks stands Forte Longone, a prison complex laid out on a pentangular plan overlooking the Piombino canal and which had been built by the Spanish at the beginning of the seventeenth century as a military fortification.

In 1963, the governorship of the prison was in the hands of a certain De Santis, a man supposedly intent on 're-educating' those in his care, but notorious throughout the Italian prison population for his harshness and evil-mindedness, and notorious to Tanino himself who had spent some hellish months at Poggioreale under his supervision. Tanino felt like Jesus Christ on the cross, sent by Providence to expiate the sins of the world, at the very start of the finest season of the year. The first two weeks weighed on him as heavily as if they had been two years. He knew all the prisoners on his wing, the lifers' wing, even though in theory he was not one of them:

he still had another twenty-two years in the dark to serve, or fewer with good conduct, and within these new walls he finally felt he had stumbled on better fortune. His cell-mate was called Montebello and had been there for a few months. They made friends at once, for Tanino could recognise very quickly whether a man was a good sort or not, and Montebello was. The man told him how, ever since he was a boy, he had done the rounds of psychiatric hospitals, his mental state had been clinically assessed several times, but with experience he had succeeded in managing it. Then Montebello had fallen in love with a woman and had soon decided to go and live with her. And then it happened that one night, in the middle of a domestic dispute, something snapped in his brain and he no longer knew what he was doing: he stabbed his companion in the chest, twice and after a bit called an ambulance. The woman died twenty days later from complications after developing bronchial pneumonia, Montebello was arrested and the magistrate Montefusco—a name already familiar to Tanino—declaring the man a recidivist and a danger, sentenced him to 'a full-life term'.

The summer sun threw its shafts through the window of the cell and Tanino began to avoid it as best he could, huddling in the dark corners where the direct heat could not reach. One morning Montebello showed him how to make a homemade telescope, which was one of the few entertainments one could get away with at Forte Longone. It consisted of two or three cardboard cylinders from toilet rolls taped in line to form a sort of tube; then you fitted inside it two lenses, which you could obtain by asking the authorities for reading glasses. Montebello knelt at the cell's small window and steadied the newly assembled telescope. After a while he said to Tanino 'look at this, you won't believe it, honestly, take a look.' So Tanino let the sun spill over him and pointed the telescope towards the beach at Porto Azzurro. He saw people enjoying the heat and the sea, children running along the shoreline, women lying down sunbathing, women laughing in the water, splashing each other, women going topless, with bouncing breasts. Before his eyes rose the figure of Ada, naked, her red hair and her full bosom, her strong and knowing hands and her broad belly and Tanino had to put the telescope down and catch his breath. Montebello laid a hand on his shoulder and said 'was I right or not, have you seen all that flesh?' Tanino made no reply, raised the device again and steadied it because his hands had begun to tremble a bit. He focused on the open sea to calm himself down, the sea always calmed him even if it wasn't his own sea. There were a few boats tied up in the Piombino canal, bobbing on the calm water and they were nearly all white. A little further out, towards the prison, there was a motorboat anchored, the colour of varnished wood. Tanino leant forward, he wanted to see better, he thrust the whole length of the telescope between the bars until he could feel the hot ironwork on his nose and cheeks. On board the motorboat were two people, the woman very beautiful, and the man also, come to that. They were making love. Tanino very nearly burst into tears, he wanted to yell, and while he held the telescope with one hand, the other clamped a window bar in a powerful grip, it was scorching hot but then the body and the blonde hair of the woman were too, and they burned his eyes, he wanted to be there on the motorboat, he wanted to push the man into the sea and possess the woman, he wanted to make love and, shit, another twenty-two years like this would be more than he could bear.

The Orlando family lived for more than thirty years in the rented apartment in a building on via Edificio Scolastico, up until 2005. The street is so called because there are two educational establishments: a primary school, the Domenico Amanzio, and an institute for commercial studies, the Manzoni. The street intersects with Piazza Trieste e Trento at via Nova, and it now seems to me clear that Tanino did not choose this location haphazardly. From there he could oversee, literally, what was at that time the busiest part of town; besides, he could keep an eye on his children, watch them entering and leaving school from his second-floor balcony.

Tanino finished the greater part of his sentence towards the end of 1971, after sixteen years—the same number as Angelo's age—of incarceration in various regions of Italy. Along with Ada and the boy, they went to live in his relatives' house on the edge of Marano. In those first few months Ada became pregnant again and it was immediately clear that they would need a larger home, somewhere just for themselves. It was then that they informed him about that apartment in via Edificio Scolastico; it was lived in by some other Orlando cousins, and when they knew that Tanino 'e Bastimento and his family needed somewhere secure where they could settle, within a few weeks they moved to another of the properties the family had in Marano. They asked Tanino if he wanted to buy the flat, telling him that they would obviously sell it for a discounted price. The money was not a problem, Tanino had speedily returned to work and in his absence the turnover of the family's business affairs had increased beyond all expectations; the fact remains that for whatever reason he said no, that the apartment was better as a rental proposition.

The Orlandos controlled the fruit and vegetable market in the northern area of Naples, they supplied commercial enterprises, schools and hospitals, including one of Naples' two largest hospitals, the Cardarelli. The expansion of the family's interests had been led by Armando and Antonio Orlando, uncles of Tanino and younger brothers of his father Angelo, the communist. In spite of their age and experience, Antonio and Armando recognised Gaetano Orlando—Tanino—as their equal. Not only did they trust him, but they recognised that Tanino's was the right face to use as a figurehead on a ship that had every intention of forging ahead. It is worth saying, too, that it is a lot easier to assert oneself if there is no one to hinder you, and if the Naples market had missed having real leaders for the last sixteen years it was down to Tanino.

On the 12th of July 1963, after more than a month inside the walls of Forte Longone, on the island of Elba, Tanino 'e Bastimento recognised a face he had already come across in his past life. Tanino was in the prison yard, in the shade, taking what little air the authorities granted him during the day. Sometimes he wrote poetry, at other times he just sat on a bench and did nothing, smoking one cigarette after another and watching the warders and the other inmates. At Porto Azzurro Tanino was respected by all the various factions because he didn't give a shit, he did his own thing and behaved well. The younger prisoners knew him by name and the ones from Naples called him *'o zi, zi Tanino*, the uncle, uncle Tanino, even though he was only thirty-three, because in prison age is relative and is sometimes confused with the number of years still to be served or already served. *The uncle* was a title of trust, and Tanino inspired it in spades, not to mention that when it came to prisons he had already known a fair number and to confirm it there were men much older and better known than him who, in the various penitentiaries of the country, had seen Tanino prove himself a man. One of these was called Raffaele La Marca, and he was known in Campania as 'the Bandit of Vesuvius'. He was awarded this title because in the post-war period he had begun a black-market operation in grain, smuggling vast quantities to be distributed all round the area at the foot of the volcano. Tanino remembered him the very moment La Marca approached him, that sultry July afternoon, in the yard of Forte Longone. 'Bastimento,' the man said; 'il Bandito,' Tanino replied, with a note of surprise that was new to him. He hadn't recognised La Marca because he was limping and it is one of the things one remembers about people, and then his left arm was rigid and almost fixed to his torso, even when he walked. Tanino recalled that he had known Raffaele La Marca in prison at Parma, in 1949. Tanino was on a two year sentence and il Bandito had said 'lucky you, they gave me life and I don't know if I'll ever get out.' La Marca had been arrested a few months earlier: some carabinieri had stopped him on the road to San Giuseppe Vesuviano, they'd told him to step down from the cab of the lorry and open the container it was carrying, so il Bandito had begun to run in the opposite direction and then left the road and headed for the open countryside. The carabinieri, there were four or five of them, had chased after him, weapons in their hands, they were steadily gaining on him and La Marca had no desire to end up in prison. He had pulled the pistol from his trouser belt—a piece of string—and fired a shot behind him, to frighten the policemen away. Fate, however, decided that the bullet he let fly should end up in the middle of the forehead of one of the policemen, who fell stone dead and La Marca had suddenly lost the strength to run. The carabinieri arrested him and il Bandito's thought was that he could never have done that intentionally even if he had wanted to. The magistrate who presided over his case was Montefusco again, and his ultimate sentence could only be a life one.

La Marca told Tanino that after Parma he too had been sent to almost every prison in the country, but things had stabilised and he had now been here for years, on the island of Elba. Tanino asked him what the hell had happened to his arm and leg and in reply il Bandito looked towards the guardhouse in the castle keep, where, at the top, the window of the governor De Santis was open. La Marca explained that one morning he was feeling pissed off, and passing near a corporal, he failed to take off his prisoner's cap as a mark of respect. The corporal had grabbed him by the collar and slammed him against the wall, and il Bandito had made the major error of pushing him away with some force. Then the corporal called for reinforcements and they dragged La Marca off to the 'magazine', the old gunpowder room underground where disrespectful prisoners were punished. They beat him to a pulp with fists and boots and clubs, they broke his right leg and his left arm and then they tied him with strips of cloth to a pallet, with the result that his fractures were never properly set and left him permanently crippled. During this punishment the screws amused themselves by feeding him while he was motionless and flat on his back. For weeks they dropped water and food into his mouth and il Bandito risked drowning every day he remained lashed to that pallet. While he was telling Tanino all this, Tanino felt the rage surging up in him, and wondered how it was possible that La Marca could talk about it with such calmness, almost with resignation, almost as if what had happened to him had been reasonable. 'What can you do about it?' il Bandito had replied. But Tanino knew that there was nothing reasonable in any of this, that a pistol shot going wrong can ruin your life, that you can't punish a man who makes a mistake in all good faith or while protecting his honour. He was surprised, too, that Montefusco didn't seem to have the first idea about questions of honour, and to discover what a 'total shit' governor De Santis was. And on top of all that, he was surprised that when you were out in the exercise yard, surrounded by all that water, the only thing you got were the whistles from the cargo ships, and nothing else, not even a little fresh air, not even the smell or even the sound of the waves. For him and the other inmates there was precisely nothing, only injustices and beatings.

I didn't go to school in via Edificio Scolastico, mamma never wanted me to. I wasn't often in that part of town at all: in the middle of via Nova square the other kids played football and I hardly ever joined in. When I was six, Bruno had once taken me to the football school run by a childhood friend of his, because he didn't have any sons of his own and he said 'my nephew doesn't "get" football, it's ridiculous, what kind of shit impression does that make with the other kids?' The coach told me to play in midfield, to try me out in a practice match. Two teams were already being sorted out and I was thrown into the mix, on the side of the ones wearing bibs. I had never seen a real football match, I had no idea what the different roles meant. I took up position in the middle of the pitch as the coach had said and stayed there. I remember standing there, not moving, with one foot always inside the white circle; the other kids ran around and I heard them panting excitedly whenever they ran past me. At one point an opponent ran at me with the ball at his feet. I tried to cover as much space as possible to stop him, he slowed down when he was a few steps away, touched the ball with the inside of his foot and slid it between my legs, dodged to the right and was away with the ball again behind my back. I turned and stuck out a hand to grab him, but he had gone, was darting off towards our goal, my goal. I don't remember if he scored or not, because I was distracted by the yells of the coach, who was shouting from the bench what the shit are you doing, why are you standing there like a statue, wetting yourself. From the other side of the field, Bruno had his face up against the green mesh fencing that separated him and the other parents from the pitch. His eyes were glued to me, one hand gripping the mesh fencing and the other his right knee, his lips tight and the pained expression of someone imploring you not to mortify him any more.

I spent the journey home in complete silence. Bruno told me not to worry, everyone can get nutmegged, maybe football wasn't one of my talents and there was nothing bad about that, not even Lello was any good but he was good at other things. Then he asked me why I had stayed there in the centre circle the whole time, and I didn't know how to reply. We arrived outside the apartment block at via Edificio Scolastico and there on the second-floor balcony was Lello, in one of the last images I have of him in my head, with his hair shaved and tubes in his arm.

The apartment itself I only slightly remember, but I have a clear picture of the corridor that ran all the way through it. Going through the front door, the first room you came to was always kept locked, the sitting room. Further along were the kitchen on one side and the boxroom on the other. When Lello played hide and seek with me in the flat, that was where I always used to hide and he came to find me there only right at the end. I liked the darkness, the crammed boxes, the smell of books and shoes, the silence which would be broken by his heavy footsteps coming ever closer and the adrenaline rush of knowing there was no escape. Sometimes, while I was waiting for him to come and open the boxroom door I would clamber up among the shelving units and rummage around in the dust. One of the boxes, at head height, had sprung open because the sellotape sealing it had come away. Inside were books, a dozen or so, all the same colour and with the same cover, which showed a black and white photograph of a man in his thirties. Above the photo was an embossed title, *Anelito tra le sbarre*, *A Look of Longing Through the Bars*, and above the title the name of my grandfather, Gaetano Orlando.

The pages were filled with words written in different ways, some in verse, some in prose, but I only became familiar with their content many years later, because every time I had a copy in my hands, in the boxroom of the apartment in via Edificio Scolastico, Lello arrived and beat on the door with his fists before I had begun to read.

The corridor then made a turn to the right, and off it were the bathroom and the bedrooms: the one shared by Bruno and Lello, then Enza and Elena's, and at the end the master bedroom, where Tanino and Ada slept, with China between them. Of the bedrooms, kitchen and sitting room I remember almost nothing; when I see myself in the apartment I am always in the corridor, alone, and the doors, in my imagination, are shut.

Longing

What is longing
it is like a radiant breath on the horizon
the only thing alive in the darkness
feeling inside that palpitation, that aspiration
because the eyes of those who look on it
speak, dream
and he, dreaming, shapes a thought
a soft thought for the wife
a bright thought for the son
and in these thoughts
he yearns.
And it is as if he hears a cry within
it is the cry of yearning.
And now his tear-filled eyes look out
ever further out
beyond the horizon.
And for these eyes filled with his tears
now they can see nothing
but a sky of lead

that beam of radiant sunlight
disappears from sight
because he lives in darkness
and now, see, he grips in desperation the bars
on his window
lowering his head he weeps and says:
"Why should that beam of sunlight not be for me as well?
Why can I not be there to see a radiant dawn?"
And now one more time
from his sad heart there is unleashed a cry
it is the cry of yearning
that yearning that is called freedom.

Gaetano Orlando, 18th August 1965, Sant' Elena's Day

On the 13th of July 1955, soon after dawn, Tanino set off for Rome. The night before he had gone to Ada's house and they had made love. She confessed she had missed her period for two months, he had put his hand to her stomach and told her you know what this means, Adaré, we must get married. The trip to Rome fitted perfectly: the occasion was a business meeting, Tanino, was due to conclude a deal to supply all the fruit to a clinic a short way south of the capital. A wedding was no small matter, and in any event Tanino 'e Bastimento did not want it to be. And afterwards he would need to find them a house, a big and beautiful house where the children could grow up, because Tanino wanted lots. Angelo, that's what his child would be called if he was born a boy; Elena, obviously, if a girl. In short, he had to ensure the maximum possible comfort for his future wife and his heirs.

That morning he climbed into Russo's Alfa Romeo 1900, on the passenger side. He was already under the restrictions of Article 1 and could no longer drive. In the back were an old man and a girl, grandfather and granddaughter. The man was the guarantor of the deal, a friend of both Russo and the director of the clinic south of Rome. The girl, aged about fifteen, had insisted on accompanying her grandfather, she wanted to visit the capital and the old man felt more secure taking her there in the company of two of the Mastroni. Russo's Alfa Romeo was only a few months old and Tanino had never been in a car that could go so fast. In the twinkling of an eye they had left Marano behind and had joined the via Domitiana, built by the eponymous emperor to link the port of Pozzuoli to the capital, and in a few hours it would have brought them to the ring road round Rome. With the windows down and the strong breeze blowing in from all sides, the girl had to shout to be heard by Tanino. She asked him why he needed to go as far as Rome to deliver fruit, she said surely there were plenty of other people who needed fruit in Naples as well. Tanino, with an arm trailing out of the window and a cigarette 'smoked' almost down to the stub by the wind, looked at the girl in the rearview mirror. At this time he didn't wear dark glasses and he had chestnut eyes, with the alluring look that according to some people denotes cunning. Tanino replied that it was important to know when to seize opportunities, that one had to look ahead, that the moment to assume the monopoly for supplying the whole city had come and that it was only a matter of waiting. 'And then there's always Pascalone,' the old man added, and Russo turned round to glance at him.

'Pascalone is a shit,' said the driver; 'Pascalone's all right,' Tanino intervened, 'a man like me and you, but he thinks everything is his and overdoes the gangster boss act.' The girl asked who they were talking about and Tanino answered 'Pascalone 'e Nola, he's the big man who runs the major part of the fruit and vegetable market at Naples. He's a decent enough fellow and lives with a beautiful woman, very beautiful. Now he's the big shot in Poggioreale prison but in a few weeks he's getting out, people like him always get out, no one messes with him.'

People were still talking about Pascalone's wedding two months after the event. It had been an enormous occasion, with more than five hundred guests, amongst whom were even Tanino and the uncles Antonio and Armando. That was where Tanino had made his acquaintance, along with his new wife, Assunta, known as Pupetta, 'the doll', because, as mentioned, she was beautiful, very beautiful.

The Alfa Romeo did not reach Rome that day, because, when they had got as far as Caserta, it crashed into a guardrail and somersaulted several times. It seems the vehicle was travelling at over a hundred and fifty kilometres per hour, but no one remembers the exact circumstances of the accident. Tanino broke a collar bone and received a severe bang on the head; Russo sustained a large wound; the old man died and his granddaughter, sitting beside him, was the only one to emerge totally unscathed.

Tanino was found in the field where the car ended up. He had lost a lot of blood from the head wound and the traffic police thought the young man was dead. He regained consciousness the next day in a room at the Cardarelli hospital in Naples, and after Russo had explained to him what had happened, Tanino felt certain the accident had not been just a chance event, he was sure destiny had ordered it, otherwise there was no way of explaining it. He understood at that moment that leaving Marano and Naples was not what fate desired of him, and that being so, if he really wanted to be a great man, he must do it there, he must impose himself and his own honour on his city, even at the cost of making enemies.

In 2005 the Orlando family was turned out of the apartment in via Edificio Scolastico and moved to an apartment in via Roma, smaller and with fewer rooms. Bruno had married and now lived with his wife and daughters; Lello had died almost a year ago; Elena lived alone, with me, in a two-room flat a few minutes from San Castrese church. So the ones who moved into via Roma were Ada, Enza and China. Even if Tanino's children no longer all lived together, they had all settled nearby, in old Marano, and continued to gravitate around the person who represented what all of them, unanimously, would have called 'home', or rather the place where Ada was. At night, only the three women slept there, all in the same room, but during the day Bruno and Elena dropped in several times, even if there was nothing they needed to do there. They put the coffee on, they changed the CD for China, they waited in case Ada needed anything. Ada, however, never asked for anything. She was usually to be found sitting on the divan, on the left-hand side, next to China, or scurrying back and forth between the bedroom and the kitchen. She would stare ahead, towards the framed photo of Lello holding a cigar and wearing sunglasses, standing in the middle of via Nova square. Normally mothers never expressed any preferences about their children, and Ada had never done so, but since Lello had no longer been there, it had quickly become clear that he had not only been the favourite in the eyes of all Tanino's other children, but also the favourite of his mother. With time, I have begun to think that this visceral love for Lello on the part of the family suddenly blossomed as a direct consequence of his death, but I don't know how much difference it makes.

There is a second bedroom in the via Roma flat, and for years it was mine. Elena was out at work every day, from morning until evening, and after school I always went round to grandmother's. I spent the afternoons partly with her and partly in my bedroom; sometimes I went down to play with Biagio, Peppe and Gennaro who all lived nearby; on occasion I brought them up to the apartment and Ada would shout from the kitchen 'no fighting, no hurting each other, I'll tell your mammas.'

The sitting room, which was locked at via Edificio Scolastico, has always remained open here. Or rather, the door is locked because it has a tendency to swing open by itself through some strange effect of air currents, but the key is in the keyhole and anyone can go in, except China, who has never understood the mechanism.

The sitting room is the room where all the family treasures and relics are kept, the pieces of jewellery, presents and souvenirs received over the years by Tanino at weddings, baptisms and first communions. There are dinner services and antique silverware, pictures and baroque armchairs, dozens of musical boxes of every size and shape. There is an upright piano, never tuned, the lid always closed over the keyboard, and on its top a decorative dagger with a twisted blade and an elaborate hilt, all curves and zigzags, in a mauve-ish colour. None of this is ordered in any particular way, all the objects are crammed in and piled on every available surface and over it all, with time, has fallen a uniform layer of dust which you only notice when you touch something. It is always cold in the sitting room, even in summer, as if the apartment knew that some things are better preserved at certain temperatures. On one of the walls of this room hangs a picture some metre and a half long by a metre high: it shows a naked girl, lying on a divan, she has her hair up, black hair, and she is revealing her breasts and the first pussy I remember seeing, barely concealed by her crossed legs and dark tufty mound. Even if it doesn't resemble her in any way, I was convinced for years it was Ada. Sometimes, in the afternoons, I would sneak out of my bedroom and slip furtively into the sitting room. I would leave the door ajar so that if grandmother got up from the divan, I would have heard the grunt of her effort and her footsteps shuffling in my direction. I was not forbidden to enter the sitting room, but if I did go in I was always asked what for. I had the impression that they didn't want me to spend too much time in there, as if I might have found something, as if venturing deeper amongst all those stacks of china I might have found myself faced with something I wasn't supposed to see.

The other object that always caught my attention in the sitting room was the life-sized gilded head of a pharaoh, set on top of a tall dresser full of blue and white plates rising almost to the ceiling. The pharaoh stared down at me from above and I stared back, I wanted to touch it and never did. So many times I could have taken one of the satin-covered armchairs, jumped on it and brought myself face to face with the Egyptian head, felt its weight and temperature, but for whatever reason I always preserved the distance between us, never trespassing on it.

On a wooden table fixed to the wall there are dozens of little frames with photos of Ada and Tanino at various moments in their lives, a few as children, before they met each other. There is one photograph that shows grandmother with another six or seven girls and a little boy, Ada seems to be the eldest.

I know that she came from Chiaiano, and had hardly ever been to Marano before she met Tanino. On some mornings, on a Saturday or a Sunday, Ada would tell me about her brief life before meeting this Tanino 'e Bastimento. She was the first of I don't know how many sisters and had just one brother who lost a leg at the age of nine, severed by a bus. Her childhood was different from Tanino's. From an early age, Ada had had to work, make herself useful, help her mother with her sisters. Her father was called Pasquale and he used to load milk on to his cart at dawn and push it all the way to central Naples, sometimes as far as Mergellina. When it was too hot, Ada would go with him and take her turn, the cart never slowed down and her father would tell her, 'Good for you, Adarè, you push as well as I do.' Then, moving on from the cart, she would tell me about Tanino, who suddenly arrived on the scene and changed everything, he took her away and within a few years she found she was a mother, of a son, Angelo, whom she had brought up alone and taken with her to prisons all over Italy, a son who had never set foot in the via Roma flat, nor had I ever seen him in the via Edificio Scolastico apartment or at the farm, but whom I would get to know only years later, a few months before I left Marano.

Once I asked grandmother if she had been the first for Tanino as well. She burst out laughing, her raucous, theatrical laugh, with all her teeth showing. She was sitting as always on the divan and the afternoon sun sparkled in her blue eyes, which she had not passed on to any of her children but only to me, somehow bypassing, she was sure, the laws of genetics. She told me that Tanino said so, that she was definitely the first and that had been good enough for her. She quoted a proverb: if you don't worry over minor stuff, your troubles will be few enough—in other words sometimes it's better not to ask too many questions.

The thing that has always puzzled me about the via Roma flat, you can see it on the main entrance door and on the notice by the entry-phone, is that there are two names. One is my grandmother's, Adelaide Manna, the other Tanino's, who has never lived in this building and never even saw it. I asked Enza if there wasn't a case for putting her name there, since the flat is in effect hers now. She replied no, it's fine as it is.

On the 6th of September 1951, shortly before midday, Tanino was released from the prison at Benevento and regained his liberty for the first time in his life. He was twenty-one years old, and the last two he had spent in the darkness, in various cells but all with the same stink of urine. At the entrance was waiting the man who for the past five years had been the communist mayor of Marano, Angelo Orlando, his father. The two shook hands and embraced. They made their way to Angelo's car, and when Tanino saw the passenger seat empty he looked at his father and both of them began to cry. Elena had died a good while back, a few weeks after Tanino's arrest, for two years he had had no mother. But they had been two years spent in the dark, alone, and in the dark the shit remains unseen. Now he was out in the sunlight, and only at this point did he understand that his mother was dead, that he had not even had the chance to say goodbye, to thank her, to reassure her that her name would live on after her.

They were on their way to the Marano cemetery when

Angelo turned off first towards Pianura and then towards the centre of Naples. Tanino asked, ‘But where are we going?’ Angelo replied, ‘It’s a surprise, a bit of air and sea will do you good, trust me.’ There was no traffic and soon they entered the tunnel on via Marina and when they emerged they were at Mergellina. The September sea still retained its summer warmth and shone, rippling in the sunlight and breaking on the rocks in a peaceful rhythm, spreading on beyond the curve of the bay and touching the foothills of Vesuvius, to the south. Angelo parked the car in front of the Excelsior Hotel and together with his son walked along the Caracciolo seafront. Tanino kept looking at the sea to his right and began to feel hot. The pair came to a restaurant, the Ferdinando al Mare, which was Tanino’s favourite, and Angelo’s too, where you could eat, according to many people, the freshest seafood in Naples. Waiting for them was a whole group of relatives, from uncles to cousins, almost all of them men. Uncle Armando and uncle Antonio embraced Tanino and ushered him with broad gestures towards the staircase that led up to the restaurant. Tanino ’e Bastimento sat at the head of the table with his father and his uncles at his side. He ordered oysters, *paccheri*—large pasta tubes—with a filling of monkfish, and fried prawns and squid. The waiter brought prosecco and the Orlandos raised a toast to freedom and Tanino, who was twenty-one and had a whole life ahead of him. But he was feeling hotter and hotter, kept turning round and looking through the plate glass window towards the rocky shore. Angelo observed it and said, ‘Go, go, but come back soon, it’s not right to keep the family waiting.’ So Tanino opened the suitcase containing his personal effects, which they’d given back to him in the entrance lobby to Benevento prison, took out a towel and a pair of mules, left a kiss on his father's neck and ran towards the rocks. He climbed over the green railings that lined the whole road and stopped on one of the large rocks, planting his feet firmly and wide apart to keep his balance. He pulled off his white shirt and threw it on the rock, along with his trousers and shoes. He saw his own body in the sunlight after those two years and was horrified at its whiteness, he had never been without his customary tan, especially in September. He nimbly made his way down between the rocks, and very soon Tanino dived in, with the sun, which had just passed its highest point, and that sea which was blue and cool and no feeble trickle like the piss in the cells but a swelling expanse, rising and falling all round Tanino in the cove. He let himself sink and held his breath while the waters of the ocean washed him clean, took away the dirt and the darkness that had lodged under his skin over those two disgusting years.

He clambered out of the water, pressing his palms on a rock to heave himself up, went to pick up his towel and scrubbed at his face and hair, he pulled his trousers back on over his wet legs and slipped his unbuttoned shirt round his shoulders. From his pocket he took out a small tortoiseshell comb and drew it carefully through his hair, sweeping it all backwards, with his fingers pressed to one temple. Then the sea chose to give him another gift and it was just then that he saw her. The girl, in her swimming costume, was moving among the rocks with such gracefulness they no longer seemed to be made of stone, since her footfall was so light, noiseless and seemed almost to lift in the air as if the girl were walking on some elastic surface. She was—like so many others before and after that moment—the most beautiful woman Tanino had ever seen. She had an expressive face, blue eyes, he could see them even from this distance, from the three or four large boulders that separated them. Suddenly the girl pointed a finger at Tanino's chest, the ribcage rapidly rising and falling as he got his breath back and the hair on his breastbone still glistening from the water. 'The comb,' said the girl, 'can I borrow it?' Tanino withdrew it from his pocket again, gripped it firmly then took a few steps towards her and she took a few steps towards him. They halted on two adjacent rocks, not quite touching, with a couple of metres between them and down in the gap a slow wash of stagnant water continuously churned over on itself along with a handful of cigarette ends. Tanino reached out, holding the comb, the girl leant forward to grab it and their thumbs touched. 'Thank you,' she said, and began to comb her long hair. Then she pinned it behind her head with a slide, saying 'why are you staring at me then, do I remind you of someone?' Tanino thought for a moment or two, then he realised that, no, she did not remind him of any woman he had ever seen, and perhaps that was what was driving him half crazy. 'You look like a nymph from the river Nile,' he told her, and she broke into peals of laughter. Then the girl replied, 'you said that in a very sad voice, are you sad?' Tanino looked at her again, her white skin, her long legs and her sharp canine teeth. Then behind him, up above, he saw his father and his uncle Armando waving their arms from the balcony of the restaurant.

'Come here tomorrow, at the same time, promise you'll come,' said Tanino, 'I'll come,' replied the girl, laughing, then she asked him his name. 'Tanino,' he said. 'Tanino,' the girl repeated, then she leaned forward again to give the comb back, turned round, and as lightly as before, she went away. 'What's your name?' Tanino yelled after her. He did not see her mouth move because she had her back to him, and it was as if the name had been spoken by the sky, or the sea, or destiny come to that. It was left to echo in the bay along with the waves and the gulls and Tanino stared at the comb in his hand, then he turned towards Ferdinando's restaurant and picked his way between the rocks to rejoin his family. In his head he had the girl with the bunched dark hair and the blue eyes. Her name was Milena.

Milena

There in that hothouse
was a flower,
a flower that outshone
all the other flowers.
It was not a rose,
nor a camellia,
it was an even more beautiful flower
blooming in its
full radiance.
That radiant flower
was called
Milena.
One day that flower
was no longer there
that hothouse
withered as if by magic,
because it lost its most beautiful flower
which by its presence
spread its radiance over everything

that surrounded it.
A monstrous hand
had snapped
Milena from her stem.
Now Milena flowers
in the celestial hothouse
of the most beautiful garden
of Paradise.

Meanwhile the monster who snapped
you from your stem
will be for all eternity
beyond hell.
He would contaminate
the others that are there.
Therefore he will pass on beyond,
while Milena
was, and you are and you will be
the most beautiful flower
whether on Earth
or in that very Paradise
where now you live.

Gaetano Orlando, 6th July 1971

Yesterday I went to see Enza and China at the apartment in via Roma. In summer, when I am in Marano, I go almost every day. Enza prepares coffee for us two in the big pot and makes China's in the small one, decaffeinated, otherwise she doesn't sleep. As soon as she hears the metallic clatter of the coffee machine she gets off her bed and comes into the kitchen. Enza makes these noises deliberately, looking at me then towards the corridor, waiting for her sister to appear in the doorway. After coffee she offered me a packet of cigarettes and we began to smoke with the french windows open. She told me she started smoking at thirteen. She says her father never smoked them more than halfway down, then threw them in the ashtray, and afterwards, when he had gone to bed, she and Elena used to pick out the half-smoked stubs and go and smoke them in the bathroom. Ada said nothing; she too stole cigarettes from Tanino because it seems he didn't want anyone in the family to take up the vice. I stuffed so much rubbish into my body in prison, he used to say, that it makes no difference if I smoke, but you, no, you must be strong, you must be healthy. In reality all Tanino's children were secret smokers, except China, in fact she did too once or twice, because Elena and Enza enjoyed getting her to do grown-up things, so they would put a cigarette in her mouth and she would suck on it and then cough, and then laugh. Enza says the only one who smoked in front of Tanino was Angelo, whose father was not around at home when he was growing up and by the time Tanino returned and they were living together he was already eighteen, an age at which parental authority has no force, even if you're the son of Jesus Christ. She explained that Tanino and his eldest child did not have much of a relationship, in fact they didn't have one at all. Angelo was jealous of his mother, they had lived as a pair up until then, mother and son, and Tanino had come back full of intentions the boy did not like. He could hear them making love every night and used to hide his head under the pillow and yell with his mouth closed, or he would take a Walkman of China's and plug it into his ear like his sister, and hum along to the songs regardless of what they were to mask the horrible sound of the springs of the matrimonial bed and the groans of his mother.

Before I left I went into the bedroom and switched on the CD player. It had a disc in it, of songs put together for China. She sat cross-legged on the mattress and waited for the music to begin. She hasn't been using Walkmans for years because she had the bad habit of throwing them on the floor when the tape ended, and until Tanino was back they used to replace them all the time, but now Enza keeps telling her they haven't got money to throw away and the CD player on the television set does the same job perfectly well. In the room are a double bed and a single bed, and in the years I lived here it was always Enza I saw using this latter one while the big one was occupied by China and Ada. Now, however, the single bed is empty and always neat and tidy and Enza has taken her mother's place in the double bed. From the TV I heard the first notes of *Aummo aummo* by Renzo Arbore.

This morning I called Bruno and he told me he was up at 'the farm'. I joined him there and we soaked up some sun on the old green plastic sunbeds that someone at work had given to Enza. I drank a warm Peroni and Bruno water from the tap, we sprinkled our hair under the pump in the vegetable patch and then he said he was hungry. In the pantry of the little house, there is always some pasta, because according to Bruno one should always keep a supply, and you can make a meal out of pasta using anything you can find. He made spaghetti *aglio e olio*, garlic and olive oil, and then from the sideboard took a little bag of *taralli sugna e pepe* left over from the last Sunday. *Taralli sugna e pepe* are little circles of baked dough flavoured with pork fat and pepper. They're *sereticci*, he said, and better like this. *Sereticcio* means 'stale' or 'past it' and usually suggests there is nothing to be done, but Bruno has always had this tendency to want to put a bold face on adverse situations, and so, as he says, better like this. He crumbled one on top of the pasta gleaming with oil and mixed it all together. We ate outside in the open, at the marble table, the pasta was delicious and under the canopy the air was cool. When he finishes, Bruno leans back in the plastic chair, rolls himself a joint and takes three long drags in silence. 'If she knew, mamma would kill me,' he says as he passes it to me.

In summer Bruno is always tanned. His hair is short and very dark and of all Tanino's children he is the one most like his father, at least from the photographs I have seen. Going by the photographs again, though, I had the impression that Bruno's hair was once very fair and so I asked him why it wasn't any more. He says he doesn't know, it was yellow coloured and then it turned black. He says it happened roughly at the same time as he gave up playing football, at eighteen, in 1990, when he broke his knee. Not that Tanino was glad about it, he explains, but football was not the path he had imagined for him. Bruno was about to qualify as a surveyor at a private college and in his last year had hardly been seen in the classroom, because he was training with La Casertana every afternoon. He had even been in danger of losing the whole year, because the day of the final oral exam for graduation coincided with an important match against Juve Stabia. Obviously he had gone off to play in the match, and Tanino had gone wild, like an animal, he says. When the results were posted on the college gates, it turned out that Bruno Orlando had failed to meet the criteria for graduation. Then, however, Tanino went to have a chat with the principal, and it seems that when he did he had a letter with him, handwritten by the then Minister for Education. It is not clear what happened, but the fact is that a week later the committee met again in one of the classrooms of the empty school, Bruno took the oral test, by himself, and received his higher diploma. After the exam, the chair of the committee approached him and said, 'I've never known this sort of thing happen before, but whose son are you?' Bruno's eyes are gleaming and half closed because of the joint, he is smiling, he puts his hands on the table, leans towards me, then continues. 'I'm the son of Jesus Christ,' he says.

Just at that moment the sun has climbed over the house and shone directly in Bruno's face. He raises his hand to his forehead like a visor to shield himself from the light, or perhaps it is a military salute to his father, I don't ask. His eyes grow even narrower and then he adds, laughing, 'And if the letter didn't work, Tanino 'e Bastimento always had the seven sixty-five.' I ask him what that was. 'The pistol,' he says, 'a Beretta, 7.65 calibre.' I don't reply and Bruno continues, 'I'm joking, your grandfather never pulled the pistol on anyone, but he always kept it to hand because he had voices in his head, like us.' Since he came out of prison in 1971, Tanino had never been without it, he had become paranoid. But, as far as I know, the last time he'd fired a shot had been sixteen years ago, in the July of '55. Bruno informs me, 'Bastimento was an absolute ace with a pistol, if he wanted to get you he got you, after prison there wasn't any shit like that any more, but before then he was infallible. In Naples everyone knew it, or at least the people who needed to know, knew.' It seems that Tanino 'e Bastimento's ability with the semi-automatic was known to Pascalone as well, and who knows whether that influenced what he did. Beyond familiarity with hunger and a ballistics skill out of the common run, I wonder whether this Pascalone knew that Tanino relied on a power that genuinely cannot be disputed: the conviction that destiny is on your side.

On the first of July 1955, a little after lunchtime, Tanino was lying on his father's bed, in the mayor's house in via Ranucci, a few steps from Marano's town hall. While Ada was easing the last bandage from his head, Tanino made his decision that this was not the right time to start a family. The car accident on the road to Rome had changed a number of things, and notwithstanding the foggy vision and the constant migraines of the last two weeks, Tanino could now see things clearly for what they were. There were business deals to conclude, hospitals and other establishments to supply and friendships to be strengthened and an appropriate kind of wedding would have consumed too much time and energy. Also because Tanino 'e Bastimento's wedding ceremony couldn't be anything but the properly stylish affair these things needed to be, and the season for such things was already half way through. To get married in autumn or winter was unthinkable and then there would have been too many people to invite at short notice, and if, by way of example, Pascalone had summoned more than five hundred people to share the occasion, then surely Tanino and Ada deserved at least as many guests. So Tanino arrived at the natural conclusion that Angelo should not come into the world just yet. Ada was in tears, she shouted and slapped her own face. 'Don't yell like that,' Tanino said to her, keeping his voice low, 'you're making my head hurt, don't you understand, you're making my head hurt?' And Ada shouted even more loudly and retorted, 'My son, don't touch my son, so help me God I'll kill myself, Tanì, I'll kill you first and then I'll kill myself.'

When they heard a knock at the front door, Ada dried her eyes on a clean part of the gauze she had just been unwinding from Tanino's head and rose to go and see who it was. 'You're not taking my child away from me,' she said before disappearing into the corridor and returning a few seconds later behind Russo, who was still ostentatiously limping and supporting himself on a metal crutch. The man removed his hat in greeting and Tanino invited him to sit in the armchair beside the bed. 'What kind of expression is that on your face?' Tanino asked. 'Have you two made a pact?' Russo looked at

Ada and furrowed his brow, then he switched his gaze back to Tanino. Ada got up and said, 'I'll make coffee,' then vanished again into the corridor, sniffling.

'What's up, Ru'?' said Tanino, leaning forward on the bed.

Russo replied, 'I'll tell you Tanì, I'll tell you, only you must stay calm and not get up, because you're still recovering and you don't want to risk making it worse.'

Tanino said nothing and looked at Russo in a different sort of way, a way peculiar to Tanino 'e Bastimento, the sort of look that says everything without need of words. It is a stare which allows no reply, a stare hard to withstand and even harder to summon up, but Tanino was tired, he had heard and spoken too many futile words and now he had no time to waste.

So Russo reached in his shirt pocket and pulled out a postcard, on the card were Vesuvius and the sunshine and the sea, Tanino laughed and said: 'So, Ru', you've been on holiday and you didn't tell me.' Russo did not smile, and turned the postcard over, he said it had come from Poggioreale. It was a message from Tanino's uncle, Antonio 'o Mastrone, brother of Angelo and one of the pillars of the family, and also a frequent guest of the state penitentiaries. On the other side of the postcard was written in biro:

> Dear Carlo Gaetano,
>
> I hope these few lines find you well. I heard you'd had that accident but that you're recovering. I never doubted it because we Mastroni have tough hides and nothing scares us. I'm fine too, don't worry about me, except that unfortunately someone did something very

bad and dishonourable the other day. We were talking quite amicably, me and another prisoner, known to you as well, then there was a misunderstanding on his part and he raised his voice and so did I, because there were so many people standing watching. This fellow came up to me and even though he's a very, very big man, I am an Orlando and I was not intimidated. He said some ill-educated words and I answered back in the same tone and he gave me a slap, he slapped my face in front of everyone there. The worst of it is, I'm very unhappy with this situation, because this prisoner has now finished his sentence and I have no way of clearing the matter up. I hope that you can. Misunderstandings are bad things and we Mastroni don't like them. But I am sure that he will listen to you because you are a respected young man. Don't worry about me, get well soon, I send you my affection and an embrace and we'll see each other soon.

Your uncle,
Antonio Orlando

Tanino's hands shook. His uncle Antonio's signature danced before his eyes and he didn't know if it was his head or if the whole world had begun shaking as well. 'You've understood who he's talking about,' said Russo in a low voice, half as a question, half a statement. Tanino handed back the postcard, summoned his forces, which were suddenly all returning, and lowered his feet to the floor. He got up from the bed and unbuttoned his nightshirt. Ada entered the room carrying a tray with two steaming cups on it. 'You should be resting,' she told him, 'get back into bed.' Tanino took a step towards her, stroked her skin with his fingers then picked up one of the boiling cups in his bare hand, without using the handle. Ada told him, 'Wait, it's too hot,' and while she was saying it Tanino had already swallowed the coffee. Then he asked her, 'Please, go and fetch my clothes.' The girl said, 'But you have to rest, the doctor said you have to rest, Tanì don't do anything rash, I beg you.'

'Ada,' said Tanino, just, 'Ada.' She put the tray down sharply on the bedside table and the other cup tipped over and spread everywhere. 'Do as you please and don't mess up, then when you're back we'll talk about this properly.' She ran her hand over her stomach and disappeared once more into the corridor, and her rich red hair scorched the air like a flame. Now Tanino wasn't thinking about babies any more, there was time to make one and to make Adelaide see that this was the right choice. Now the priorities were the members of the family already living, the honour of his uncle to redeem at any cost and the name of the Mastroni to defend, a slap in the face, it was unthinkable, a slap, laying hands on someone in that manner, a gesture intended to dishonour one's adversary, to demonstrate one's superiority. Tanino respected people who, like him, harboured no grudges against anyone, but not at the expense of someone of his own blood. A slap in the face, his thoughts continued, the face of uncle Antonio, you don't let that pass unanswered, this shit of a man, I'll teach him to behave with due respect.

From the corridor, without coming in again, Ada tossed Tanino's clothes into the bedroom and they landed on the floor. He picked up his trousers and pulled them on, then slid the belt through the hoops. Russo rose from the armchair and Tanino realised his friend was still there. 'I've been finding things out, Tanì, they're letting him out from Poggioreale next week, there's no point in all this effort now.'

Tanino drew air into his lungs and then sat on the bed again. He saw the coffee dribbling over the side of the tray, running down the bedside table and pooling on the floor, the cup lying on its side in a dark puddle, then he felt the coffee he'd drunk still burning in his throat and stomach.

'Take me to the sea,' he said, 'I badly need to go for a swim.'

I've been down to the sea with Biagio and Gennaro. I don't go often, but up in Marano I'm dying of heat and every time they go they call and ask me. They came to fetch me in Gennaro's Panda at ten in the morning and before I went off mamma said make sure you put some protection on and don't spend money on useless things. I've always slapped on factor fifty because of my fair skin and also because part of my father's genetic inheritance includes a predisposition to melanoma. One of my uncles died from it. On top of that, I was born with an elliptical shaped stain in the middle of my back, halfway between a birthmark and a gigantic mole. It makes, at least according to my mother and the dermatologists we consulted over the years, a bright red target for the rays of the sun and for anyone walking behind. For that reason I don't usually go down to the sea, but this time, yes. We were caught in traffic for nearly an hour and a half and then we arrived at Miseno, which isn't very close but at least if you catch a good day the sea is clean. We went down to the empty beach, we laid out our beach mats next to each other and Gennaro got out the music box. I asked for a hand to rub some suncream on my back and Gennaro said, 'Bro' you are my life but you know that touching that thing gives me the creeps,' so Biagio spread it on for me. We went for a swim and I swam under the water because then I hear everything muffled and see things more slowly and clearly and I like the sensation. While I was in the water I thought about Tanino and the nymph of the Nile and I realised that these things never happened to me, and that if a similar encounter had occurred I would never have managed to make anything out of it and that some people are magnets for chance encounters and I am decidedly not, perhaps because there is hardly anyone here left to encounter. We stayed in the sea for a while, crouching with the water up to our necks, Gennaro said, 'What I fancy is a screw,' and Biagio replied, 'What I'd like is a million Euros.' We came out again and I lay on the beach mat, they passed me a joint and I smoked and we relaxed in the heat of the sun. We repeated the same routine two or three times and then decided to go back. On the way home Gennaro said he fancied a pizza, Biagio responded he didn't like going into pizza houses in his flip-flops and so I suggested getting the pizzas and going up to the farm, because when I'm home in Marano I always have the keys on me. So that's what we did. We also took a few beers and I opened the iron gate as the sun was setting over the city. We sat round the marble table and ate the pizza, it was nice and cool. Gennaro noticed that the grass at the farm is higher than usual, in a few places it now comes up to your knees and it's not well looked after. I told him what they had told me, that the farmer hasn't been round for a while, Biagio asked me if I was with anyone now, in Turin, and I smiled at him and I answered no, he said good for you, just thinking and partying. Gennaro nodded vigorously in affirmation while biting into a huge slice of pizza which left oil dripping from the corners of his mouth. When I finished mine I drank the last drop of beer and settled in the swing chair to look up at the sky, which was starless. Then Biagio suddenly proposed looking inside the old ruin that stands on the farm's land to see what was there, because we had been coming here for ten years but we'd never gone in. Mamma didn't want us to and even Bruno has never encouraged me to do so, they say it's in danger of collapsing, that its stone structure is *fràceto*. *Fràceto* means something like 'wet through', 'eroded by time and by the ingress of water'. Usually that is not a good thing. They have always said there's nothing inside of any value, it's not worth the risk, at the most you might find adders and rats. But I was pretty pissed off with all that as well and so I said all right.

The ruin is a two-storey barn and it is covered in a tangled mass of climbers and branches which makes even approaching it difficult. There is an underground entrance which you access through a sort of grotto lower down the sloping land of the farm, but it seems as if that route is more dangerous. So we decided to get in by the main entrance, which stands not far away from the little house and seems easier to get at. We lit the torches on our phones and plunged into the jungle. Biagio led our little group. We bent our heads to pass under the scratchy branches of the trees and we skirted a clump of bushes that came almost up to the walls of the ruin. We flattened ourselves against the wall and edged towards the entrance, because the gap between the level ground and the building is uneven and seems even more so as you approach the door. The entrance is a small archway—with no door—which is completely invisible from the other side of the screen of foliage. We went inside and I felt a little anxious because disobeying makes me feel guilty, even now I'm grown up and I know there's no real danger. We stopped on the threshold and shone our torches inside, the barn was vast and empty, with no rooms, no floors, no doors or stairs. High up, at the level where an upper floor should be, there's a timber framework of sorts, half ruined, but no cement or tiles. Then I pointed the torch downwards and found myself confronted with an unusual spectacle: the whole floor of the barn was covered with stones fallen from above and which looked to all intents like books. Books everywhere, maybe hundreds of them, scattered on the bare earth. I looked closer and the dimensions and colours of the books were all identical, the same book, hundreds of copies of the same thing, chucked in this ruined barn, but why? I squatted down and picked up a copy that seemed less dirty and *fràcete*. I stood there for a moment staring at the cover before realising that these books were the same as the ones in the boxroom in the apartment at via Edificio Scolastico, the boxroom I used to hide from Lello in, and I recognised this book by its title, by the black and white photo of the thirty-year-old and by my grandfather's name just above. *Anelito tra le sbarre*, I read again, *A Look of Longing Through the Bars*. 'What the hell does *Anelito* mean?' Gennaro asked. Now even I know that, I thought. '*Anelito*,' I replied, 'means sort of "desire", "craving for something", but also "panting for breath" or "your dying breath", so in other words something you want very badly because it's fundamental, something bound up with life.'

'Bound up with shit,' Biagio retorted, and we started to

laugh. I hastily leafed through the book, I half caught names and events and things, and I wanted to read it.

'But this book is by your grandfather,' said Gennaro as he too picked up a copy from the ground, 'I'd heard he'd written one, he wrote it after he killed that bloke, right?'

THE FIRST DUEL

Very early on the morning of 16th July 1955, Carlo Gaetano Orlando rose from his bed in via Ranucci. He hadn't slept all night, or hardly, but the moment his feet touched the ground he felt filled with a strange energy, and took his first steps of the day with no feeling of tiredness, as if driven by an invisible force in a clearly defined direction. His head did not hurt, nor his eyes, for the first time since the accident. He went into the kitchen and started to make himself some coffee with his mother's Neapolitan-style coffee maker, which she had always preferred to the moka pot. Once he had drunk a small cup he went to the telephone and lifted the receiver. He opened the leather-bound address book where his father kept all the numbers and dialled one. The person who answered was a woman: her name was Giovanna Sica and she worked as an obstetrician. Giovanna berated Tanino for the earliness of the hour, it was seven o'clock and at seven many people were still sleeping, but that morning Tanino 'e Bastimento didn't give a damn about other people's timetables. What he wanted instead was to have a precise schedule and to confirm when they would be meeting. They made an appointment for her house, at 12.30. Tanino ended the phone conversation by saying, 'I'll call Ada and tell her, half past at your place, or even a little earlier.' Giovanna Sica let a few seconds pass and then asked, 'but are you both sure, Tanì? You realise there's no going back, maybe the two of you want to think about it a little longer, no?'

Tanino hung up without answering. He leafed through a few pages of the address book and dialled another number. After it rang a few times it was picked up at the other end by Russo, whose voice suggested he had only just woken up, and he kept clearing his throat every two seconds and sounding like a simpleton. Tanino made arrangements to meet his companion at eleven, at the railway station, and repeated several times 'eleven' and 'station' because Russo was barely awake and seemed unable to grasp anything. 'This is just a scare,' said Russo, 'a scare and then we're off, Tanì, an arm or the legs, nothing more, that's what you promised.' 'That's what I promised,' Tanino replied, then hung up. He drank another cup of coffee and then dialled Ada's home number, without needing to check in the address book. Tanino was expecting to be told to go to hell for the third time that morning, by Ada's father or mother, instead it was Ada herself who answered after just a few seconds. He recognised the scratchy tone in her voice and was surprised to find she was already up and about, like him, and from the short time it took her to answer he realised that she had been waiting for this very call. 'I've contacted Giovanna,' he told her, 'she's expecting you at midday.' 'And isn't she expecting you?' she asked. 'Are you sending me alone?' Tanino replied that they would meet there, at Sica's place in via dei Tribulani.

He said, 'I've got an errand to do at the market, I'm with Russo, don't worry, we'll see each other there, kiss.' This time it was Ada who made no reply, she hung up after a short sigh, and Tanino couldn't know, but he felt certain she would have slammed the receiver down, would have wanted to shout wretch, you shit, I'm not going, but her parents and her sisters were asleep and no one yet knew that Ada was pregnant, and they wouldn't ever have known, no one would ever have known and her son would have forgiven her, he would be born at a later date, when the time was right, when the waters were calmer; of this Tanino was convinced. He drank a last coffee then went to take a shower. He washed carefully and returned to his bedroom, opened the wardrobe and took out the clothes he meant to wear and on one of the doors there was a mirror almost as tall as himself. He pulled on his beige-coloured lightweight cotton trousers. He put on and buttoned the white shirt with care, right to the top, and then tied his tie. Tanino held in faint contempt men who didn't wear ties because of the heat, because decorum, doing things the right way, doesn't recognise heat, and if you're going to be a man you must be one at all times. He slipped on the jacket, the same colour as the trousers, and then the wristwatch, in gold. He sat on the bed and put on his shoes, brown Oxfords, then he opened the bottom drawer of the bedside table, and under the white cotton vests, there was the semi-automatic. He lifted the 7.65 out and felt its weight in his hands, then with a swift and elegant movement spun it and slid it into his waistband, over his left hip. He rose from the bed and before going out passed the door of his father's bedroom, which was ajar, with its occupant asleep inside. Tanino looked at Angelo and then made his way to the outside door. Before leaving, he slid on his near-black Carrera sunglasses, ran a palm over his hair and kissed the small golden cross he wore at his neck, hidden underneath his shirt.

Tanino got off the tram at the Arenaccia stop, lit a cigarette and then walked to the station as the July sun rose ever higher and stronger. He saw Russo sitting on a bench, hat on his head and his hand resting on a wooden cane he had taken to using since the accident. The two men greeted each other and set off towards Vasto, the site of the fruit and vegetable market and the place where the traders of the region met every week. Everyone in the market knew the Mastroni and had learnt to recognise Tanino 'e Bastimento, who was clearly a Mastrone as well but also something distinct. He was twenty-five years old and was treated as if he were double that, for his shrewdness and his experience. Tanino made his rounds, deliberately ignoring the central area of the market, where certain characters were in the habit of meeting late in the morning. Before a fruit stall, a man named Corvino bowed his head in greeting, passed on his respects to the Orlando family and held out an apple to Tanino, saying as he handed it to him, 'You've got to try this, sweet as honey, tell me if it is or isn't.' Tanino bit into the apple and tasted the juice and sugars. 'That's special,' he said, and then walked on. He checked his watch and it was five to twelve. He said to Russo, 'We're going in a moment, because I've got to meet Ada in via dei Tribulani.' Russo looked down and sighed, because he didn't agree with Tanino but after all he hardly ever did, and yet he had understood that the situation, one way or another, justified Tanino to a degree, and he therefore decided not to protest. The two men peeled off into Corso Novara, which was the market's main artery, and Russo had to work hard to keep up with his companion, who was striding rapidly towards his goal. They came to the intersection with via Firenze, at the centre of Vasto, and Tanino took a moment to look round for him. The figure of Pasquale, known as 'Pascalone 'e Nola', was there in the middle of the crowd, towering a good ten centimetres above anyone else standing round him. Tanino felt his heart begin to race; he felt the adrenaline released by his nervous system course through his body, to every part of it. Then he drew in his breath, thrust his chest out and his shoulders back, as his mother had taught him. Russo was at his heels, two paces behind, gripping the head of his stick tightly, gripping it with all his energy, his lips compressed in a tight line. Pascalone was eating an orange, he had thick black hair and a pair of sideburns in the same dark and bushy style. He was leaning against a stall selling vegetables and salad and chatting with the man standing behind it. Tanino stopped at the stall and without looking at Pascalone said to the stallholder, 'You've got some good stuff here, my compliments. On the other hand,' he added, 'your clientèle's rather more fit for the sewer.' The man thanked him and glanced at Pascalone and then Tanino and then Pascalone again. Tanino checked his watch and it was exactly midday, he raised his head and the sky confirmed it, because the sun was at its highest point, halfway between the Mastrone of Marano and the giant of Palma Campania.

The man turned to Tanino and Russo, looked them up and down and said, 'The two of you put together make half a man, a lame one and a dwarf,' then laughed loudly and nobody laughed with him, except the owner of the stall, who nodded a nervous smile and then began to rearrange his cherries. Tanino said to his companion, 'Let's move away from here, it's getting hot.' Then he walked past Pascalone without looking into his face, brushing against his arm, and when he had gone by the tall man turned round and said, 'What's all this, doesn't Pascalone even get a hello?' Tanino halted, his back to the other man, he smiled and understood that this was the way the thing had to go, that the moment had arrived and that he would finally expunge that slap to his uncle's face, the slap in the face to his family and the name they bore, there should be no mark left, not now nor forever afterwards.

So the thing was decided. Tanino turned round to face the other man, looked him up and down with a look of total contempt and replied, 'Why, would you be Pascalone then?' Pascalone opened his eyes wide, his face twitched and he moved his hand immediately towards his belt, under the jacket, grasped the pistol and Tanino took a step back, shoved Russo aside, making him lose his balance, brought his right hand to his left hip and in a flash whipped out the Beretta and the sun glinted on the dark steel while Pascalone was still going for his own; then Tanino slipped the safety catch and took aim, with all the calmness in the world, a world that had come to a standstill, that had stopped and Tanino saw everything clearly, and it was the easiest thing in the world, from that close it was really too simple for an expert like him, indeed the shot went off and the shot went where it was meant to go and that is straight at the wrist of the hand that was holding the pistol, and that hand, by the natural law of things, opened. The pistol fell to the ground and moments later Pascalone fell too and the world began to turn again and Tanino couldn't understand what the hell had happened. The man was sitting on the ground and pressing his hand to his abdomen and Tanino said to himself no, Jesus, please, no don't do this to me. Pascalone's white shirt was beginning to be tinged with red where he was pressing his hand. The bullet had gone straight through his wrist and lodged in his abdomen. The giant kicked out at his own pistol and sent it spinning under the fruit stall. Russo grabbed Tanino's arm and shook it, Tanino was standing there motionless, rooted to the spot with his mouth open and his head who knows where. 'We need to get out of here,' said Russo, 'we need to go now, for God's sake what a disaster.' People were beginning to come running, they were swarming round the fallen giant, and someone was looking at Tanino and muttering something. Russo moved in front of Tanino and slapped him twice on the cheeks. 'We need to go, Tanì, wake up.' Only then did Tanino 'e Bastimento come to himself and start breathing again, he looked at his adversary one last time and he and Russo marched briskly away from Vasto and merged with the hundreds of people bustling about and arguing over fruit and vegetables under the limpid midday sun.

At 13.00, Tanino arrived at via dei Tribulani, outside the apartment of the obstetrician Sica. He told Russo to go home, to phone the other members of the family and explain what had happened. He added that he'd be in touch soon, and that he didn't know if he'd be coming home that evening.

He opened the door to the entrance lobby and climbed the two flights of narrow stairs and realised he had not stopped for a second since the moment of the shooting. So he lit a cigarette on the landing and took three long drags, one after the other, and then dropped the rest of the hardly burnt cigarette down the stairwell. He knocked on Giovanna Sica's door and after a short pause she opened it. 'You're late,' she said, and then she saw Tanino's white face and her eyes withdrew the accusation. 'I thought you'd changed your mind,' said Ada when she saw him. 'Come with me,' Tanino said, 'I have to talk to you,' and they went into the sitting room and Giovanna disappeared. 'I'm in trouble,' he told her, and then he explained what had just happened. 'Now I have to get away for a while, we need to find out what's happened to him.' Ada gave a cry of alarm, called out invocations to the Madonna and baby Jesus and Sant'Anna and then she hugged Tanino. 'It'll be all right, you'll see to it,' she said, and stroked his cheek, 'there's nothing that can't be sorted out.' Tanino said he had a phone call to make and then he had to get away at once. He found *signora* Sica in the kitchen, sitting at the table by herself, and said, 'Your services are not needed for now,' then asked where the telephone was. He dialled the number for uncle Armando, brother of uncle Antonio. 'I've had a run-in with Pascalone,' he said, 'and it's serious, uncle Arma'. I have to go now, I can't wander round Naples like this, we'll see each other in Marano, and after that it'll be in the hands of Almighty God.'

Before going, he said to Ada that they couldn't leave together, that it was dangerous, that he'd sent for someone to pick her up, and then he kissed her. When Tanino was on the stairs, she appeared above him in the doorway of the flat. 'I told you you'd never take my child away from me,' she said.

No one remembers much about the next few days. Tanino disappeared and wasn't seen for a week. After the shooting it seems that Pascalone made it back to his car on his own two feet, supported by a couple of his companions, before the carabinieri arrived. Obviously nobody had seen anything, and the police returned to their barracks to wait for further news. He was taken to the Incurabili hospital, where, by an ironical coincidence, he was operated on by a doctor called Tufano, a newly qualified surgeon. The ironical coincidence lay not so much in the fact that in mid-July the senior surgeons were all on holiday, or in the fact that Pascalone's wound was easily curable. It lay in the fact that doctor Tufano, who also came from Palma Campania, was the son of a man who in turn was the son of another man who, it is said, was killed years before by the giant he was due to operate on. The surgical intervention was completed without any particular problems, but as for the stitching of the wound afterwards, the easiest part, it was not done properly. Pasquale died alone, in the night of 17th to 18th July, from a haemorrhage.

His wife Assunta was left a widow after just a few months of marriage, she too with a child in her belly, a baby who would be born a few months later. There was talk of premeditated murder, of the *camorra*, of the monopoly over the market and many other things. The one thing that was clear to everyone was that the person who killed Pascalone was Carlo Gaetano Orlando, known as 'Tanino 'e Bastimento'. Tanino would have to face a major trial, a trial with wide media impact. Whatever the case, he thought, he'd come out of it with broken bones. In many versions people had already started to call him a hired assassin, and this was the thing that annoyed him most of all. He felt he could bear all manner of accusations, but not that of having taken someone's life at the behest of a third party, whoever that third party might be. Tanino did it on his own account, and this had to be made clear to everybody. He gave himself up to the forces of order on the 25th of July, ten days after having disappeared from the world, and found himself back in prison waiting for judgement to be passed, waiting on destiny, waiting for a child.

This is the known story. The moment at which Tanino decided he would outlive his own century is the moment of the duel in Corso Novara. His children's memories are welded to that moment, which they never witnessed, the shot that opened the way to a series of events that have led, in the end, to the present we are in now, the only possible one, a present I too am wading through. And so I too am to be found in that shot, in that pierced wrist. Maybe that is the motive that has urged me to come back, to trace the outlines of who I am. Because who I am I still do not know, I cannot grasp it. I used to think I could be anything at all, except not Tanino's grandson, and yet I have found myself siding with him. I have realised that this legend makes even me proud, someone who never knew you and who, in all honesty, until now never wanted to. Your honour, your name, your creed, all things that I have always rejected, I considered them superfluous, I considered you superfluous. Because ever since I have been able to listen, your name leaps out, your deeds are repeated over and over until I am sick of them. I used to ask myself the reason for this and my answer was that it was the only thing to do, because that is the only thing left of you. I was wrong. Your name is far more than mere memories. I realise that you are everywhere on the streets I walk, in the scorching summer that is upon us, in every footstep I take and in those of the people who taught me to take them. I find myself smiling, because I have realised that in your past I am looking for something that belongs to me, something I have not yet found. We are bound together by something more than simple genetics, this is what I believe, and if you don't agree it is of little importance, because this is my version, and for the first time I intend to follow it to the end, to go beyond the legend, beyond Corso Novara and that pierced wrist. I must delve deeper.

In the Silence

At evening's fall
in the world of
the buried alive
silence descends.

So silent a silence
it seems almost sepulchral
and in these silences
one meditates all the more.
And things are thought:
there are those among us who think
of the grief enfolding us
of the harm we have done
to others and to ourselves
by making errors.

Who think of the children
and the woman we love
think of the elderly parents
we have left in anguish.

And in the silence of evening
I think always of the years
of my youth
destroyed
years that will not return
and each time I ask myself
Why?

I am constantly waiting for an answer
and sometimes in the silence
I seem to receive it.
And I hear like a distant echo
answering me:
it was destiny.

Gaetano Orlando, 4th January 1970

On the 7th of September 1951, shortly after noon, Tanino made his way to Marano cemetery to greet his mother and receive her blessing for his newfound liberty. Only a day before he had been in one of the grey waiting rooms at Benevento prison, waiting for his father to come and collect him and put an end to those terrible two years, the first he had spent in the state penitentiaries. The mayor had taken him down to the sea, at Mergellina, to eat fresh fish, to clean his mouth of the dark and the dust. In the green meadow, he knelt before Elena's gravestone and no tear fell from behind those nearly black Carrera sunglasses. He had shed them all during the nights shared with his fellow inmates, now he was determined to leave the unhappy past behind him, and the youth of his twenty-one years stretched out before him. However much life had already submitted him to the severest of tests, Tanino was confident in the future and in himself, sufficiently so to leave the cemetery with his head held high, and was even able to direct a smile towards his mother's marble slab. Russo was waiting for him outside, leaning against the car door. He was chatting with the cemetery manager, about light and gas and other bothersome things which in a cemetery affect only the living. When he saw the young man, Russo gave the manager a hasty smile and sat in the car. Before following his companion, Tanino saw to the left of the forecourt the florist's barrow. He went over to it and the florist took two steps back, as if to show his wares, then said to Tanino, 'The dead deserve our respect, our consideration, and these flowers are exceptionally fresh, they last for ages and they don't lose their scent, and that's God's truth,' he said looking up towards the Creator for an instant. Tanino stood thinking for a moment, then asked for a bunch of red roses. The florist wrinkled his brow, for no one presents roses to the dead, Tanino guessed what he was thinking and said, 'They're not for a dead person, they're for a woman.' The florist granted the unusual request and collected a score of blood-red roses, wrapped their stems in glossy paper and handed them to Tanino, who dropped a handful of money on the barrow and turned towards the car without bothering about the change. He climbed into the passenger seat and placed the bouquet on his lap. 'If we leave now, maybe you'll be able to get something to eat,' Russo said, and started off. The car joined the road that goes in the opposite direction from Marano, towards the centre of Naples. 'What's the girl's name?' Russo asked, 'Marianna?' 'Milena,' Tanino said, 'she's called Milena and she's as beautiful as they come.' He had met her the previous day, on the rocks at Mergellina, during the lunch organised by his father to celebrate the end of his sentence. They had made an arrangement for the next day, at the same place and time, Tanino had thought about it all night and had been counting the hours that separated him from their next meeting. Now there were only a few kilometres of road keeping them apart, he experienced a certain restlessness that made the air effervescent, he had not enjoyed the warmth of another body for two years and only he knew how much the question had tormented him. The car drove on without any hold-ups and in a few minutes they were already on the main road to Chiaiano, which led to Capodimonte and then to Colli Aminei, Corso Amedeo di Savoia and down eventually to piazza Dante. As Tanino was looking to his right, with his head out of the window, to try to spot Milena's body, Russo slowed down and stopped the car, because a gaggle of youngsters began to wander across the road in front of them, all heading in the same direction. The crowd was straggling out from beneath a tall wooden door on their left, the door of the Chiaiano teacher training school. Russo sounded the horn, stuck his head out and shouted at the unheeding youngsters, 'What's all this? Come on, get a move on.' In sole response, one of them held up his middle finger, causing his little friends to laugh and Russo made as if to reach for the door handle before he was stopped by Tanino who glared at him without saying anything. But while he was looking at him, Tanino saw, framed in the window, a small group of young people still hanging round outside the building, and in the middle of the group a flash of something flame-coloured. This is the way some things happen, you suddenly find yourself on an unexpected course, something inside you is triggered and in an instant you are aware of everything that is about to happen. The past, the present and the future coalesce in a single instant, uncertainty no longer exists, all that exists is that patch of red, that flash of flame you have to get to at any cost, there's nothing else you can do, you do it. 'Everything okay?' asked Russo, Tanino replied, 'Everything's okay,' and then, 'Pull in for a moment, there's something I have to do.' The car went backwards and then to the left towards the pavement, off the main carriageway. Tanino got out of the car and Russo shouted, 'Where the fuck are you going, uh, Jesus,' then he clapped his hands over his mouth. Tanino shut the door, strode across the forecourt outside the institute and reached the group of young people standing in a circle and talking. The flash of red had come from this group and it turned out to be nothing more than the fiery hair of one of the girls: simple skirt and pullover, a leather rucksack slung over the right shoulder, hands not very well cared for and eyes of an absolute blue, not toned down, not nuanced, a perfect contrast against the colour of the hair: a fire at sea. The little group fell silent when it was clear that Tanino was coming straight towards them, there were a few strange looks, a couple of muffled laughs, but Tanino 'e Bastimento paid no attention to any such distractions, he had his eyes on the girl and in Chiaiano and in the world and in the entire universe, she was the only thing that existed. 'What's your name?' he said, and a boy coming up behind him said loudly, 'Here we go, the registry office has turned up.' There were a few laughs, stifled almost instantly by the expression on the face of Tanino, who turned on the youth a single rapid glance of indifference, but intensely serious nonetheless, before turning back to scrutinise more closely the face with the blue eyes. 'I'm Ada,' the girl eventually replied, 'Adelaide.' 'Adelaide,' Tanino repeated, savouring the sound of every syllable rolling between tongue and palate. He asked if she was from Chiaiano and she answered yes, he said, 'I can escort you home,' and the jokey youth replied, 'There's no need, we're all going the same way.' Tanino again turned on him a fleeting glance, like someone who doesn't know the language and thinks that trying to translate it isn't worth the bother. After a few moments of uncertain silence the girl said yes, Tanino offered her his arm and she took it, linking it in the crook of her elbow. The two of them began to walk towards the street and the rest of the group stood where it was. Russo leaned out of the window and sounded the horn again, because he saw his companion was going off in a different direction. Tanino said to the girl, 'Wait for me here, I'll be back in a second,' then he went over to the car and bent down at the window. 'Are we going or not?' Russo asked, and Tanino said, 'You go, go back to Marano, don't say anything, I'll explain later.' 'What does that mean, I'll explain later, you're not well, there's that girl waiting for you in her swimming costume on the rocks and you're playing some foolish game with the little girls.' Tanino held his palm out towards his friend and looked down at the bunch of flowers, the other sat there with a look of disbelief, ran a hand through his hair then gathered up the roses, thrust them in his friend's hand and without even glancing at him, started the engine, shook his head once or twice, executed a U-turn in the middle of the road and headed back towards Marano. When she saw him approaching with the bunch of flowers, Ada said, 'That's what I call express delivery, but what about you, who are you?' 'A man like everyone else,' Tanino replied, and offered her the bunch of roses. The girl took it between her hands and lowered her nose into its petals, shutting her eyes, and asked, 'But are these for me, had you already seen me before somewhere?' Tanino said, 'Yes, they're for you,' linked arms with her again and said, 'Show me the street where you live.' The two walked along like a couple, arm in arm, while families were sitting down to eat lunch, the moment when everyone stopped to rest and then carry on, stomachs filled, towards the evening. Tanino did not often visit Chiaiano, and it was a rare thing for him not to be familiar with the street he was on, but his inner self sensed no danger, only a powerful curiosity to go on further.

'Ada, how old are you?'

'Sixteen, you?'

'Twenty-one.'

'That's a lot.'

'Just right. Will you come out with me one of these days?'

'I don't know if I can. I have to ask mamma and papà.'

'You can see I'm a nice boy.'

'I have to ask.'

'If you have to ask it means you're not really interested.'

'I'm interested, but there's no way I can go out with someone I don't know and who says he's twenty-one.'

'You'll have enough time to get to know me.'

'That's not enough for my parents.'

'I'm a nice boy.'

'You've already said, you're repeating yourself.'

'Have I also already said you're extremely beautiful?'

'Don't be silly.'

'You are. Don't you believe me?'

'I believe you.'

'And am I handsome, in your opinion?'

'You're unusual, it's hard to tell. Wait though, take off the sunglasses.'

'What do you think?'

'You've got dark, dark eyes.'

'And you've got blue ones.'

'I know, but yours are nice as well. You look good without the glasses.'

'Thank you, but I don't see too well without them. The sun bothers me.'

'But everyone likes the sun.'

'What can you do? There's lots about me to find out.'

'Look, we've arrived, this is where I live.'

'Got it, I'll come and pick you up tomorrow morning.'

'But I've got school tomorrow morning.'

'I've already done school, I'll teach you.'

'Even maths?'

'Even maths.'

'Are you going to tell me your name?'

'Gaetano, but everyone calls me Tanino. Tanino 'e Bastimento.'

'Bastimento? That's a strange name.'

'It's an extra name. It refers to a little goat that used to live out in the country, at Marano.'

'You don't say, it sounds like a good story.'

'I'll tell you all about it tomorrow. It's a good story all right. Pretty good.'

Buried now in the cemetery at Marano are Tanino 'e Bastimento and two of his children. He didn't witness any of their deaths himself, Ada included. I went with her there just once, fifteen years ago, when I was seven, or just about eight. Mamma worked on Saturday mornings and I stayed with grandma, and sometimes Enza was there and sometimes not. Lello had died a year ago and Ada still wept for him every day and at first she went up to the cemetery as often as she could, even if she was tired and her back was bent and she had swollen legs that hurt all the time. The cemetery was a beautiful place, always fresh and sunny and scented with flowers, and it was quiet there, which it never was in the apartment in via Roma. That morning everything was fine, and when we arrived at Lello's grave, grandma's tears began to flow. I was used to it and lowered my eyes when it happened, because the suffering of people I love has always made me feel uncomfortable, and I have never been able to face it. 'Say hello to uncle Lello,' grandma said, and I said, '*Ciao* uncle Lello,' to the circular photograph of him, big and round and smiling, straddling his grey motorcycle in the middle of via Nova. Under the photo was written RAFFAELE ORLANDO and under that his dates: 1973-2005. The tomb was white marble and on it were loads of assorted flowers and letters and bracelets and dolls and soft toys in the form of teddy bears: uncle Lello's nickname in Marano was Orso, because he resembled a bear. Grandma told me that he and Tanino didn't get on, that Tanino teased his son because he was fat and he wanted to be a painter when he grew up. Ada always defended him, she sometimes shouted in Tanino's face and she was the only person who could do so. Except for his father, Lello was respected by everyone in Marano and perhaps among all Tanino 'e Bastimento's children he was the best known, because as a boy, with Bruno, they fought everyone and he never lost. He defended his elder brother and his sisters on several occasions, it seems he even took on six or seven people at once, all by himself, and he always returned home on his own two legs. When Enza went into Year Four she was picked on by a gang of fourteen-year-old kids, she was fat too and they told her so, they teased her and then they started pushing her about and jostling her outside school. Tanino was hardly ever at home in the mornings and he had never seen them from the balcony of the apartment in via Edificio Scolastico. One day the kids had put a bag over her head and began to push her around and laugh in loud voices. They were seen from the balcony by Lello, who went to the middle school and had stayed at home that morning because he had a temperature. He was out of the flat in an instant, crossed the street and outside the front door of the school he set upon all three of the kids, kicking out, they were older than him but not as tall, not as strong and not as angry. 'My children have always protected each other,' grandma said, 'but Lello wouldn't let anything go, my son, my soul.'

After she had changed the oldest flowers and the water in the vases, we walked along the boundary wall enclosing that wing of the cemetery until we came to a set of gravestones embedded vertically in the wall. At a certain point we stopped and Ada pointed to a spot in the top row. It was Tanino's stone and this time grandma did not cry. She had a half smile on her lips and I clearly remember she seemed about to say something, with her mouth half open and her eyes flickering between him and me. The photo of Tanino portrayed him, needless to say, elegantly dressed with his hair swept back, his sunglasses on, his back straight and his face unsmiling. '*Ciao* Tanino,' she said after a while and I understood we were going. 'Aren't you changing his flowers?' I asked. 'I don't go up there because I'm old and you because you're only a little boy. Enza changes them when she comes, or even Bruno, don't worry.' A little further on there was a kind of ladder with steps made from wooden pegs, old and crumbling, which was used for getting up to the graves set right at the top. Ada took my hand and together we made our way out of the cemetery, back into the world of the living.

The grass is longer now, up at the farm. I went to meet Bruno, who had just finished eating, and beyond the little house the grass was almost up to my knees. The cement platform the table stands on seemed overwhelmed on all sides by long stems of grass growing up over it. The sun was very strong, and Bruno told me he'd had an argument with the peasant farmer who looked after whatever was grown on the land, the vegetable plot and the trees, and who took half the produce in payment. He doesn't explain what the argument was about, which makes me think he feels he is in the wrong. In any event, the man, known as the 'pilot', has taken offence for some reason and has decided to leave. And he has taken the lawnmower with him, which was his, and so Bruno hasn't been able to cut the grass. 'We'll get on fine without it,' he said. Then he rolled himself a cigarette, a tobacco one, and continued, 'We Bastimentos don't have green fingers, unfortunately, think how stupid that is, we're sons and grandsons of people who made a living off the land, people who work the market, and with a pair of shears in our hands we're as useless as shit. It makes me laugh but I should be crying,' he said, shaking his head. He seemed incredulous. He remained silent for a few seconds, leaning back in his chair looking for the right words, his hands clasped behind his head, then he leant quickly forward, placed his feet firmly on the ground and said: 'My father passed on to me only one thing. Love child he used to call me, love child, what crap. The truth is Tanino 'e Bastimento spent half his life in gaol and all sorts of filth stuck to him, inside, the beatings he took, all that repressed rage, thoughts of killing himself, the shit they gave him to eat and the other sort of shittiness he discovered when they kept him in isolation and starved him. This is what I am, this mixture of disgust and dead insects and rancour that my father had festering in his body for years and which he infected mamma's body with, and straightaway after that I was born. Logically even my brothers and sisters got some of it, it was inevitable, but a big part of that filth came down to me. Angelo, God rest his soul, was born before any of this but not even he escaped the curse completely, because the Bastimento foulness had already got into him. Love child, I don't think so.'

Then Bruno falls silent and we both collect our things, we shut up the little house and lock the gate. I feel the wind on my face and in the sky black clouds are moving fast. Before leaving I took a closer look at the kitchen garden, lots of the fruit there was ripe by now; some of it was beginning to go black as well and dissolve into shapelessness.

Me, mamma, Enza and China have been to see aunt Michelina, one of Ada's sisters. She lives in one of the most panoramic spots in Naples, in Corso Vittorio Emanuele, just above the Spanish Quarter. We went by car and Enza drove, as always. Mamma put one of the prepared CDs in the Clio's player and out came *Don Raffaè* by De André, the version with Roberto Murolo, holy monster of Neapolitan music in the last century and, needless to say, a friend of Tanino. Elena and Enza say that besides the familiar voice, it's the song itself that brings back memories of Tanino 'e Bastimento, and for all I know, they might have no other reason than that. Then mamma suggests changing it and Enza at first objects, then lets her, because she knows that Elena always makes these things a matter of principle and insists on them, whereas she hardly ever does. China is sitting in the back with me and watches them arguing, then gives a yelp of distress when she senses the tone of their voices has risen too much and so the two in front lower their voices and kid her along. We arrive at aunt Michelina's a little before dinner time and the person who comes to open the door is Chitra, the new home help. Chitra is Indian and speaks little Italian, her skin is dark but her hands and parts of her face are patchy, because a year ago she had an accident with boiling oil when she was cooking and the burns left her with big pale marks.

Aunt Michelina is sitting at the kitchen table, waiting for us with her chin on her hand. When she sees me she makes a big fuss, and says she's always thinking about me and she loves me and I don't understand why given that we hardly ever see each other and she knows practically nothing about me, but in certain families love resides in genetic inheritance, and if she is the sister of my grandmother, then there's nothing else she can do but love me as she does. She looks a lot like Ada, but more slender, and has deep black hair, she is more foul-mouthed and smokes like a chimney, or 'like the Turks' as we say. Then the children and grandchildren arrive and they all have something to say, they ask me about university, the holidays, the seaside and the weather in Turin and I reply mechanically, accustomed to giving more or less the same answers, with a few variations here and there. At a certain point Valencia comes out of her room. Valencia is Tanino's fourth child, she is autistic and schizophrenic and she is my mother's twin. When she and Elena were born, in August 1975, Tanino had his first two female offspring. The first one to be born he named after his mother and the second, who did not cry as she came into the world and who weighed only half as much as her twin, he named after the Spanish city, because the infant was very pretty and very far away, like Valencia. It appears that whatever her problems were, they only presented themselves because she was not immediately transferred to an incubator, and so she emerged into the world when she was still too weak and the world left its mark on her in an instant. The twins lived together in via Edificio Scolastico for almost three years, until the birth of the last Orlando daughter: Asia Rosa, or China. In those years Tanino was in and out of prison for short periods and his mind was beginning to become less open than before. Perhaps the reason is that having two children out of seven unable to express themselves or to grow, was too much. After a few days, when Ada and China returned from hospital, he telephoned Michela, who was married and had two children and a much more stable situation, and asked this great favour of her. It was rare for Tanino 'e Bastimento to ask anyone for anything, but when he did ask, no one ever said no, because if he asked you for something it meant he had already done something for you, without making an issue of it. That same evening they brought Valencia round to the house where Michela and her husband lived, in Corso Vittorio Emanuele, and there she would stay. Valencia does not talk much, uses short phrases and in response to questions, answers only "No" or else "Eh", she keeps her eyes lowered all the time, and the eyes resemble mamma's. She too grew up with a Walkman plugged into her ear but she doesn't get on well with China because China seems a little jealous of the attention Valencia gets from Enza when we go to see her. She is fat too, like her sisters. Elena embraces Valencia and points at me and says, 'He is your nephew, what's his name, he's called Francesco,' and she repeats, 'Francesco' and mamma laughs, looks at me and goes on to say, 'You have the same blood.' I nod. Then the pizzas or *panini* arrive and aunt Michelina pours me a beer with her old woman's hands, all knotted and speckled with brown spots and she does it to make me feel at ease, she doesn't know me well but she has understood that I don't feel very comfortable in these sorts of situation, and then I swallow down the beer and she winks at me and mamma doesn't say anything because woe betide anyone who displeases my aunt. With my stomach full and my head lighter I feel better, so when we have finished I get up and go out on to the balcony for a smoke, and aunt Michelina's balcony has one of the finest views I can remember. Just below me the cars and motorbikes are flowing along the Corso and making lots of noise, then a parapet separates the road from a long slope, a slope that carries on down and brings you to the Spanish Quarter and still further beyond, the sea, and all the lights of the city curving round it in a gentle arc that links me to the volcano we revere, and there Vesuvius stands and it is the most banal of images of the city, but it is beautiful enough to disgust you and so I light another cigarette straight after the first and smoke it slowly, as calmly as could be, and things don't seem so bad. Below, on the pavement, there's a boy, younger than I am, he is leaning back against his scooter, a Liberty 125, and there is a girl sitting on it, all I can see of her is her sleek blonde hair and her brown legs contrasting with the white of her very short shorts. They are kissing. I turn back inside and they are all still at table, and seem to be perfectly happy, this is all they want. This is all they want not because they were born with few expectations, but because they have learnt to be content with eating pizza around the same table, because the world is slowly but steadily weeding them out, reducing their numbers, and they have accepted the fact, we all have our turn under the sky, they always say, at one time or another. We are under the sky, and the sky is well capable of being a piece of shit: they don't say that but I do, because they never allow themselves to contradict Providence and what it takes from us, they are accustomed to believe in a higher design from which they cannot escape, and so there is nothing to fight against, nothing to object to, only wait and stick together as much as they can, put a good face on a bad joke and eat pizza and *panini* on Sunday evenings around the same table. In aunt Michelina's sitting room is a bookcase and in the bookcase nothing but old books, encyclopaedias or good, sensible volumes, which no one reads. Amongst them is a copy of *Anelito tra le sbarre*, *A Look of Longing Through the Bars*, and I had never noticed it before. I take it in my hand and turn the pages and this copy is in a much better condition than the one I took with me after the visit to the ruined barn. Inside, on the first page, there is a handwritten dedication from Tanino. To Michela, it says simply, nothing more and nothing less. A fine present, I think and then look at Valencia, who has risen from the table and is staring at me. I ask her if everything's all right. She replies 'Eh,' then disappears into her bedroom and her footsteps make no sound.

In 1977, Carlo Gaetano Orlando was sentenced to internal exile in a distant part of the country. He was sent away to live under the supervision of a priest in Valdastico, deep in the heart of the Veneto, at the beginning of winter. Over the years Tanino's hide had learned to withstand more or less everything, but real cold he found it hard to bear. He had spent the hottest summer months of his youth in thick-walled cells exposed to the sun, he had sweated like a pig for years, he had shared rooms with dozens of men and had been locked away in windowless isolation cells, and so after a while heat had ceased to be a problem, on the contrary it had become a companion, something to remind him he was alive and that he had to resist, something akin to the pains of martyrdom. But the cold was another thing altogether. It got into his rotting bones, *fràcete*: eroded by time and dampness, and the pains he felt at fifty made him lose his clarity of mind. In winter, when the wind blew, his back would seize up and he felt as if someone was stabbing icy needles in his spine, he seemed to be back on one of those pallets where they tied him down for punishment at Forte Longone. But at Valdastico, at least, he was partially at liberty. He spent the days writing poetry or letters to his relatives, and when it came to relatives he had plenty to write to and so when he finished one round of missives he promptly started all over again. The majority, obviously, were for Ada and for Russo, who took care of the family's needs when Tanino was absent. In the small town the people showed little trust in him and he, in turn, showed even less in them, he would remain until mid-afternoon in the little room assigned to him, in the highest part of the local church.

He had made friends with the priest and often chatted with him, because he respected men of God. But in the town there were two or three thousand souls and they all knew that the thin, sun-tanned man, who wore sunglasses even when the sky was dark and in the evenings, was there to do his time, and dozens of fantastic opinions circulated about what he had been sentenced for, because few people dared approach him and the priest always retained a decorous reserve when faced with the townspeople's questions. Tanino's winter had been the most severe he could remember, and on some nights, his shivering and shaking was not even muffled by the straw mattress in his loft room, and then the priest would come and knock on the door. He knocked only for form, because Tanino was locked in at night, to prevent him from running away under cover of darkness. He was huddled under the inadequate blanket, but when he heard the rattle of the lock he sat up at once, forced his limbs to stop trembling, because he would never show any signs of weakness before the priest. So the priest, with a lamp in his hand, would invite him downstairs, to warm up a bit in front of the woodstove in the vestry. Tanino smoked cigarettes and sometimes they would drink wine. They spoke little and the priest pressed his prison guest to make his confession. Tanino laughed it off and said his sins he would only divulge to God, without benefit of intermediary, or to the soul of his mother Elena, in his dreams. When he had warmed up enough, he patted the priest on the shoulder and asked him to lock him in the loft room again, he needed his sleep. When the first snow began to melt, Tanino grew stronger, but he was still alone and he still had a summer and another winter to get through in this valley. He decided to invite young Bruno for the summer season: he oughtn't to spend too long away from his father; he ought to understand what it meant to be on your own and far from home. Bruno was excited at the prospect of going to see Tanino and was put on a train by Ada one morning in June. By sunset, the six-year-old child was collected by the parish priest and taken to the church, after a swift tour of the town. Tanino saw him arrive from the small, barred window of the loft room, and noticed at once how many centimetres Bruno had put on over the winter. He hugged his son and ran his hand through his golden curls, then sent the priest away and said they'd be going out for a walk in the town. Tanino showed his son the cobbled lanes of Valdastico, took him to the bar and bought the child a Coca-Cola and the barman did not smile at either of them, possibly irritated by his typically Neapolitan attitude, or to be exact the excessive self-assurance shown in his body language and gestures by someone who is not part of that place, as demonstrated by his free and easy ways, leaning his back against the counter, his arm waving aloft to attract attention, the loud voice and the constant use of dialect terms incomprehensible to the many Veneto shepherds. But someone like Tanino necessarily had to be at his ease everywhere, because feeling at ease was a condition he had learned to deem precious, and just about everything counted as ease if the standard you judged by was being held in solitary confinement and beaten up by prison warders. But Bruno did not like the place and after two weeks he had not spoken to a single other boy. He had seen some in the square playing football, and had been pleased because that was a language he could speak pretty well. They had played at taking penalties and Bruno had placed every one of them in the corner, brushing the goalposts which were two plastic bottles filled with pebbles. Up above, from the barred window of the loft room at the top of the church tower, Tanino's eyes had followed Bruno and the other nervous children, who had taken to communicating with Bruno only by puffing out their cheeks and scowling. They hadn't dared touch him because they too had noticed that the dangerous man was watching them and they were afraid of him. Their mothers had turned up to call them in for lunch earlier than usual and had carried their little puppy dogs away in their arms, whispering in their ears and directing rapid glances at the boy from Naples. When Bruno sought the window at the top of the church tower again, the figure of Tanino was no longer there, and so he went back inside too.

From then on, the little boy spent his days alone, wandering up and down the town, kicking a ball against the church walls, impaling lizards on fence posts, with the priest crossing himself whenever he walked past these massacres of the cold-blooded creatures. All this caused Tanino pain, his favourite son was alone and the sound of his native Marano voices were so far away, and in the valley there was fear but no respect, respect for the name they bore, for the deeds accomplished and for the good done in the streets of Naples.

Tanino decided to write another letter to Ada, to tell her once more about his grief and feelings of martyrdom, and the burden of his son, which had added to his own. He began to write at night, with Bruno asleep in the narrow bed and a moth fluttering about, attracted by the room's only light: a candle the priest had brought up from the vestry. Tanino was sitting on a stool, bent over the small table that he used as a writing desk as well, half his face illuminated by the light of the red candle. While he set down his troubles, the moth flew round and round, coming closer to the flame. Tanino waved it away and continued writing, the pen firm in his right hand, but he lost his thread and couldn't concentrate, and then he swore under his breath and the moth continued to seek its death. Tanino couldn't understand the instinct of this living creature, which suddenly dived towards the flame and yet again he wouldn't let it: flicking his wrist, he knocked the candle over and it fell forward on to the sheet of paper. He had the quickest reactions of anyone, as we know, and instantly extinguished the flame with the flat of his hand, snuffing it out against the writing desk, but he couldn't prevent the red wax from splashing everywhere, including, inevitably, the paper as well and the half-written woes. In the darkness Tanino could now see perfectly well. He took the spoiled sheet, rolled it into a ball and threw it into a corner of the room, away from Bruno. He heard the moth fluttering about again and he thought for a moment he saw it fly out through the little window of the loft room, towards the crescent moon and into the sky over the valley. He had to laugh at himself a few moments later because he found he had begun to sing under his breath, a song he loved, and the song was called *Night moth*, written by Salvatore di Giacomo and sung by Sergio Bruni and by Roberto Murolo, and the words exactly matched what had just happened to him.

Enza began to believe in God at around the same time I started secondary school. Her discovery was gradual, with no before and after, no significant event, miracle or catastrophe. She went to mass, week after week, and every time the after-effects of the Sunday sermon she had heard stayed with her a little longer. She attended a different church, not San Castrese, where all the family had been through the various rites, but San Ludovico, one of those churches built in modern architectural style, with straight and simple lines, and the people who prayed there were also like that. Enza had begun to quote Don Massimo, she preached the same beautiful things that he preached, and soon she had taken to going on the retreats and pilgrimages organised by the church. Enza always made a summer trip and a spring trip, and to begin with I stayed with grandmother and China, and China was beside herself when her sister went off: she howled and sulked and grandmother kept saying Enza is coming back, she's coming back soon and she'll bring you something nice, Enza's coming back. Sometimes Enza would ring me and ask me to hold the receiver to China's ear and she would say the same words, I'm coming back, mamma's lovely girl. With Enza's gradual conversion, travel for pleasure had become travels for faith, and she went to Assisi or to the Holy Land. When she returned you could read the peace in her expression and she began to call out China's name even from the stairwell, and when she burst into the apartment she sent the wheeled suitcase skidding away over the tiled floor and rushed open-armed towards her sister, surging forward like a caricature figure, head held high and wagging from side to side, as if imitating the wild impatience of certain Neapolitan dramas. Then she clapped her hands in rhythm and China did the same, she began to sing and put her fingers in her mouth and whistle loudly and grandmother would mutter curses.

She would always bring back masses of presents.

Magnets for Elena, who arranged them carefully on the fridge door to make a frame round the letter magnets that spelt out the name Francesco. For her mother she brought colourful fans, big rings bought in the markets or voluminous white summer dresses. For China however she brought sweets or CDs or large flapping multicoloured trousers and T-shirts, which she had bought from sellers on the beach or from the street markets, haggling for every item, and she used to tell me it was essential to haggle because if you don't they'll rip you off, you have to be hard-nosed about it but you have to believe what you're saying, otherwise even if you try to bargain they'll always say no. For me she always sought the prettiest and most precious kinds of thing and Enza was determined to dazzle me most of all, even at the cost of doing things that were barely legal, sometimes. She might pilfer a bracelet from the bigger souvenir shops, that objectively was not worth the price being asked, or she might pinch a piece of coral hidden under the fine sand on the beaches, and if she bought eight fridge magnets, a couple of them might be considered complimentary. Mamma and grandma would get mad as hyenas, Enza would tell me you must never do this, then she would wink at me and slip whatever bracelet it was over my wrist. Some of the best souvenirs she had brought back from the trip to the Holy Land, again with the church, and she continued to talk about this journey for months. She had also brought back some holy water that came from Jerusalem and was therefore holier than any other sort, in a transparent bottle in the shape of a praying Madonna, and for a number of Easters my grandmother blessed us at table with this water, sprinkling it on us with an olive twig, because she and Enza said that ordinary holy water wouldn't do the trick now, like when you take too many doses of medicine and the body gets used to it and the pain doesn't go away and so you either stop taking it altogether or you move on to some more powerful medication. Amen.

I went to have lunch with Angelo the Twin, because it's hot up in the hills all right, but you don't feel you're dying of it quite so much. I also went because Angelo knows lots of things about the family, he can disentangle the names and deeds of three generations and explain everything without too many frills. The twins are the cousins of the seven—not the kings of Rome, not the seven dwarves, but of the children of Tanino—and they are the sons of Raffaele Orlando, the eldest of Tanino's brothers. They often come to 'the farm' in summer, and they are among the few relatives my mother can stand. The twins are called Angelo—*supponta* of the mayor—and Giuseppe, who is, like me, not a *supponta* of anyone in the Orlando family. *Supponta* means linking a child to an older relative, or one from a previous generation, by giving him the same name, in the hope that along with this personal identifier the new child will inherit something beyond simply the name he bears, so that the values of the family will be kept alive from generation to generation. And indeed, for example, Lello bore the name of his uncle, who was Tanino's favourite brother. Getting back to Angelo, he has always been outside the family's affairs. At thirteen he was sent, along with Giuseppe, to a middle-class school in Posillipo, and then to study away from Naples, and the two of them returned to Marano years later, their personalities already shaped and with a different outlook on things, but they know all there is to know about the family. Angelo owns a piece of land in the upper part of Marano, almost at Camaldoli, and mamma never goes very near him because she says he uses the same aftershave as Tanino. He leads a life one could call 'rural self-sufficiency', he eats what he grows and when I go to see him he takes me round his vegetable plot and shows me his preserved fruits. At table we drink the wine he makes himself and eat gnocchi with a ragù of marrow, and the marrow is extremely succulent and is grown a few metres from where I am sitting. Angelo tells me about great-uncle Lello, his father, who has been ill for years and in my memories of him he is an old man sitting in an armchair in an apartment in via Ranucci. But in the Twin's stories he is a fundamental figure in the rise of Tanino 'e Bastimento, because Lello took care of the family and the market when Tanino was away. His temperament was calmer and produced better results in discussions with the handful of men who weren't prepared to bend to Tanino's overbearing ways. The two brothers were fond of each other and guarded each other's backs because they knew they shared the same blood, unlike their younger brothers. Angelo *il Mastrone*—the communist mayor—had had several children himself, but from two separate marriages. The first of them, among whom were Tanino and Raffaele, were his first wife's, Elena, known as *'a Valencia*. Then Elena died of a broken heart, Tanino had ended up in prison and by the time he came out his father was already thinking about getting married again to another woman, Carmelina, mother of a younger generation of Orlando children. By now Tanino was a fully grown man and he did not see in this new woman a substitute for his mother, and Raffaele thought the same way. Then my uncle Angelo concludes by saying the Orlandos all share the same characteristics and they have a latent defect or illness which sooner or later breaks out into madness, or makes them crazy at certain moments and they lose control: 'Orlanditis'. He says this laughing, but the lesson continues. According to him, Orlanditis makes you hear Voices and the Voices you either give in to or else you shut yourself away at home to suppress them. Gaetano *'o Mastrone*, Angelo says, the forefather of the family, who lived a century ago, he listened to the Voices and ended up splitting his wife's head with an axe. Tanino 'e Bastimento, he continues, did not let the Voices overwhelm him, and he spent the latter part of his life at home, not wanting to see or listen to anyone. We carry on drinking wine and Angelo makes a spliff, which he calls a 'trombone', rolled in a rough and ready manner and finished off with a fat filter pushed in at one end. He lights it and says, 'Even your mamma and your aunts suffer from Orlanditis, but you know that already.' And indeed I do know. Angelo says the *Feroci* (the Furies, that's what he calls Elena and Enza) have never done anything good for anyone, they were terrorists, and I think that because of the father they had, they learnt how to make themselves equally tough and coarse in an extended family almost all of whom were men. Within this vast Orlando tribe they raise their voices when they need to raise them and show respect only to those who merit it. In Angelo's house, a light-filled open-plan space furnished in modern minimalist style, there is a biggish wooden bookcase containing two principal categories of books, that correspond to their owner's passions: entomology and Ufology, UFOs. Ever since I was little the Twin has talked about the Greys, abductions, signals left on the earth we inhabit over the course of the millennia. Usually, if a particular archaeological discovery arouses suspicions, or if an ancient stone structure comes to light, or if the writing of some ancient civilisation has not yet been deciphered, Angelo finds the answer in extraterrestrials. In the same way, speaking of a particular aspect of human nature, he will drag in the behaviour of some dangerously-coloured Hymenoptera. I have always had an incapacitating fear of wasps and bees, and Angelo was partly responsible for my terror. Until six or seven years ago, Angelo kept hives, and inside the hives thousands of bees went about their business undisturbed. Then it so happened that one day he took me with him to collect the honey. I remember feeling uncomfortably hot when I put on the kind of space suit and the gloves, I remember the mesh over my eyes and the pungent smells of the fumigator, and the first bees coming out to defend their nest and falling dazed in the clouds of smoke. 'Now keep calm, they can't do anything to you,' he told me as he opened the white-painted hive. Then the buzzing drowned out every other sound and the thousands of bees charged out to defend their home. They were everywhere, they crashed against the mesh protecting my eyes and all over my chest and legs and arms. Meanwhile Angelo was squirting the smoke all round and I stood there motionless, terrorised by the determination of that black and yellow tornado which was intent on driving me away at all costs. Angelo passed me the smoke dispenser and pulled from the hive a wooden frame set vertically, the middle of it entirely covered in bees, looking like a single, pulsating fur coat. With a spatula-like implement he started scraping them delicately off the frame, and soon I saw the intricate hexagon design, the cells of the honeycomb, with the honey gleaming on it, grainy and dark and viscous. Angelo scraped the honey into a large glass jar, and what fell in was a mixture of dead bees and pieces of honeycomb and tiny flies and the thick honey, which seemed to cling to the honeycomb with all its might, and as for dropping into the jar, it didn't want to know. He repeated the procedure another five or six times, until the container was not quite full. Then he signalled me to come closer and he had to urge me forward because my legs were lumps of wax. I stepped forward slowly, aware—without feeling any contact or pain—of the stinging of the bees hurling themselves at me. I was standing over the hive and I looked down, and Angelo pointed with his finger to the biggest bee, the queen, which was double the size of the others and was picking its way among the little cells quite calmly, less scared than its daughters who were swarming chaotically around. The queen didn't seem to mind our presence even though she was only a few hands' breadths from our faces and the drifts of smoke were still in the air nearby. For an instant I forgot the terror, something about the colours of her back held me spellbound and I wanted to put my fingers out and touch her, to take her away with me and see how the rest of them would react. Angelo closed the hive again. The black and yellow tornado calmed down and gradually the bees began to return inside. When we were under the porch of the house again, I pulled off my helmet and asked Angelo if the bees would follow us, to reclaim the honey or anything like that and he answered no, that battle was lost now as far as they were concerned and the only thing that counted was defending the hive, always that one thing, and at any cost. Then he began to filter the honey of all the impurities and now it had a colour similar to gold. 'They're too scary for me,' I continued, and he replied, 'You shouldn't be scared, if you don't bother the bees they won't bother you, you've seen how it goes, provided you don't threaten the hive they leave you alone, but if you threaten it they react, they react as any animal would, no one likes it when someone bursts into their home, when they put you and your family in danger, and they're scary because there are so many of them and they'll defend their nest to the death, but they're peaceable creatures in the end, which is why we don't test their patience.' After which Angelo broke off a piece of white honeycomb and held it out. It was gleaming with fresh honey. 'Eat,' he said, 'it's a delicacy.' Without making too much fuss, I put the honeycomb in my mouth and it was very sweet, packed with honey, but I had difficulty getting it down, because however much I chewed, the stuff wouldn't dissolve and remained stuck between my teeth and the roof of my mouth. Angelo went out into the open to take his protective suit off and I remained inside and looked at mine, which I was still wearing. Dozens of dead bees, still attached by their hook-shaped stings, were hanging from every part of my body, from just under my neck right down to my legs, while the piece of honeycomb I had in my mouth refused to dissolve.

In 1971, Tanino had all but reached the end of his sentence. In spite of the fact that he had been dispatched from one prison to another over a period of almost seventeen years, far from the world of the living, everyone knew who Carlo Gaetano Orlando was. The duel and the consequent death of Pascalone had made him something of a celebrity, even discounting the brilliant light reflected back on him by Pupetta, who, following the death of her husband, had become a public figure. She too had ended up on trial. The greatest debate surrounding the killing of Pascalone concerned its nature, what sort of killing it was. There was a great deal of talk about the murder being premeditated and it resulted in Tanino 'e Bastimento being labelled a 'hired assassin', mandated by others to carry out the execution of a man. Not everyone thought so, but Assunta, known as 'Pupetta', had no doubts. Six months pregnant, she had walked into a bar in Posillipo one sunny morning, knowing she would find Tonino 'e Pomigliano there, head of the market and big chief of the rural camorra in the fifties, and according to many people, the man who ordered her husband's murder. The smiles on the faces of the men in the bar on seeing such a beautiful woman come unexpectedly into the bar quickly gave way to expressions of terror, staring eyes and open mouths. Pupetta was holding a black Smith & Wesson semi-automatic, whose full magazine she discharged in a few seconds at the chest and face of Tonino 'e Pomigliano and the man died on the spot, sitting on a chair, killed in cold blood by a woman six months pregnant, out of pure, blind revenge. For Pupetta there followed a period of enormous media attention, including foreign newspapers, the *New York Times*: everywhere people were talking about the '*lady camorrista*', the woman who respected absolutely the mafia patriarchy and had followed the rule 'kill or be killed.' The absurd thing was that Pupetta didn't seem to hold any grudge against Tanino, to her mind a simple pawn, just an inconsequential hand that pulled the trigger at the opportune moment. Tanino could not tolerate this. He hated the idea that someone might think he had not acted on his own account, because Tanino 'e Bastimento took his orders from destiny alone and no one else, so help me God. In any event he, Gaetano Orlando, was preserving his honour, a noble thing that should remain unblemished, and in the society he found himself living in after his incarceration, it was a commodity widely recognised. The world had changed, Naples had changed, and with the new system that was taking shape, corrupt and oriented solely towards profit and to the detriment of the poor, someone like Tanino shone out for the honesty displayed over the years, he was one of the few men everyone spoke highly of, and to confirm it he had the support of the whole of Marano, the city which, after his father, he had helped to make greater to the detriment of nobody, or hardly anybody. For Tanino 'e Bastimento there ensued a period of prosperity, of gratitude and dinners out, of beautiful women and songs sung in rousing voices, of jewels and '…no way don Tanino, it's on us.' One day in the middle of September he was in Milan on market business, because even that was going very well and Tanino was a great man to deal with, because for a customer, getting down to business with him standing in front of you was like starting to discuss prices with the crazy frontman of a band, the sorts with bare torsos and long hair who launch themselves into the crowd in the middle of a song that everyone knows. On a free evening, Tanino visited a nightclub, La Vecchia Milano, where scores of people in jackets and ties, grouped around tables scattered across the nightclub floor, were drinking from glistening champagne flutes and smoking cigarettes in old-style cigarette holders, while in the middle was a stage and on the stage just then a band playing light blues music, as a background. Tanino was not used to alcoholic drinks, it wasn't his habit to have a glass of wine at the table, a grappa after dinner, still less a cocktail or spirits. He only enjoyed Campari or sparkling wines, which he could barely distinguish from a champagne or a prosecco. He liked the effect of the bubbles in the glass and the moment when the light shone on it and the liquid turned into white gold. Tanino's palate had grown accustomed to swallowing down the worst and most disgusting stuff, and so he had not the slightest pretension to refinement: for him, appreciation was immediate, and a thing was either good or it wasn't good and his impression was virtually instantaneous. Strolling through the nightclub, at a certain moment he felt a hand on his shoulder, and then his name and his own special name pronounced in tones of amazed respect. It was an old acquaintance of Tanino, Tony Dallara, a nationally famous singer who had been at San Remo in 1960, and obviously Tanino had only been mentioned in some conversation, because in 1960 he was locked up on Elba. But they had got to know each other some years later, in the prison at Alessandria, when the singer had stayed there as a guest for a concert, and they had met and become good friends. Dallara had been impressed by Tanino's coolness and poise at being detained within these prison walls, it seemed to him that he was there by choice and not because he had to be, he knew the names of the warders, and amazingly even the warders didn't think badly of him, and almost all the other inmates referred to Tanino as Don Gaetano. Photographs were taken of him with Tony Dallara and then they promised to meet up again whenever fate turned in his favour. The singer grabbed Tanino by the arm and escorted him through the crowd to a table, set away from the stage and in a kind of private nook, with red velvet curtains hanging from the ceiling decorously separating them from the rest of the nightclub. Sitting at the table were two other faces Tanino recognised as being famous: Minnie Minoprio, co-star with Tony in the club's evening shows, with bouffant hair and a dazzling smile, and Mirna Doris, according to Tanino *the* female Neapolitan singer of the moment, with eyes like a panther's, full lips and wearing two massive gold earrings. He had seen her too for the first time in the prison at Alessandria, but only on a television programme. Tanino kissed the *signoras'* hands and sat down with them. They drank champagne and Tanino was the centre of attention: they asked him about prison, about his wife and son, the aftershave he was wearing and his favourite songs. Then they went to do their turn on the stage of La Vecchia Milano, leaving Tanino sitting behind the curtained screen, his eyes keenly fixed on it all, and especially on Mirna, who was sitting beside him and was still drinking, leaving pink stains on the rim of the flute she twirled between her fingers. Tanino asked if he could see her again and the woman answered yes.

They met during the Christmas holidays, on New Year's Eve, at the home of Sergio Bruni, who was far and away Tanino's favourite artist, not just from Naples but in all of Italy. Meanwhile, in those weeks, Ada was pregnant for the second time and spent those festive days at home with Angelo, her first child who at this period was beginning to feel disturbed and annoyed by his father's behaviour. Since leaving prison, Tanino had started going out in the morning and returning late at night, at most he came home for lunch and for an early afternoon rest. However, he had become great friends with Sergio Bruni, because Tanino's way of operating pleased people of the élite: he did not seem to have that ostentatious flippancy of the rich artists, he was only frivolous in the shallower moments of conversation and, when he was not wearing the sunglasses, he looked you straight in the eyes. He was one of those people who do not encourage you to discuss life's weighty subjects, who don't make too many demands on you or leave you feeling out of it, instead he was the sort who talks to you straight, presents you with a credible vision of the world and that suits you, it's comforting. At Bruni's place Mirna was also there and Tanino did not waste the opportunity to voice his admiration for the lady. They ate fish and played cards and Tanino was not all that good, but he didn't hold back, because every time he hesitated over a bet Mirna smiled at him and urged him on with remarks like: 'So this is what Tanino 'e Bastimento's courage is really like, is it?' Faced with challenges of that sort it is hard not to give way, because they play with your self-image and put it to the test, and then if you add in the few too many glasses and an unspoken wish to humiliate, probably linked to sexual submission, it becomes clear that Tanino could not take a backward step. He won. As a prize, in addition to his monetary winnings, he asked his two companions to sing together for him, then he said to Bruni, you know which song gets me going, and soon the singer closed his eyes, raised the fingers of one hand to settle himself and launched into *Carmela*. After a couple of verses Mirna joined in as well, and her voice gave the piece a new balance and Tanino sat there leaning back in his wooden chair, a cigarette, an MS, between his fingers and satisfaction flowing through his body at having before him two great artists, a good friend and a beautiful woman, and at home Ada was waiting for him and waiting also for a new heir, the love child, living—almost—testimony that his wife had waited seventeen years for him. On the chorus, he too began to sing Carmela, *Carme'*, still sitting in his chair, and outside it was Christmas and the New Year on the way and Tanino, for the first time in who knows how long, was at peace.

New Year's Eve

Tomorrow is New Year's Eve. The life begins
of a new year.

All those who are free
wish each other a better year.

They wish each other happiness and joy,
while for the man in prison
there is little to wish for.

He ends the old year
in the sombre walls of a cell
and begins the new one
in the same walls.

And thus even the prisoner
exchanges mournful wishes
with his other prisoner friends.

And for many of these
like the undersigned
for years and years
it is always the same chorus
saying: For you I wish
the new year may bring you freedom.

I too will await in the gloom
of a dark cell
the year 1971, I will await it,
yes I will await it with every atom of myself
because my heart, it seems,
has a different beat.

Already sixteen New Year's Eves
have passed in this
Hell of buried lives.

I hope with all my being
that the seventeenth New Year's Eve
is the year of my freedom
and of my happiness
which now I know longer know.
What does happiness mean
the happiness which only exists
in freedom.

Gaetano Orlando, 30th December 1970

Over the winter and spring, Tanino met Mirna at various times and they became good friends. He flirted with her a bit and she allowed him to. Ada had begun to come along to these encounters as well, because although she came from a far more humble family than Tanino's, she was different in having a natural inclination towards a more worldly way of living and her husband had noted the fact. He had begun to buy her mink coats, shiny rings and outsize earrings. Before going out, Ada sprayed her wrists and behind her ears with generous amounts of Chanel N°5 and would look at herself in the mirror, arrange her red hair and apply lipstick like a grand lady, savouring the moment of drawing it across her half-open mouth and imagining herself already having dinner. She would be sitting at table with a whole crowd of people she could only ever have dreamed of meeting during the long years of Tanino's imprisonment, during all those sleepless nights she spent, changing from one slow local train to another to visit him in prison; and she would give herself an extra squirt of perfume to mask the stink of piss in those prisons, which always came back to her every time she thought about them. Sometimes Angelo went with them, at other times he preferred to remain at home by himself, or to go out with his fiancée Gaetanina. He couldn't see a way to marry her until he had found a place of his own, a place with his own rules and values, a place where he would be indisputably the head of the family. Then Russo would call in to collect them and take them wherever they wanted to go, and Mirna often stayed in Naples at the Hotel Vesuvio, at Mergellina. The singer had introduced Tanino to her trusted dressmaker, a designer from Florence, whose clothes were the height of elegance, and Tanino had commissioned a suit for himself and several outfits for Ada. Mirna's hotel suite was all in tones of yellow ochre and blood-red, with comfortable divans and a beautiful and valuable table. Often she arranged it so that they found her propped on the four-poster bed, cigarette holder in hand as if imitating a figure from the 1920s. They spent the evenings singing, drinking and playing cards, rummy and *teresina*, an Italian variant of poker. Under cover of the table Tanino held his wife's hand or stroked her thigh, and at such moments she forgave him for the life she had been living on account of him. One morning in May, her swelling stomach now becoming visible, Ada received at the apartment in via Edificio Scolastico a telephone call from Mirna Doris informing her that the Florentine designer had this time excelled himself and that the "stuff", that was the word she used, was ready. They arranged for the dressmaker to call at Marano with the new clothes that same evening, when even Tanino would be back. The singer decided to come along herself as well, since she had never been to Tanino's home before. They came up to the apartment and had coffee and were laughing amicably together, when everything happened in a rush. Thunderous knocks at the front door and a harsh voice said, 'Open up, police.' Tanino went to open the door and there was a whole squad on the landing, all with their hands on their pistols. Tanino put his hands up and asked rhetorically, 'But is this the way?' at which the carabinieri strode in and began to search everything and everywhere, opening drawers and pieces of furniture. Mirna was deeply upset, and the dressmaker too. They looked at each other, terrorised, with the expression of people who find themselves in the wrong place at the wrong time, the home of a murderer which they should never have set foot in, what a stupid mistake to trust a criminal, that was what Tanino read in their eyes, while a corporal frisked his jacket pockets. Ada's face expressed shame and embarrassment, her gaze shifting from the police to her guests and back to the police again. She put her hands to her face and said, 'But what are you looking for, there's nothing here, I swear there's nothing here.' The policemen turned the apartment upside down: all the furniture pulled open and the contents scattered, the clothes the dressmaker had brought lying on the floor, bags and pockets rummaged through. Tanino, as usual, seemed imperturbable. When there were no more places to search, the Major in charge said, 'We're done here, we can go,' but he said it to his search squad not to the owners of the apartment, who had been ignored throughout the whole thing. The only dirty look was for Tanino, who shook his head with a half smile. He accompanied the carabinieri to the door. Not long after, the guests wanted to leave and the dressmaker took his clothes with him. Mirna Doris was distraught and refused to talk to Tanino, even when the explanation for what had happened came to light. It transpired that *signora* Doris, on the telephone, had referred to the clothes with the term "*roba*", in other words "stuff", as well as "clothes", and someone must have intercepted the call or overheard, maybe someone at the Hotel Vesuvio who knew Tanino and knew the circles he moved in. During her call Mirna had given the time and place of the meeting, nothing simpler for the forces of law and order. Both Tanino and his wife made frequent telephone calls to the hotel room where their friend was staying, but she hardly ever answered and when she did her response was evasive. The outcome, in short, was that they didn't see each other again for years. Ada was sad because those evenings had given her a new lease of life, and the jewellery had made her feel valued, the expensive clothes as well. But Mirna's friendship was soon replaced by other new acquaintances of Tanino, who continued to attend the most "in" parties and evenings taking place in town, unknown to most people, but very quickly someone in the crowd would recognise him, remember some detail seen on TV or read in the papers, especially the sunglasses worn even late into the night. At some point the name Tanino would come up, it was almost natural, and then questions would be asked and he would respond, having a way with words. In this way he would find himself the focal point in the room, surrounded by many of the nation's élite people. And they, like children, couldn't help but be left fascinated, even open-mouthed, after one of Tanino's stories since, it has to be said, he knew how to tell them.

Mamma has shown me some family photographs, from her childhood. I asked her about them myself. She hesitated a bit, diving into the past is not a favourite sport as far as she is concerned, but then she let herself be inveigled into a little bout of nostalgia. We were in the via Roma apartment, it was late afternoon, and Enza was on the bed beside China, resting for a moment before preparing dinner. The photo albums are in the sitting room and we went to look for them together. Every time I go in I get the impression that the presiding rule of chaos has changed things around, and nothing seems to be in its rightful place any more, except the old painting with the nude—whom we now call Milena—and the golden pharaoh's head, which sees everything from its vantage point and seems to stand guard over the sitting room, perched on the display case that contains countless trinkets. The photo albums were under a table, protected from the light, and bound in heavy covers that made them look more like the volumes of an encyclopaedia. Elena heaved a number out, and then chose two, the ones she remembered as containing the best photos. Then we returned to the kitchen and began to leaf through them, in fact she began, and before turning each page hesitated for a second, with a faint smile on her lips, a smile in which I could read both melancholy, and so it seemed, a degree of relief. The photos were grouped according to events, like birthday dinners and Christmases or days at the seaside, and along with them images from life up at the farm, and in the apartment at via Edificio Scolastico, where the background is similar to that of via Roma, because the furniture is the same, as are the colours of the walls and the tones of some of the floor tiles. There were photos of Tanino on the beach, at every age, by himself or with friends or with the family. In one he is squatting on the sand beside China, the colours of their skin almost as much in contrast as the level of awareness in their eyes. Tanino is about sixty, wearing swimming trunks, his watch on his wrist and his gold chain falling across his chest. His hair is wet from the sea and his hand is on the shoulder of his youngest daughter, whose mouth is half open and who is looking towards some vague point in the opposite direction from the sea. Then another, from the same day, of Enza with Tanino: in this picture she is thin and wearing a multi-coloured one-piece bathing costume. She is as tall as her father and they are standing arm in arm. Then there are pictures of via Edificio Scolastico in the Eighties, with the cars of the time and different signs above the shops. There are lots of photos up in the green heights of the farm, with Elena and Enza in early puberty. Elena is dressed all in denim, with a terrible old gilet and an even worse mullet haircut; Enza is smiling and could be mistaken for a boy, from the way she is standing, her hair and her clothes. Mamma says that this is part of the reason why Enza was much more free to do as she pleased, when Tanino was around. He had brought her up like a boy, she had no mischief in her and therefore Tanino felt at ease allowing her to go around with her girl friends, letting her come home late and giving her presents, like travelling to America, while Elena stayed at home doing the ironing and helping Ada with the housework, because she was unmistakeably female and therefore not to be trusted and mischievous by nature. Which is why Tanino would keep her at home until she was fully grown up, when a respectable young man from a good family would materialise—a prince charming in a jacket and tie—and marry her, relieving Tanino of the responsibility for bringing up his eldest daughter without any risk of her turning into a whore. Next, a medley of beauty contest photos, all flash-lights and bright colours, scanty costumes and high heels and the most dazzling of smiles on Tanino's face, his hands round the waists of women and men alike. I realise that even in the family album, he always steals the scene, and he appears in at least half the pictures. Another photo shows him and his father, Angelo the mayor, at around the beginning of the Nineties. I had never seen a photo of Angelo il Mastrone, and until now I had maybe not even wondered what he looked like, and I realised his features could not have been anything different from what they were here. I can't connect him with any other relative in particular, but he has the unmistakeable features of the Orlandos, in fact maybe he has them all, all the things I have seen dispersed among uncles, nephews, cousins: the large mouth with expressive lips and a square jaw, the straight and slender nose, the broad shoulders. In the photo he is sitting next to Tanino, and rather than father and son they look like business partners, with their grey suits and sunglasses—indoors—and lighted cigars. Elena says there was never any love between them, only the ties and obligations of the name. She adds that she could never stand her grandfather, that he gave his other grandchildren ten thousand lire when he saw them but never her, because even though she bore the name of his first love, she was the daughter of Tanino 'e Bastimento, the black sheep of the family, who casually takes for his special hallmark the name of a real black sheep, black in terms of his fate rather than his looks. 'Insult piled on injury,' mamma continues, 'as if it wasn't already enough for me to be my father's daughter.' She says these words in a quieter voice and turns towards Enza's bedroom, because if she heard she would spring to Tanino's defence.

Another photo of him, this time standing between his eldest two children, seventeen years separating them, the first born from the next, Bruno on the right, identical with his father, hair at that time black, like the dress suit he is wearing, which again matches Tanino's. On the other side Angelo, wearing a yellow suit over a blue shirt and a multicoloured tie. The older one is staring at the ground and not at the camera like the other two, who are standing with their heads held high, hands in their pockets and feet set wide apart on the terracotta tiles. Then I see a different photo, and of all the ones I have seen of Tanino this one is unique: a head and shoulders snap of him and Ada, sitting cosily together at table, caught by the camera with natural, relaxed smiles on their faces, Ada with an arm round his shoulders and him in a short-sleeved shirt and no sunglasses. The smile shows his even teeth, with a slight gap between them, like Valencia's, who is pictured, as it happens, in the next few photographs, a series of photos taken of her and mamma on her twentieth birthday, again up at the farm. In the album there are also several images of Lello, but he is never captured for posterity alongside his father. The last photo in the album seems to have been put there by chance and Elena and I start to laugh heartily, because it's her, in the foreground, at eight years old, on a bicycle, and in the background, sitting on the balcony at via Edificio Scolastico, is China, with her legs crossed and her head in a box of *pandoro*, the special Christmas-season cake, in summer. We closed the album and just at that moment Enza entered the kitchen saying, 'I'm hungry, why don't we order a nice pizza?'

At the end of July 1955, after turning himself in to the police following the killing of Pascalone 'e Nola, Tanino was escorted to the prison at Poggioreale to await trial. He was put in an isolation cell, in the most remote wing of the gaol, to prevent him from seeing other detainees from Naples during this period of confusion. The cell was dark, with a tiny barred window high on the wall, which Tanino couldn't reach even by stretching his arms. Along one wall was the thinnest of mattresses and on the other side the latrine, a hole in the floor with a water tank which was emptied once a week so that the prisoner was obliged to sleep four paces away from his bodily excretions, the smell was appalling and not a breath of air came in through the tiny window. Then, at night, it was invaded by mosquitoes and bedbugs. He felt the things crawling over his face and body and he spent all his time slapping himself, and itching. In the morning his face and body were covered in blood, and red stains soon began to appear on the walls. He washed the blood off with a wet rag, the same one he used for chasing away the insects that invaded the cell. Even the warders were of the worst sort, and having a powerful person by the balls made them feel powerful in their turn. When they brought his food, they found it amusing to toss the tray into the cell and make it tip over, and Tanino was forced to scrape the disgusting slop off the cement floor after they had gone, because for the first ten minutes they stood there, waiting for the prisoner to crawl towards the food and humiliate himself in order to stay alive. Instead, Tanino waited, and if they made fun of him or provoked him, he remained silent, tried to remember that animals of that sort feed off the satisfaction you give them, and if you don't give them any then there's nothing they can do. When the warders went away, spitting into the cell, then Tanino reached for the tray and bolted down whatever awfulness they were giving him. In the meantime he fantasised about the most gory ways he could kill a guard, and he would never have done so but there was no way they could have been sure of it, the malice of the men scared him to death and made him malicious in turn. Seeing Tanino refuse to respond to provocations, in mid-October they began to bring him water only, twice a day. He could not understand whether the hatred directed at him was something the guards genuinely felt or whether it came from higher up, or indeed on governor De Santis' orders. Very soon Tanino saw his ribs beginning to protrude and spent the nights weeping with his face to the wall, in the absolute silence of the special wing, where there didn't seem to be a single other prisoner. And at times he would yell and shout, make demands and no one would respond and, fuck it, he couldn't make out if he was alone or if he was the only one to have a tiny scrap of life, and hunger, left in him. In the meantime, he was exchanging letters with Ada, and Tanino's relatives used to go to Poggioreale to make sure these letters reached the intended recipient and that he, the recipient was able to reply. Since Ada was pregnant and the plan to terminate the pregnancy had failed, now they needed to get married, establish a union that was at least legal and recognised in the eyes of God. Tanino knew that a baby now would be good for him, would keep him bound to the woman he had married, that he would be motivated by pride for them both, and it would represent, for himself, a distraction, someone new to think about and direct his love towards through all the years he would have to spend in prison, and he didn't yet know how many that would be because he had heard nothing at all about the trial. Since they didn't allow paper and pens inside the cell, it was the priest who wrote Tanino's replies and read out those of Ada. Tanino stood with his shoulder to the corridor wall, his eyes on the little window and his back resting against the iron door and the priest, on the other side of life, listened to his words as if in the confessional, but instead of replying he wrote, suggested a few turns of phrase and he complimented Gaetano Orlando on the correctness of his language and the purity with which his feeling seemed to find expression. In any event, they fixed the date for the wedding for 25th November; even though he would have preferred to be going to meet her, in a month's time Ada would be entering the walls of Poggioreale to leave again as a married woman, ready to become a mother. The hours spent dictating letters and organising the ceremony did Tanino good, but in all other respects he continued to get through them with difficulty. When he was alone he began to be frightened, his hunger didn't allow him to sleep, in spite of the ends of bread that the priest took from the pockets of his tunic and gave him in secret. The warders would enter the wing in the middle of the night and shine their flashlights through the hole in the door, or shout to wake him up and beat their weapons against the iron door. Tanino had begun to pinch his own stomach to distract himself from his rage, so he inflicted pain on himself as well, and around his belly-button, itself very sunken, was a mass of purple marks. One night towards the end of October Tanino started to have hallucinations, a powerful burning sensation in his stomach kept him awake—whilst sleep, when it came, and diminished energy plunged him into a catatonic state of constant drowsiness. In this state he muttered things anyone listening would doubtless have thought mad, but there was no one to listen, for Tanino was as solitary as a dog. Suddenly, through the window grille flew an insect which began to flutter round the cell and Tanino's eyes were by now accustomed to the pitch dark and he could follow the wanderings of the flying insect, a moth. The moth began to circle near Tanino, who kept a close watch on the creature and simultaneously started to sing, with the little voice he had left: *Moth, this is a lamp/It's not a rose or jasmine/And you insist on flying/Ever closer to it*. He was fascinated by insects of this type, which go crazy in the presence of a light source and begin to follow it, and even if the light comes from a living flame it doesn't put off the moth, it has to fly straight towards it even at the risk of its life. But there is no naked flame here, he thought, reflecting on the words of the song. There was no light and flying in empty darkness carries risks, Tanino knew. Even in those conditions, and with his strength weakened, his wrist was still what it had always been, quick as a viper. As it flitted past his nose, Tanino raised his forearm and caught the creature in his hand. With tears in his eyes—he couldn't tell whether it was from hunger or at the desperation of his action—he lifted the moth to his mouth and bit into it twice before swallowing it, while the insect crunched damply between his teeth.

Over the next few days his stomach pains grew worse and Tanino had to ask to see a doctor. The doctor prescribed pills called Rabbro, and he was given one each morning. He told him he had an ulcer and that he must be careful, especially about what he ate. What a fucking joke, Tanino thought. In any event, the pills reduced the pain a little. Autumn was moving on and nights in the cell were becoming cold. Ada wrote to Tanino that she had chosen her wedding dress, she had ordered something plain, and Tanino replied what a shame, the plain style isn't for a lady like you. The lady had also ordered a suit for him, with his measurements, and Tanino did not tell her that two of him could have got into that suit, that his size now was considerably smaller than it had been, after all these months. While all this was happening, his tongue had been getting darker. He could see it if he pulled it out beyond his jaws, and when he was able to check it like this he began to feel even more worried, because he didn't know much about anatomy but he was fairly sure a tongue was supposed to be red. Halfway through November it became almost black and so he asked to see the doctor again. The doctor asked if he felt any pain or discomfort and then concluded that the peculiar colour of Tanino's tongue was due to the stomach pills. There was nothing to worry about, but he should continue to take them if he wanted to feel better with his ulcer. Just then the doctor was summoned to the office of the governor, De Santis. Tanino was escorted back to his wing and with a none too gentle shove the warders sent him stumbling into the cell. The day before the wedding, Tanino managed to get his hair cut and tidied. He had to ask the priest, because for prisoners in solitary confinement a periodical buzz-cut was the only procedure available. The priest cut his own hair and kept scissors and comb in the prison chapel. He managed to bring a degree of order to Tanino's hair, the parting was fairly precise and the cut more or less symmetrical. There was nothing much that could be done about the tongue, which was now black and remained so for as long as he continued to take Rabbro.

The 25th of November eventually arrived and it was a rainy day, far from what Tanino had imagined and certainly Ada as well. A wet wedding is a blessed wedding, the priest had told him that morning, handing over the suit which Raffaele, Tanino's brother, had deposited a few days earlier at the entrance lodge. The suit was elegant and grey, with a black tie. On top of the shirt and under the jacket he also wore a dark waistcoat, which served both to make him look a little less thin in the over-large suit and to protect him from the end of November cold, which had begun to penetrate the walls of Poggioreale and all its cells. Tanino was escorted to the chapel, a small room with cement walls and four low-quality strips of wood panelling along the sides. In the middle, a handsome white altar which hardly went with the rest of the room. The few wedding guests and witnesses arrived. Raffaele for Tanino and Michelina for Ada. From her side there were also her mother and two sisters, Tanino had no one else. Then she entered the chapel, on her mother's arm, and she was extremely beautiful as a twenty-year-old might well be. Tanino was surprised because Ada was wearing a long black coat, fastened up to the neck, and there was the hint of a smile on her face, in contrast to her eyes which were noticeably dull and lifeless. She advanced up the aisle and stood before the man who was about to become her husband, holding her tears back with difficulty and her belly by now quite large. The wedding march rang out through the room and was sung, unsteadily, by the assembled voices and Tanino asked the woman in a whisper why wasn't she wearing white. 'Because there's little to celebrate,' she replied with deadened eyes and then she stroked Tanino's cheek. 'There's this to celebrate,' he said, placing his hand on Ada's stomach. 'Yes, a child with no father, how it'll grow up I don't know,' she said, then added, 'Show me your tongue, the governor told me, he said you were ill.' Tanino put out his tongue, black as tar. 'It's all right Adaré, really it's nothing, whatever rubbish the governor's told you.' Ada managed with some effort to hold back her tears and all

Tanino wanted to do was go to De Santis' office and pin him to the wall, because the man wasn't satisfied with ruining a whole life, he even wanted to poison a wedding. The priest waited for the music to end and began to recite the office in a low voice that conferred on the ceremony a certain aura of intimacy, a murmured solemnity that was privileged to few engaged couples, with no loud appeals to the wider world, at least on this occasion. When the moment came Tanino and Ada exchanged kisses and became man and wife. This time she did not hold back her tears, tears which seemed to have little to do with the immediate emotion. He kept repeating, 'I'm fine, Adaré, don't worry,' but sometimes facts speak louder than words, even if the words are true and the facts not, and the fact was that Tanino looked like a corpse already, pale and emaciated as he was, and with the black tongue. After the kiss they were allowed another half hour for refreshments and to talk to each other before Tanino was escorted back to his cell, and he made the most of it to fill his belly as full as he could. There was a small buffet prepared by Ada's sisters, who had brought a selection of *antipasti* that were easy to make. He ate an enormous quantity of salmon and fish roe on bread, Russian salad and half a plateful of salami and cheese. Ada stood to one side talking with the priest, her hand obsessively held to her stomach. Tanino sought out his brother and they embraced and Lello looked very like him. Tanino thought he had grown, even though it was just a few months since he had last seen him. He looked healthy, with his head held high and his back straight, the Mastroni's large mouth, damp and shiny with the sparkling wine. Tanino asked his brother to stay as close to Ada as possible and to keep her calm, that whatever the governor had said was a load of bullshit, he would get through whatever had to be got through and would return to her in Marano and to the child. Raffaele told him that De Santis had called them in not long ago and announced to them that Carlo Gaetano Orlando had cancer of the tongue and that he didn't have long to live, perhaps a few months. 'All bollocks,' he said, 'honest to God, Lellù, you have to believe me, I've spoken to the doctor and I'm fine.' He could have said all that to Ada himself, as he knew, and he was shocked at himself. He had faced up to all manner of people and very few times had he come away defeated, as his past record showed, but with Ada it was different and maybe he had discovered a flaw inside himself, a weak point in his usual fearlessness that made him cowardly, but it was not love, no, it was something that had to do with the blood they now shared, and which in their children would tie them forever to their destiny.

A warder entered the chapel, announced that the ceremony was over and that the newly married man was going off on his honeymoon to suite thirty-three at the grand resort of Poggioreale. No one laughed. The relatives left the room and Ada was last to go, her blue eyes looking deep into Tanino's. She kissed him one more time, running a hand through his hair, and despite her self-possession her kiss was one of despair, and then she touched his hollow cheek. 'Listen I'm fine,' he said, and again she made no reply, just a sigh that had something of a laugh of resignation in it. In the middle of the reception room their ways parted, the Orlandos and the Manni going in one direction and Tanino in the other, to be plunged once again into that profound darkness, and who knew for how long. At the entrance to the special wing, Tanino touched his tongue and wondered whether the blackness coating it could be transmitted through one's saliva or by touch, or through a loving gesture such as a kiss. De Santis had lied to his family, it was not cancer, it was an illness like any other, which would pass along with the years in his cell. The governor liked his little joke, but Tanino was in no hurry, he put his trust in the swift passing of time and in the certainty that he would have the last laugh.

Of Tanino's sons, only the first two married, and in the case of Bruno, it turned out badly. He had four children, three girls and a boy, the youngest. Then, ten years or so ago he and his wife had their last big row, she took the children and whatever she could and moved to a small town near Milan. Over the following weeks Bruno switched between periods of great energy and confidence and periods of blackness, between moments of 'life is shit' and catatonic apathy. He moved house and went to live in a studio flat near the apartment in via Roma, by himself. It was there that he gave up drink, because he said that alcohol is either something you can take or something you can't, and he belonged to the second group. After a couple of years Bruno's eldest daughter decided to return to Marano because life in the north didn't suit her, and her father was grateful though he never said so. Her name is Adelaide, like her grandmother, and she is twenty and always perfectly amiable. We were good friends when we were little, and maybe we still are, even if we don't see each other very often, nowadays pretty much only when I'm back for the summer, at Enza's apartment, and sometimes at Christmas on the days she isn't spending at her maternal grandparents. She dropped out of secondary school in Year Ten and wants to be a tattooist. She does them already in fact, for herself and her friends, and on the pork skins she manages to bring away from the charcuterie where she works from time to time.

Bruno's last and youngest child is called Raffaele, named after Bruno's brother. He always wanted a boy and managed to produce one only after three girls. In his plans, when a boy came along he was going to be called Gaetano, after Tanino, but the death of Lello changed everything and Bruno, who badly wanted to feel the name *Rafé* on his lips still, decided on this name instead. He promised himself he would be his son's best friend, because he felt he was still young and he could get up to all sorts of games and mischief with this Lello, a new Lello, a young one whom he could set on the right path. And he felt, too, that it was a name that would define him, because the Raffaele Orlandos, the Lellos, are always well-liked, behave in ways that earn people's respect, yet they enjoy a certain freedom, very far from the enormous responsibilities borne by any member of the family called Angelo or Gaetano.

It could be said that the second and third of Tanino's children had a carefree youth. In Marano they could do more or less as they pleased, they were friends with everybody and those who weren't friends soon became so, even if they had recently come to blows. Sometimes they would walk drunkenly through the streets, laughing uproariously, always arm in arm, always with their heads held high, arrogant, confident in their own capabilities and the strong arms of Lello. In fact, it rarely happened that anyone provoked them or went looking for them, but it did happen. Lello was according to everyone, even the tough guys, a good man, almost devoid of malice, and fundamentally treated people he didn't know as his mates. On occasion it did happen, though, that someone would get too sure of himself and start to laugh or make fun of him for his way of speaking, for Lello had a noticeable stammer and found it hard to get his words out. Even if he laughed good-naturedly when his brother or his close friends pulled his leg, it wasn't the same thing if strangers did it, and if by misfortune some people did imitations of him more than once, or exchanged glances amongst each other, taunting him with silent smirks on their faces, then Lello gave them a slap in front of everyone and went back to laughing and drinking with Bruno, who would meanwhile tell the poor idiots spreadeagled on the ground, 'I warned you, I told you not to make fun of him, did I tell you or didn't I?'

The little house up at the farm is full of photographs of them together, right in the middle of the crowds, the other Marano lads they used to make merry with. The picture of Bruno with red eyes is the one I remember best, because behind his back the bonfire is blazing away. The Saint Anthony's day bonfire is on the 17th of January every year. In the days leading up to it, the young men of via Nova divide up the tasks to be all ready and prepared for one of the most eagerly anticipated evenings in the district. Bruno and Lello would borrow a van from anyone who would let them have one and would go knocking at every door in the old part of Marano, asking for unwanted furniture, tables, planks, the discarded bits from any carpentry work, just about every sort of wood possible, then they loaded it all into the van and unloaded it in via Nova square, just at the corner with via Edificio Scolastico. It was said that replacing your furniture once in a while brought good luck, and more or less everyone wants fate to be a friend, even those who don't believe in it. Then along with the others living near the square they set about breaking up all the wood with axes and hammers and Lello enjoyed himself hugely and even though it was winter he sweated out every drop of fluid in his body. The wood was all piled up together ending in a neat point, forming a sort of pyramid, the tallest pyre they could build. In the best years it could reach to eight or nine metres. They went to drinks wholesalers and spent as much as a hundred thousand lire on beer, and on the afternoon of the 17th they put it on ice in the square, under the guard of someone trustworthy. They cooked up large quantities of beans in aluminium drums to make pasta for everyone who was coming, there was the table piled with *panini* and also a stall with sweets and plastic toys for the younger children, who were included in the celebrations. The last essential element of the bonfire was the dummy, a construction made from old rags and dry sticks, commissioned from the dressmaker's, and which was collected on the actual day. When the sun set, the youths of via Nova lit the bonfire, the flames leapt up and the party began. Towards the end the fire swept over the dummy, which was tossed into the middle of the blaze and was devoured in scenes of delirium and excited shouts from the square. Someone sang out: *you know why my heart is beating, I've seen Maradona, oo-ay mother I'm in love*, the children ran around with toy swords and guns and the older ones lit joints and twisted the caps off the beer with their teeth and lighters, the juices from the meat that had been cooked beside the fire ran from people's mouths and Bruno and Lello found some stool or other saved from the bonfire, sat down, watched their town as it partied and toasted their youth, the most wonderful of any there could be.

Lello's last bonfire was in 2004, and he did not go down into the square to join the festivities because he had an IV drip in his arm and he was no longer strong enough, but he watched everything from the balcony of the second floor of via Edificio Scolastico, because from there one can see the whole piazza and via Nova sang and chanted for him. Someone from the street made a short film with a video camera and the cassette is still in the sitting room somewhere, heaven knows where. Lello laughed and waved to his brother who was celebrating down below with death in his heart, forcing himself to appear carefree but unable to take his eyes from the balcony and from Lello. At a certain point Lello went back inside and the young people in the square thought he was tired, that he must have gone to bed, he had had his fill of entertainment, poor Lello. Instead, after a while he emerged again and in his hand he had a vast contraption in gleaming metal, his legendary hooter, plugged into the mains in the apartment on a long black cable. Lello lifted the siren and set it off and the sound tore a gash in the night and rose above the voices of the square. Everyone turned and stared towards via Edificio Scolastico and began to yell and leap, and in the meantime, from the kitchen, Enza was rhythmically connecting and disconnecting the other end of the cable, so that the siren really was chanting with the boys of via Nova, with Bruno and with Lello for one last time on the night of the bonfire.

Summer is advancing and Marano, as usual, is rapidly emptying. The town is almost deserted and the only people still there are the elderly and those who work all year round and can only afford to take a break in September, or can't afford to take one at all. In the Orlando family Bruno is one of those; Enza has to look after China and Elena doesn't go to the seaside because she doesn't want to see herself, or be seen, in a bathing costume. In addition, in the evenings they go and visit aunt Michelina and Valencia to give them some company, because their aunt is slowly getting worse and isn't very strong. Even she is fast becoming worn out.

It has been the hottest summer I can remember and at the end of the month I have decided to go away for a few days, to the seaside. Beautiful places in these parts are plentiful, the Tyrrhenian offers crystalline waters and the further south you go from Naples the more places there are. This time, however, I have finished up on the Adriatic coast, in Romagna, where the sea is fairly disgusting like the waters round Naples. My host is Lorenzo, who studied at Turin with me and is one of my closest friends, one of the people you choose when you are old enough to understand whether you genuinely like someone. The train journey to Bologna took six hours, then from there we took another train to Ferrara and from that point a bus to Comacchio. For the journey I downloaded a couple of films and took with me one of the tattered copies of *Anelito* I found up at the farm. In its pages, Tanino recounts, in the first person, his version of the events surrounding the killing of Pascalone, but before getting to that point he takes you on a sort of journey through his life, a sketchy journey, non-linear, made of sudden recollections and moments that are not always clear and others that could easily have been omitted. Every so often there are spelling mistakes and other minor slips, but the voice of Tanino is clear and credible at every point, you can feel his anger at the injustices he believes he has suffered and in the end this is what counts. He must have written these pages quickly, both in and out of prison, and there is no room for fine words and turns of phrase. Most care is reserved for the poems, you can sense that he is proud of these and they all hammer away at the same point, the ill luck that has stalked him ever since he took his first breath, the sufferings he endured, both physically and in terms of his destiny, which tried to shaft him in every possible way.

Lorenzo and I arrived at the house by the sea and settled into our rooms, he let me have his parents' double bed and the handset for the air conditioning. The first evening we ate *piadine*, wraps, smoked a joint and watched a film, exchanging the occasional word and a few laughs. The next morning we went to the beach and I slept in the sun on the beach lounger. I smeared on sun cream several times, being especially generous when it came to the mark on my back, because mamma never stops reminding me in the messages she sends that you don't joke with the sun and it can get you without your noticing it. In the evening we bought pizzas and then went dancing with friends of Lorenzo from the beach, I drank more than usual and my sight became a little misty, I felt I was floating and under the flickering lights of the disco on the beach my eyes kept falling on a girl who was dancing with her friends, she even glanced my way and smiled and then turned away again, she had a beautiful bronzed body and was dressed partly for the seaside and partly for the evening, in shorts and with a tight iridescent top over her small tits. Her spangled sandals stirred the sand up and I realised that bit by bit we were edging towards one another. It is a fascinating phenomenon, there is something very ancient about it that I don't understand, the thing that pushes two people to seek each other out in a crowd, their movements ever more subtle and leading towards one single point, and gradually it becomes clear one last effort is required, one of the two has to expose him or herself, has to take a step which amounts to signalling I admit it, I like you, you've won. Her eyes grew more insistent and her smile flashed white in her suntanned face and there was a barely concealed mischief in it and I realised I wanted to get closer, see her properly, I felt excited, I felt my blood pumping harder, but I was still too sober, too sober to forget my responsibilities, my fears, the complications. *A timid man doesn't get to sleep with beautiful girls*, is a saying I've often heard and it applies to so many different situations, not just sex but life in general, but now these words had a literal meaning, the most instinctive one of all, and it made me laugh. I asked Lorenzo to go with me to the bar and have another cocktail, I drank it down in one gulp and returned to the dancefloor, the alcohol rose to my brain and I no longer knew what the hell I was doing, I was floating more than ever and swaying forward. When I got back among the crowd, at the exact same spot as before, the dancing girl wasn't there any more, nor were her friends. I lit a cigarette and looked around, looking for those eyes, those small tits, suddenly vanished forever, the opportunity to be young and act without thought thrown away again, drowned in a Negroni I don't even enjoy, not just this one in particular but all Negronis, which are as bitter as anything but help me achieve the 'high' of courage needed to get laid by beautiful women, which I don't have, but have always wanted to have. After a while Lorenzo and I left and took his bike for a spin along the coast; I was standing up behind him, with my hands on his shoulders trying to keep my balance in the dark, with the wind from the sea in my face and the mosquitoes pursuing us. Back at the house I collapsed, I went to bed and I slept until the afternoon, I read more *Anelito* in the sun and we got up only to drink or eat. Then in the book I arrived at a point in the story I didn't know, Tanino was talking about how things were when he was around twenty, and about his father, and there in the middle of it all I found a confession, a truth semi-articulated about a particular event, dated 1949. He was talking of another duel, one I had never heard mentioned before, one which even Tanino seemed reluctant to talk about. It mentioned another death before 1955, another murder, more blood spilled by Tanino by mistake. My hands started to shake and I realised I had joined up dots where there had previously been none, and the picture of the Orlando family now appeared more clearly before me. I phoned my mother and asked her what these pages were referring to, this ex-fascist who was mentioned and this sort of assassination attempt on Angelo the mayor. I asked her what death had occurred, whose blood was spilled and mamma remained silent for a while, then I heard sobs and her strangulated words, 'It happened so long ago, papà was young and there was an accident, we never talk about it in the family but we all know, I couldn't sleep for years when I found out, but there's nothing anyone can do, that's the way it went and that's the way it had to go, my papà got into so many scrapes, Francé, but this one he didn't deserve.' When I hung up so many things were swirling through my mind, and in that instant, that instant dated 30th September 1949 when the curse on Tanino and on his children began, I found the original sin which opened the way to everything that has followed and which carries its consequences right up to the present day, creeping silently underground to me, and now everything seems clearer and makes sense. Lorenzo entered the room and asked me if I fancied going to the beach to drink something cool, I said yes and I left the book on the bed, undressed and put on my swimming trunks, then we went out into the sultry heat and the deafening chatter of the cicadas.

In 1948, towards the end of spring, Carlo Gaetano Orlando—Tanino—was eighteen years old and relishing the cool, fresh air of Marano which, being on the slopes of the Camaldoni hills, had a perfect climate and a healthy breeze that blew all day. There were few streets at that time and the countryside stretched gently, green and yellow, for miles and miles. Tanino spent his own days doing very little: in the mornings he helped his uncles load the fresh fruit into the vans heading for market, went home to shower and change and then went down into the town again. Tanino had four younger brothers, all of whom were still at school, and in the apartment in via Ranucci there was only Elena, his mother. The two had a special rapport, as the *mammà* always has for her male children, and especially the first: they were inseparable. Perhaps she still had feelings of guilt, a guilt she would never completely expiate, that of having abandoned him for three years in the hospital's orphanage, with no parents and no name. But this was an old story and Elena had demonstrated many times that sincere mothers' love, Tanino had forgiven her when he was still a child and all was well. Deep down, he was proud of this story, born twice, two different names, in short he had always felt himself to be special and he had understood that historic suffering makes you wise in other people's eyes, especially if you don't complain, because if you do complain you can awaken feelings of pity, and Tanino at eighteen didn't yet know much, but one thing he did know was that no one should feel pity for him. After his thorough wash, Tanino put on a shirt and rolled the sleeves up to his forearms because summer was on the way. He couldn't bear ties and so he never wore one, and no sunglasses either, because he liked his eyes and Elena told him that there was something predatory in his gaze, a power that even other people recognised, and it was something he should be proud of. Tanino left via Ranucci to walk through Marano, and already everyone knew him. He was a Mastrone and the son of the mayor, a well-liked mayor because he fought for his town like a man condemned. Every Monday Angelo went to Rome to request funds for the commune: at the time the minister for Public Works was himself a communist, he was called Emilio Sereni and he was friends with Angelo, what they saw was an Italy that was great and a South that was ever more stuck in the past. The mayor was having a proper drainage system constructed for Marano, which still lacked one and when it rained it created chaos. Wherever he walked in the streets of the district Tanino felt at ease, he bestrode the creation of his father and he did so with his head held high. He greeted the shopkeepers and went into the bar to drink two, three, five coffees, and sometimes he paid for them and sometimes they paid for him. He made love regularly, several times a week with a girl called Rosaria, the pretty daughter of a herdsman out in the country who bought boxes of fruit from the Orlando family. He undressed her in her barn or out in the fields, with the sun on his bare back, the strong smells of the country mingling with the smell of their bodies. It was not a true and proper relationship, Angelo was a man of the old school and in his view Tanino ought to get married as soon as possible, that way he would be free to do as he pleased. He knew his son was a hothead and in his heart he was longing to have the responsibility for him off his hands. For his part, Tanino was well aware of his own origins, of the fact that he had been brought into the world by two good Christian people, unmarried, whose relationship was secret. So Tanino allowed his father to say what he liked, let him lament as much as he wanted the ever more corrupt ways of the world and all that; but then he and Rosaria disappeared for hours on end, secretly shagging, and everything was fine, Tanino was in no hurry to get married and change his life, aware that great things lay ahead of him anyway and that his moment would come, one way or another.

As mentioned, Angelo the mayor was well-liked in Marano, he carried himself like a true First Citizen and the poor people appreciated what he did for them. But he did have some political opponents, and one in particular had proved himself to be a real troublemaker: he was an ex-fascist militant, called Castrese D'Angelo. Besides espousing ideals in sharp contrast with those of the mayor, D'Angelo was at that time the *guappo* of Marano. A *guappo* is a swaggering type of thug who thinks he owns the streets, not quite a *camorrista* but not far off. The result was a constant, low-level power struggle with the mayor over local affairs and with Tanino a battle of honour and words. Admittedly, at that time Tanino had shown nothing yet, but his ambitions were already in clear focus, and he would have been happy to go along with any other man on Marano's streets if he had any merit about him, but D'Angelo did not, not by a long way. He was older than Tanino by about ten years and was genuinely feared in Marano. With his companions, his acolytes, they did what they wanted and sowed terror, at night, in the streets. He blamed the lack of security in the town on the mayor and on communism, he incited the mob against the dominance of the Mastroni who in one way or another had always been the leading lights in Marano's affairs. On his side D'Angelo had numerous angry young men, poor people who were hungry and didn't think that waiting for Angelo Orlando's funds would really lead to anything. He had acquired the title of *guappo* through a variety of circumstances, it is something you have to earn through strength, because it is measured on the streets and on the streets favouritism counts for very little. And also, it did him no harm that he bore the name of the patron saint of Marano, Castrese. All in all, the young man had more than one point in his favour for his claim to power on the slopes of the Camaldoni hills. When Tanino encountered him in the street he greeted him, lowered his head without meeting his eye or smiling at him and walked straight on without comment, but he had to acknowledge him and couldn't do otherwise and this fact made him all the more hostile. Whenever he bumped into D'Angelo his mood changed, he became disagreeable and responded badly, he made love to Rosaria without saying a word to her and left her sprawled in the barn when he had finished, going off without a parting caress, without a kiss. Every now and then at night he was woken by noises in the street, and he would then go and stand on the balcony and see the ex-fascist and his friends smashing a few windows, or pulling down the posts at the side of the road, they would throw empty bottles and laugh loudly and Tanino would grip the rail, glance inside the apartment towards his father's room, where he must be awake too because of the uproar, but he didn't get up, he didn't say anything and anyway he couldn't have, because he was the First Citizen, but Tanino knew that as a man of honour he was weak, he had too much faith in institutions and in people's goodness of heart, and his son considered his attitude to be foolish, idealistic, cowardly.

One morning D'Angelo went to the town hall, which was a few steps from via Ranucci and the Orlandos' home. He asked to see the First Citizen and had the brazen cheek to propose himself as the *Comune*'s watchman. It was obvious that he was aiming to set himself up alongside *il Mastrone* and who knows what he had in mind, he knew it was a request that stood no chance of being accepted but all the same he pretended to be astonished at the mayor's refusal, and at his counter-proposal that he should sign up with the employment office to find himself some proper hard work. D'Angelo left the office of *il Mastrone* with a little smile on his face and the mayor knew this was not the end of the story, that the *guappo* had something in mind and in that sick head it could be anything. He reported the incident that evening at dinner, over the table, and Tanino raised his voice and told him he needed to take precautionary measures before it was too late, he said, 'It's not a case of doing nothing, he's a hotheaded shit and he must be punished, papà.' Angelo replied 'I'll deal with it, you mind your own business, we don't bandage a head before we've broken it.' Tanino hammered his fists on the table and said, 'If something happens it's your fault,' then he got up, left the table, put on his shoes and went out. He walked briskly out of town, up and up, towards the open countryside, past the church of San Castrese. He arrived at Rosaria's farm and threw stones up at her window to attract her attention, asked her to come down, told her he needed company. 'Papà will kill me because of you,' the girl said, and he said, 'I can handle your father, I don't give a shit about him, come down.' Rosaria put on her dressing gown and slipped out of the house, followed by sudden yells and the heavy footsteps of the herdsman, who shortly appeared on the doorstep with a shotgun in his hands and his fat chest heaving in alarm. 'Where the fuck are you going?' he said, then he saw Tanino. He was standing there with his hands in his pockets and he looked over towards the man, who pushed a cartridge into the gun and pointed it at the young man, closing his left eye to take aim, but his hands were still trembling from his sudden fit of rage. Rosaria went and stood behind Tanino, crouching down and with tears in her eyes. The herdsman recognised Tanino, made as if to put his finger on the trigger and Tanino stood there unperturbed, he stood where he was and for answer merely lit a cigarette. The man with the gun gave a cry of anger, lowered the weapon and spat on the ground, 'You're dead,' he said to his daughter, then he turned back inside, slamming the door.

'Don't worry, he won't do anything to you, you know he respects me,' Tanino told her, to calm her down, as he pushed her against the henhouse, took her clothes off and kissed her sweating neck. The girl was crying and Tanino repeatedly stroked her as he came into her, he told her that soon she would have nothing to fear, that no one would stand up to him when his moment came, not even an ignorant herdsman of a father like that one. He said his moment would come and that he would be respected and feared by everyone, in Marano and beyond. He swore it, not to the girl but to the heavens, the night and the stars.

I stepped off the train at Piazza Garibaldi station in the early evening, with the August sun stubbornly hanging in the sky until a late hour. Enza came to meet me and China was in the car with her, sitting in the back, and they were both full of smiles as usual. Enza always welcomes me with the same enthusiasm when I return, it makes no difference whether I have been away for months or just a long weekend, to return and all be here together again is an excuse for celebration. Caught up in central Naples' traffic there is always time to gossip, and she asked me how the holiday had gone, she wanted to know about Lorenzo, if we had enjoyed ourselves and so on. I said that better than enjoying ourselves we had been able to relax, that I felt better for having baked in the sun and indeed she remarks that I am browner than she is. In the past Enza used to go down to the sea at least once a week and she developed a really deep tan, as her father had recommended. After making sure I was genuinely better and calm after the week at the seaside, she told me she had some news. Aunt Michelina is no longer with us, she said in her delicate way, the funeral and all the rest has already taken place, your mamma and I didn't tell you because you were on holiday and you needed to enjoy it. I was a bit upset, I told her: 'But what the hell are you saying, why don't you ever tell me anything.' The truth is that she and Elena have always tried to protect me and keep me at arm's length from death and other unpleasant things, they've been doing it for years, they didn't want to show me the end of life before I was old enough, but now they've begun to die off like flies in our family and keeping me distant from it all had become too difficult. Death has always been part of the family, it has always hung over the homes of the Orlandos like some distant relative who you know will return and pay a visit at some point. Yes, you know, but this doesn't mean you can face up to it without all the inevitable consequences. Each death that I didn't see with my own eyes I saw in the eyes of my mother and aunt, in the lines on their faces and in their hair which is no longer the gleaming colour of old. I have seen it in the extra kilograms they put on by way of emotional compensation, out of sadness, and I realise that this fatness has something primordial about it, like mother bears that accumulate fat for the winter, for the harder times ahead and which the cubs, by themselves, would not be able to survive. And I, for them, am still a cub, something to be preserved, something that has to be kept away from troubles, from the curse that hangs over them, even though I am more grown-up and maybe ought to get by on my own, to expose myself to life more, even if it means facing squarely up to death and danger. I believe this is the biggest difference between me and Tanino, one of us an uncertain spirit and the other always swift to act, a boy who doesn't know what to do and a man who has taken on full responsibility for any issue, even those that don't affect him directly. I sensed a certain anger rising in me, an emotion I rarely feel and one which was hardly suitable for the present situation. I imagined Tanino's mocking smile, his eyes examining me from behind his dark glasses without a trace of pride in me, an absence of any faith in me, blood of his blood.

The death of aunt Michelina did not upset me in itself, I have always been rational about these things and my aunt had been suffering not just from old age but from the disease that was eating her away from inside, and to be honest I had had few memories of her. As always, it is not the act of dying that is frightening as much as the consequences it brings, and the consequence of this death had already been clear for some time. When we are nearly at Marano, having negotiated the 'Titanic' roundabout, Enza has confirmed that now Valencia will be staying with us, she said even she is returning to the fold; after forty-five years in another house with another mother, a daughter of Tanino is now returning to the place where she belongs, and I wonder if, in his time, Tanino had foreseen this as well. We parked beneath the apartment block in via Roma and went up to the flat and Valencia and mamma were waiting at the door, the twins truly united at last. Elena hugged me, smiling, with tears in her eyes, I held Valencia tight too and asked her if she was well and she answered, 'eh', her gaze lowered and the same neurotic smile as always. The female children of Ada and Tanino are still all fine, and living close to each other gives them strength. In the evening we dined together and even Bruno came, who never absents himself on occasions like this. He teased Valencia and China as usual, in his affectionate way, he danced with them and made them laugh. Then with Enza's help they moved half the kitchen furniture, because it was a small room and with another very large person in the apartment it was hard to make ourselves comfortable and the table in the middle alone took up half the space. We moved the furniture and we were sweating, and Enza said we didn't need it anyway, it doesn't matter, and we distributed plates, pots, cups and glasses pretty much anywhere we could in the kitchen. At the end we were tired but at least there was extra space now, and so we all ate an ice cream together to cool ourselves down. Bruno went back to his own place and I left too, mamma stayed behind to sleep with Valencia in her new room, the little one that had been mine for years and then Bruno's after he had separated.

While I was going home I thought of all the other times we had had to reorganise ourselves after the death of someone. The mad rush of telephone calls, funerals, people coming to the house to offer condolences, all those remarks about eternal sleep, tiredness and hunger relegated to second place, until you don't know who you are and then you eat like an animal and sleep like a child.

The next morning I woke late, and after looking at myself in the mirror with half-closed eyes, I told myself I needed a haircut. Over the last few months it had grown too long, down to my shoulders, and the healthy effect of the sea water was beginning to wear off, it had gone dry and frizzy, a dullish yellow. So I left the flat and went round to Nello's, the barber just round the corner, a few steps from San Castrese church. I've been having my hair cut there since I was seven, but since I've been living away from town I have rarely been back. Nello is in his forties and he welcomed me with his customary friendliness, which some barbers seem to do for every one of their customers, they can remember all manner of stuff about them, and so you feel that every time you go to get your hair cut or your beard trimmed, you're resuming the conversation from last time as if there had been no gap at all. I waited my turn and then Pietro washed my hair. I kept my eyes closed while Nello talked to me and asked how I was and I said fine and he said me too. I sat in the chair, he put the sheet round my shoulders and he began to thin out my hair as I'd asked. He circled round me as always while talking either with me or the other regular customers and Pietro, commanding the situation with enviable calm and precision. He asked about Enza and I told him not bad, I explained a little of the new situation and he said, '*Ua*, what a *ciorta*, that family of yours.' *Ciorta* is '*sorte*', fate, and the Orlandos' fate has always been clear and all of a kind. Nello explained who I was to a man of about fifty, 'Tanino 'e Bastimento's grandson,' he said and in the mirror I saw the other's face register an expression of vague astonishment, as if he had suddenly appreciated that I was a fellow with balls, but he didn't say anything. 'A Christian chap like your grandfather, Francé,' he said as he smoothed out a tangle with scissors and comb, 'comes along once in a hundred years. There was always a place at Tanino 'e Bastimento's table, if you were dying of hunger he put a plate in front of you, and the amount of money he gave away with nothing behind him, you could go to him and he'd say you can give it back later, don't worry, and loads of people never gave it back at all, but that man never cared about money, what mattered to him was that Marano should be all right and people should respect him, *grand'omm*, the big man. But then he did all those years in gaol, how many did he do?'

'More than twenty in all,' I tell him, '*More than twenty*,' he repeats, turning to the small crowd waiting their turn while my hair drops to the floor. 'A great gentleman,' he says expansively, 'but your uncle Lelluccio…' He stops and removes the scissors from my hair, puts his thumb up and looks at me in the mirror and says: '*Number one.*' He does a quick imitation of his stammer and then goes on to mention various evenings round the table at the farm where he was present as well, the laughs and the insults and the demijohns of wine that would enter the scene full and leave it empty. 'Tanino was a great gentleman but Lello was the real staff of life, he was the leading spirit of the *Fucarazzo*, the great bonfire, he was Marano.' He does the last details round my neck with the razor then lifts the sheet away. He asks me if it's all as it should be and I say yes as always and I thank him. I pay him and as I'm going out the little group of men waiting nod at me in acknowledgement, dip their chins, as if I deserve respect for the blood that's in my veins. Outside the sky has clouded over and I can feel the air cool on my skin and in my hair which hasn't been so beautiful and glossy for a while.

My mother and I have always enjoyed going out by ourselves. Family occasions and obligations are things she hates and she has never done anything to hide the fact. Among her relatives, some have never been her sort of people, and when there was a lunch or an event she would send Enza and me along, saying I must stand in for her, and she would make me tell them she was unwell, she had a bad headache or her hernia was playing up. The Orlando cousins have always treated me well, in part from a certain wariness they felt in dealings with my mother, because there was nothing they could do about it and she has always gone face to face with everyone, responding harshly if they said anything against people who weren't there. As a joke the cousins called me *TheSonOfElena* or Milord, for my somewhat unusual colouring and for the fact that I was always quiet and when I did speak I spoke in a soft voice and in Italian. At weddings and celebrations in restaurants I enjoyed myself, they would secretly give me wine to drink or let me puff on a cigar, they slipped me a few coins and told me to buy myself an ice cream and when I left after a session with the Raffaeles, the Armandos and the Angelos it was always with full pockets and a light head.

With Elena though we treasured the moments we stole together. She worked and has always worked, from morning until evening from when she was eighteen, at the same place the whole time. It was Russo who found her the job in this small diagnostic centre he had recently opened in Marano, and over the years it had grown to be a big concern. Tanino had put her to work as soon as she had finished high school, in 1994, because you weren't allowed to stay at home doing nothing and because in those years they were beginning to need the extra income, because Tanino was old and had virtually nothing left and Ada had never been obliged to work. Elena was glad to be out of the house and away from her siblings and parents for a few hours a day and then they paid her, she began to be independent. After a year or two she got to know Daniele, who had been employed at the same place as a radiology technician. He had blue eyes and he made her laugh, all the time. They had met almost from his first day and had fallen in love, they made love secretly in the clinic's empty rooms and went out secretly, because Tanino mustn't know a thing. He would never have accepted a boyfriend he didn't know, not even one from Marano, and he would not have allowed his eldest girl child to start having sex without the prospect of marriage. For her part, Elena's one desire was to be her own woman and escape the asphyxiation of via Edificio Scolastico, which is why, after a while, she found accommodation of her own. It was a one-bedroom flat in a block Tanino had built but which belonged to the Mannas, the relatives of Ada.

When we went out together, just the two of us, mamma used to take me to the prettiest parts of Naples she knew, to see the *Veiled Christ* or to have lunch in a restaurant she had been to years before, perched on the cliffs. Her favourite place was the Pozzuoli seafront, where she had gone with Daniele on the first few dates and where he had bought her roses and they had smoked joints together sitting on the rocks and had clinked bottles of ice-cold beer. After a couple of years, in the summer of '98, she found herself pregnant. Tanino knew nothing about Daniele, let alone any grandchild, but at that time he was not well, keeping to his bed, his head wasn't right and for quite some time it was easy to conceal the pregnancy. In the meantime, however, Elena and Daniele were hastily making arrangements for the wedding, which would have been the only solution that allowed Tanino to accept the situation. One evening, Elena, Ada and her sister Angelina, a midwife at the Medical Centre, got in the car and drove to Pianura, to the house of Daniele's parents. They needed to discuss the engagement and come up with a plan to smooth everything out, but within a short time frame, if possible before Elena gave birth. Daniele's mother was called Adelaide—another one—but everyone called her Adele, the husband was Antonio and they were both radiology technicians, an educated family in other words, and had never had anything to do with personalities like those of the Orlando family. And then Adele was a churchy sort of woman, but in the true sense, one of those who go to mass every afternoon and are always involved in the parish church or on retreats, people who read the Gospel and the Bible and whose sense of catholic morality is genuinely strong and bows to no one. The result, that evening, was that Daniele's mother couldn't believe her ears, she had had to learn within a few seconds of imminent grandchildren, surprise weddings and relatives whose names now and then ended up in the papers. Adele rose from the table and drove her visitors out of her house, the pregnant Elena, the anxious Ada and even Angelina. She said the whole thing was totally absurd and she didn't want to hear another word about it, there was no place in heaven or earth for such things. Ada didn't know what to say, nothing like this had ever happened to her in all her life, she had never been invited to leave a house where she was a guest and she was rendered speechless. Elena began to cry and Daniele swore at his mother. Antonio chased after the women to apologise and told them there was nothing to fear, that he was mortified, that everything would be resolved and Adele would come round. 'I'm very pleased to have a grandchild,' he said to Elena, 'really pleased.' Daniele left the house in tears with the Orlando women and apologised several times on his own account, with his hands in his hair and his face bright red. Ada didn't utter a word during the whole journey back to Marano and Elena held her stomach, her head even more messed up by the knowledge that two out of the four parents were never going to accept this pregnancy. She thought of her grandmother Elena, that poor girl who had been forced to give her son away for the first three years of his life, because she was not married. She wondered if the fact that they shared the same name meant something, if she too were destined for the same outcome, but that doubt blew away in an instant. Now the mother was her, and she would do it in her own way, the baby would be born and would be at the centre of everything, never mind Adele and her God; never mind Tanino.

On the 18th of September 1948 Tanino woke up when it was still dark. Summer was over and the first chilly winds were beginning to sweep the night streets of Marano. Tanino was in bed and toying with the good luck charm, a cross, round his neck and unable to get back to sleep. The affair with Rosaria had ended a few days before, she had decided not to see him any more and had begun to refuse to leave the house. More than once Tanino had stood under her window at midnight, whistled and thrown stones and the girl's only response had been to turn out the light in her bedroom and close the curtains. So Tanino had stopped trying, he wasn't short of female company anyway and he knew very well Rosaria was only a distraction and to be honest, she wasn't even a good match, she couldn't read or write, and attaching oneself to a family with an old-school peasant farmer such as the herdsman had never looked like a good idea to anyone. And yet the idea continued to keep him awake, he was not used to being rebuffed and it was not a sensation he enjoyed. Meanwhile the sun outside was rising in the sky and daylight was flooding his bedroom. He heard his father getting up and then his mother. The metallic clatter of the Neapolitan coffee maker came to his ears and the smell of coffee spread stealthily through the apartment.

His brothers were still sleeping peacefully in their rooms and soon they too would be up and off to school. Tanino, on the other hand, would be making his daily rounds in Marano, and perhaps go into Naples to cast an eye over the market. When it was almost eight, Angelo, on the other side of the door, put on his coat and hat in front of the mirror in the hallway. He was due to go to Rome on the train, he had an important meeting with the minister Sereni at Termini station and he wanted to make a good impression, as always. Elena came up behind him, adjusted his hat and brushed the back of her husband's coat. 'May Our Lady go with you,' she said, then she kissed him on the shoulder and followed him to the door. Angelo smiled at her and asked, 'What are you giving me for dinner tonight?' She replied, 'We'll see.' He repeated, 'We'll see,' and descended the building's main staircase. He walked along the path beside the building and noticed that Elena was now on the balcony watching him, as she did every time he had to go and catch the train. Angelo opened the metal gate and closed it behind him again, and at that precise moment Castrese D'Angelo came round the corner of via Ranucci, walking rapidly, in his right hand, thrust forward, he was gripping a revolver and in a flash he fired a shot that sent Angelo's hat flying and the mayor heard the whistle of the bullet past his ear, he put his hands up and then turned round to open the metal gate which had now clicked shut. Elena was watching from the balcony and she felt her legs give way, she gripped the railing in both hands as hard as she could and shouted her husband's name. D'Angelo's quick strides brought him closer and he fired another shot which sent sparks off the metal of the gate, Angelo was struggling to find his keys in his pocket and found them in his shaking hand while all the time trying to stay clear-headed and act quickly, the figure of D'Angelo was coming ever closer, he would be unlikely to miss his shot next time. The mayor thrust the key in the lock and turned it as hard as he could, with too much force, and the gate didn't open and he snatched a look behind and D'Angelo was six or seven metres away. Angelo glanced rapidly up at his wife, in case it was for the last time, then managed to release the gate while out of the corner of his eyes he saw D'Angelo's arm lift. He hurled himself with all his strength at the main door which opened at the moment the ex-fascist fired a bullet that smacked into one of the iron bars of the gate. Elena cried out, Angelo dropped to the ground on the path and kicked his feet back to slam the gate shut again, then looked up towards the balcony and saw his wife slump to the ground and he no longer knew where to look. D'Angelo came still closer and his face wore the expression of the devil, he seemed out of his mind and Angelo thought he was going to die, but Tanino came out of the building just at that moment and he had a kitchen knife in his hand, he shouted, 'You shit, you're dead, I'll kill you so help me God.' Angelo scrabbled back on the palms of his hands, still lying on the ground, and his son helped him to his feet. D'Angelo stopped at the gate for a second, looked at Tanino with something that was almost a smile, as if he had been expecting this, as if it was a challenge, then he turned calmly round and set off running, back in the direction he had come from, disappearing round the corner. People were out on their balconies and beginning to jabber, someone pointed to the balcony and Elena, who was lying on the floor, helpless, Tanino said, 'Mamma,' just 'Mamma', then picked his father up in a flash, propped him against the wall and ran inside.

At the Cardarelli hospital the doctors told Angelo and Tanino that Elena had had a heart attack and that it was a miracle she had survived, but she had slipped into a semi-comatose state and her condition was very serious. In the waiting room Tanino's brothers all sat with their eyes lowered, the youngest were crying and Raffaele didn't utter a word all day. They were able to bring Elena home, to bed, though only after they had spent a week sitting at her side in hospital. In the meantime Castrese D'Angelo had been found and arrested, but Tanino knew that this was far from the end of the matter, and no reason to rest easy, because the man he'd shot at was a communist, and doing the calculations, the *guappo* wouldn't remain in prison for long. There followed months of worry, with Elena's condition inexorably worsening, interrupted by intervals of lucidity lasting several days during which she did nothing but cry. She woke at night calling out Angelo's name, and Angelo would take her in his arms and say, 'I'm here, I'm fine, don't worry.' Tanino heard her from his room and he was consumed with rage, he had never felt this way, he burned with the injustice of it and he cursed himself for not having had a gun on him at the time. Inside, he began to hatch the idea of a vendetta: it was the only thing that enabled him to get to sleep at night, that prevented him from going mad. D'Angelo had no idea of what awaited him when he was released, that would be the real pay-back, and he would pay in blood, Tanino only had to hit on the best method but now he had no further doubts. You don't attack the family, he was thinking, especially mine, and you don't attack unarmed people. He prayed his mother would be restored to health and in his head he advised D'Angelo to pray for the same outcome as well, because otherwise, my God. My God.

On the 15th of August, we were supposed to go up to the farm, it is where we traditionally celebrate the Feast of the Assumption.

But now that the peasant has gone, the undergrowth is too neglected, the grass is rampant and the country spiders have woven their webs in every corner of the little house. So Angelo the Twin has invited us to his place and the family lunch went ahead just the same. Not that it was all that important usually, but with the arrival of Valencia there was a need for some sort of distraction, to make her feel at home and to get through a day without too many worries for Enza and Elena. We went by car, with me squeezed in the middle between the two sisters, who didn't speak. Angelo welcomed us enthusiastically and as soon as he saw the four sisters he pretended to be terror-struck, he called out the Furies have arrived, every man for himself. Sitting at the table were Bruno, Giuseppe—the other twin—with his wife and little daughter, and Lucia, Enza's and mamma's best friend, who grew up in the same building in via Edificio Scolastico, but on the floor below. It had a large terrace, which their second-floor balcony looked out over, and from there the young Orlando sisters laughed with Lucia and played tricks on her dog when she was inside the apartment. When Tanino was in a rage, they often sneaked down to Lucia's flat, played cards and waited for their father to calm down or go out on his rounds.

We sat down at table and Angelo brought out the cold meats and the mozzarella cheeses, white and gleaming and succulent, and the milk was soon dribbling from the corners of our lips. Giuseppe started refilling my wine glass every time I looked the other way, and I knocked it back with pleasure. Bruno noticed that no one was talking and asked, ‘What’s this silence then?’ Elena said what Bastimento used to say, and all the others responded in chorus, as if it were a mechanical reaction drilled into them by time: ‘When you eat you’re keeping death at bay,’ there is no need to talk.

Enza brought out the pan of ragù and the container with the cold pasta, in this way we could decide whether to choose between something lighter or have a taste of everything. She and Elena had their glasses filled a few times and I saw them finally relax, because they haven’t slept for days; they haven’t even been going in to work because they’re trying to see to both China and Valencia and help the recent arrival settle into her new home. Then they started talking about the 15th of August celebrations in the old days at the farm and began to bring out their memories. Elena mentioned grandfather Angelo, the mayor, who never gave her or her siblings money or presents, because they were the offspring of Tanino and Tanino was a black mark on the family. Only the first-born was well treated by his grandfather, because he bore the same name and perhaps because he too had shown that his ideas were very different from Tanino’s. For the twins, however, it was a different tune, because they are the offspring of Raffaele, the one his father loved most, and of all the Mastroni they have always been the most favoured. They say that relations between the mayor and Tanino changed when the son ended up in prison for the first time, in 1949. They had different ideas about how to make Marano a better place, and Tanino’s close friendships during the Eighties were almost all with people on the right. Disappointment in the children is an arguing point that often comes up at family meals, and this middle generation, the one between me and the mayor's children, was born in a period of affluence that was always in the balance, poised between strong ideals on the one hand and ill-favoured destinies on the other, and they consider themselves the most unlucky, because none of them has been able to match up to expectations, no one has continued with the fruit business or has made himself a *guappo*, a popular leader, and so over the years they have lost their sense of well-being and their resolve, they have remained as they were, framed within ideals they were never sure about, but grew up in. And a Neapolitan education is like this, blood carries too much weight, and is hardly something one asks for, but once you have it you have to get on with it, carry it forward with all the consequences, and unless you have your own ideals, new ones, you have to operate within the ones that have been imparted to you, because the important thing is to have values of some sort to preach, to propagate one's own truths and not fall into a void. But here everyone is anchored to a seabed that is too solid, they go round in circles and run the risk of taking on water and sinking below the waves, indeed someone has already done so and didn't even realise, and yet they carry on in the same way because they are the children of Tanino and of Raffaele and of Angelo and of whoever, and blood has to be honoured, which makes it all the more vital to have these get-togethers.

Then we ate the meat from the grill and on the side we had all sorts of aubergines, roast or with mushrooms, in oil or with parmesan; then fruit and sweets and liqueurs. It suddenly began to rain, hard, and we retreated under the terrace for shelter. Giuseppe asked me to pour him a couple of fingers of limoncello and while he was still drinking it he fell asleep in his chair, his head thrown back, as peaceful as a lamb. Elena was smiling and humming little tunes, laughing with Lucia and Enza over some past event, because these days they only remember nice things from the past. Meanwhile the downpour vented its fury on the grass the plants and the earth. Angelo showed me a new book he had bought, it accounts for the works of our ancient human ancestors, such as the pyramids or some Greek temples, which must have been created by extraterrestrials because no human could have either the tools or the capacity to build some of the world's marvels, nearly all of them connected with the divine, something up there which can't be seen, which governs the lives of women and men from on high, while we carry on believing we are alone, believing we are making our own choices. Who knew?

For a few seconds we were all silent, looking out at the rain which was soaking the ground. Bruno broke the silence, saying, 'Would you believe it, on Assumption Day,' and accompanied the remark with a gesture of finger and hand as if to say go away. Pretty much all at the same time, we got up and left, promising to see each other again before September. Enza went with mamma and me in the car and it had stopped raining, but water was running through the flooded streets like an untamed torrent and the car sent up little waves even when it was going slowly. I helped Elena out of the car and we were standing in water up to our ankles. We climbed up to the apartment and she was still a bit tipsy. She took off her shoes, left them on the balcony and disappeared along the corridor towards her bedroom. She emerged again with her eyes gleaming and a transparent plastic bag in her hand, and in the bag was a cassette tape. We went into the kitchen where there's the stereo that Daniele gave her twenty years ago and she removed the cassette from the bag. I took it in my hand and on it someone had written in biro Gaetano Orlando—poems. I slid it into the tape compartment and after a couple of mechanical noises and a long silence it started to play. I heard the voice of Tanino for the first time and tried to make it out. He was reading one of his poems, it seemed to be called The Cry, and his voice was calm, it had something of the quality of Bruno's voice and a tone like Enza's, the slowness and the clear way of articulating the words were similar to Ada's. In the meantime Elena sat down beside me, with a strange smile on her face, the saddest I had ever seen, her eyes lowered, practically on the floor, and her head moving from side to side in a slow and everlasting no. Meanwhile Tanino's voice, scratchy given the passage of time, comes to our ears, but in the end it sounds like any other voice, the voice of an old man who is reading the words he has written, the pain he claims to have endured, the wrongs he has suffered and a thousand battles won or lost with honour, but always just the voice of an old man. Mamma has had her eyes closed for a while and her head has fallen back against the backrest of the divan, so I've taken the cassette out and replaced it in its little bag, I've turned off the stereo, the lights; I looked at mamma from the doorway to the hall and I went off to get some sleep.

The Cry

As they declared him guilty
he heard a cry.

A shrill cry
that pierced his heart
more than the verdict itself.

The judge was reading out
his sentence
but now he heard
nothing, he heard only
the echo of the despairing cry
of his woman.

She had come there,
to that dark courtroom,
to bring him, after so many years,
home with her.
Instead she had to return alone.

Another long calvary,
the odyssey of a woman
was not yet over,
the reverse, it was beginning again
whilst he would be put back
between the freezing walls
of a freezing cell,
with the sole difference,
that now it would be not just
pain that kept him company,
but rather,
the despairing cry also
of the unfortunate
woman, his beloved.

Gaetano Orlando, 12th February 1964

THE SECOND DUEL

The winter of 1948 was a long, slow one. Tanino could not remember so cold a winter in all his eighteen years, with such persistent rains and even snow, which lay on the streets of Marano for some days, to general amazement. There were children who played in it for the first time in their lives, they made slides wherever they could, they threw snowballs, they put the stuff in their mouths and rubbed it into their skin. Tanino had watched his brothers from the apartment windows, whilst trying to care for his mother as well as he could, while Angelo was out at work.

Spring arrived and Elena's condition grew no better, rather the reverse. She had grown thin, there was hardly any flesh on her bones any more, her breathing was weak and halting, and words were almost a forgotten memory. Doctor Caniglia called every week and it seemed to Tanino that after each visit the doctor's expression was ever more grave. Tanino would stand blocking the doorway and say Doctor, speak plainly; the medical man would reply and what am I supposed to say, isn't what's wrong with the *signora* obvious. During the attempt on Angelo's life, Elena had been convinced her husband was dead, she had seen him collapse after the shot was fired. Her heart had failed her and reduced her to these circumstances. She no longer ate, she spoke in monosyllables, her words were disjointed and never made whole sentences, she did not laugh. Mainly she wept, she woke from sleep full of nightmares and called out her husband's or her children's names. Then Angelo would appear, enter her room and sit on the side of the bed, stroking Elena's hot and perspiring brow a few times, until she closed her eyes and went back to sleep.

Out in the country, green shoots began to break through the earth again and grow, the farmers resumed their hoeing and planting and at the end of March Castrese D'Angelo was released from prison. It was uncle Armando who warned Angelo and Tanino of the fact, the mayor was surprised and Tanino not at all. Not a day had passed without his thinking about the man who had nearly ruined his life, who had succeeded in just a few seconds in destroying life for his parents and who was at liberty again, still a *guappo*, a boss-man, and still more dangerous. D'Angelo started to patrol the streets of Marano once more and the people greeted him as they had done before, as if nothing had happened, as if he had not dishonoured the name of the Mastroni. He still walked about armed, the pistol visible, stuck in the back of his velvet trousers and it was a display of power, because there were no wars and he had no other enemies. When he toured the streets he always passed in front of the town hall and not far from the vicinity of via Ranucci, so that either Tanino or his father might easily run into him. When that happened, D'Angelo was all smiles, he sought eye contact, he made loud mocking comments. If he was with one of his followers and Tanino was crossing the road they would start laughing, spit on the ground and whistle. Tanino felt ready to explode, something inside him caught fire, he hated his father for not taking any precautions and he hated himself because he hadn't managed to do anything either, and there was little he could do against a man always armed and surrounded by friends. Tanino had his own friends as well but they were all young like him, still boys, still more scared of dying than of anything else. Tanino began to go more often to the places where D'Angelo habitually hung out, he walked along Corso Europa in the middle of the road, throwing glances to right and left. He didn't exactly know what he was doing, the reason behind his wish to come face to face with him, defenceless. But if he didn't catch sight of him on his rounds, he was restless at dinner, at night he didn't sleep and his thoughts were all directed towards the former fascist, he had become an obsession.

One night, at the beginning of May, Tanino was returning home after a drink with some friends and cousins. They had been out in the country, high above town, so Tanino had to descend the steep roads that led back to the centre. He was fairly drunk and to keep himself steady on his feet he leant against the walls lining the sides of the road. For a few moments he thought about turning round and going back up, to go and say hello to Rosaria. He hadn't seen her for months: she wasn't often in Marano, she didn't have any friends from school because she hadn't been to school, but spent the days helping her father with the sheep and hens and the harvest. On a few occasions Tanino had gone up to where their land began, hiding behind some fig trees, from where he could watch her throwing out crumbs of old bread or hanging washing on the line. He was not in love, he didn't even feel the loss of her for most of the time, but there was something sweet about her, a sweetness Tanino found he liked. The idea of having a womanly hand to look after him was beginning to grow on him and there was something maternal about Rosaria, even in the way she looked after her father.

When he reached San Castrese church he was still thinking about these matters, so that he did not notice that round the corner were D'Angelo and two of his acolytes. Grabbing Tanino by the arm before he had time to react, they began to attack him with kicks and punches. D'Angelo stood to one side, with a cigarette in his mouth, as if he had staged similar scenes many times before. Meanwhile Tanino was trying to wrench himself away, hitting out blindly, and he made contact with a nose, and indeed one of the two kids laid off him to put a hand to his face and Tanino seized the moment to dash past the *guappo*, but he, the *guappo*, caught him by the trouser leg and Tanino fell to the ground. The kids pulled him to his feet again and pinned him against the wall, pinioning his arms. D'Angelo strolled up close and laughed, there was something abnormal about him, no one acted that calmly in such situations. Always there was a rush of euphoria, or adrenaline, the urge to move fast and lash out, but D'Angelo seemed to be savouring the moment and Tanino felt a wave of loathing. The *guappo* put his face a hand's width from Tanino's, drew on his cigarette and said, 'Okay, go and change your trousers, you shit-faced wimp.' He opened his mouth and belched in his face, blowing over him—to make Tanino's greatest ever humiliation even worse—a mouthful of smoke. The other two started to laugh and it wasn't just to provoke him, they were properly laughing, tears in their eyes, they were doubled up with laughter and in that moment Tanino could have escaped, but he remained where he was, he let himself slide down to the ground, against the wall, while the two of them jeered at him and went on their way with D'Angelo, one leaning against the other's shoulder from laughing so much at what they'd done to him.

Tanino returned home without saying a word, everyone was asleep. He undressed in the bathroom and he was still shaking, he had bruises on his chest and abdomen but he felt no pain, he felt only Castrese D'Angelo's breath in his nostrils, it swirled in his brain. He thrust two fingers down his throat and vomited into the lavatory pan, keeping the tap running to cover the sound of his retching. He slid into bed, naked, buried his face in the pillow and let out a yell, with his teeth clenched and his mouth closed. He punched the mattress and the pillow, he beat his fists against his own body and pinched his stomach as hard as he could, until tears came to his eyes. His head and his eyes were bursting and after a while, exhausted, a sense of damnation filling his soul, he fell asleep.

The following day he woke late, the sun already high in the sky. Angelo was out attending to the business of the Comune and the younger ones were at school. Elena was in her room, breathing softly, and her son entered the room to greet her, say hello and ask if she needed anything. There was no reply.

Tanino made himself some coffee, and after slowly smoking a cigarette, set about emptying every drawer in the apartment. He opened the cupboards and turned out the bedside cabinets, he checked under the beds and in the shoe boxes; he went downstairs to root around under every plant in the garden and look inside the letter box. He was sure it was there somewhere, Angelo had it, for certain, he had even seen it once. Then he realised the answer was obvious. He returned to the flat and went into the bedroom where Elena was sleeping. Tanino hovered in the doorway for a few seconds wondering whether she was awake or not, but these days it didn't make much difference. Tanino squatted down near his mother and stroked her stiffened face, her breathing was almost imperceptible and smelt stale, old, smelled of something more not here than here. Meanwhile he slid his other hand under the mattress, swept it rapidly over the bedsprings, cold beneath his fingers, then suddenly felt something soft, silky. He got it in his hand and drew out a box covered in red velvet, with his father's initials on it. He concealed it behind his back so that Elena wouldn't see it and carried it from the room. Tanino settled in the kitchen and opened the box on the table: the inside was partitioned into wooden sections and in the middle, disassembled in four pieces, was Angelo's pistol. It was a Beretta M35, it was around fifteen years old but it still looked like new, the black metal gleamed brightly in the sun. He sat there for a moment, working out how to reassemble the gun, trying to fit the pieces together. Finally he managed to attach the barrel to the body, with a *click*, then he mounted the whole thing on the handgrip and pushed in the magazine, empty. There were no bullets. Tanino raised the pistol, it felt just the right weight, like all well-made things, and it was black and quite small, elegant in its proportions. He pointed it towards the window and closed one eye, then held his breath to stabilise his aim. Beyond the window he could see Corso Italia, the longest street in Marano, where people were walking up and down, going about their business and living their lives according to the paths assigned to them, without stopping or questioning themselves, and Tanino couldn't understand that. He had a desire to change things, and now he had the means, an object as small as a pistol was enough to make his voice heard, to follow a destiny or go against it, to reverse the fate of the town and re-establish the Mastroni as the leaders of Marano, more firmly than ever. He picked up the phone and dialled Russo's number, waited for him to answer and then told him you have to teach me to shoot. They arranged to meet out in the country on the Arecca hill, where the roads climb towards Quarto and towards Camaldoni, where there are few people and plenty of wide open fields.

Russo brought his own pistol and a tin box with a collection of lead projectiles in it. He was a few years older than Tanino and had fought in the war, managing to sneak his weapon home when everything had calmed down. The May sun was fierce and Tanino had to roll up his sleeves and undo his shirt buttons halfway down his chest. He also put sunglasses on, because they had set up the targets with the morning sun behind them. The targets were bales of hay and glass bottles, the green ones containing the country wine that almost anyone produced who had a bit of space on his land. The first thing Russo showed him was the proper stance, the supporting leg firmly on the ground and the shoulders rigid.

He warned him about the recoil, that he mustn't suddenly take fright at the instant of firing but hold the pistol firmly in position. The first shot was fired by Russo, and it went and buried itself in an oak standing several metres to the side of the targets. He said, 'We're too far away, we need to get a bit closer, Tanì, you don't have to be a crackshot.' Tanino, however, had already taken up his position; he put two bullets in the magazine and snapped it home, took off the safety catch and lowered the hammer; he gripped the pistol firmly in his hands, so that all his fingers were in contact with the metal, then he pointed the barrel at the targets and after taking a quick breath pulled the trigger; the silence was shattered, the birds rose flapping their wings, the sun and clouds continued to hang motionless in space and a bottle twenty metres away exploded in a thousand pieces and in every direction, like drops of water from an emerald green pond after someone has thrown a stone into it. Russo did not speak, but the expression on his face was unequivocal, it said as plainly as could be: 'Shit, man!' He fired again at another bottle and succeeded in knocking its top off, leaving the rest standing. He hadn't aimed precisely at that point, he was merely trying to hit the bottle, but after his two shots it was evident to him that he had some talent for it, or at least that it came to him quite naturally, and even Russo said the same, he said, 'Tanì, that's brilliant,' but he also warned him that it was one thing to hit a bottle, which was standing still, don't forget, and another thing to fire at a fellow being who moves and breathes and who might not do so any more. Tanino replied, 'Let's hope so,' then reloaded the Beretta. He succeeded in hitting almost every target and only two or three shots flew off into the distant thicket of trees. Afterwards, he and Russo sat on the trunks of two fallen oaks, ate bread and prosciutto and shared a large bottle of Peroni. Russo asked him if he was being forced into doing this and Tanino answered no, he was under no obligation to do anything but he wanted to do it, he wanted to damage D'Angelo in some way, but he had not provoked him, he had not attacked him first because there were people who respected him in Marano, not everyone hated him, and if Tanino wanted to kill him he had to do so for a reason, even if both he and Russo agreed that the attempt on Angelo's life and Elena's condition were already more than enough pretext. When the afternoon air began to shimmer through the trees and the long grass, Russo handed his friend a small bag containing six bullets, he said, 'These should be enough if you shoot the way you shot at the bottles, and I definitely didn't give them to you, understood?' The two parted with an embrace and Tanino told him, 'When it's done, you will know, a lot of people will know.' 'Amen,' Russo replied with his eyes turned to heaven, then he departed in one direction and Tanino departed by another way.

On the 15th of May, at ten in the morning, the storm showed no sign of abating. The rain had begun to fall the previous evening, while tables were filling for dinner, then it had turned to hail and then to violent rain again. Marano was totally awash, the drainage system, still under construction, regurgitated grey-coloured water and sewage into the streets, the roads and tracks that came down from the countryside above had become torrents of mud and scum, and the flat part of Marano, including Corso Italia where all the town's activity took place, was a lake of dirty water up to the knees. From his bedroom window in via Ranucci, Tanino could see people using buckets to try to clear the water from their shops; on the street they were trying to keep their umbrellas upright as they were lashed by the wind, a wind not so much cold since it was by now late spring, but wilder than anything that had been seen for years, even in the harshest winters. Tanino was holding the Beretta between his hands, he had been polishing it every day for the last week. At night he kept it under the sheet, along with a bullet, and played with it to help him get to sleep, he had learned to put it together and take it apart in a few seconds, even without looking. He could empty and refill the magazine in a second and now he knew the weapon intimately he had only to make it talk and this rain, so different from what was normal, so exaggerated for a Sunday like any other Sunday, confirmed his conviction that this was the day. He wouldn't kill D'Angelo because it was raining heavily, it was raining heavily because he had decided that D'Angelo should die, destiny was giving him a scarcely veiled sign and Tanino always looked out for signs, above all else, and this, in the long run, was what would make the difference, would draw the sharp line that separated Tanino from other men.

Just after eleven he got dressed, white shirt, trousers. On top he wore his camel-coloured raincoat, a present from uncle Armando, and pulled the belt tight. He didn't want to get his hair wet and so he put on the fedora belonging to his father, who never used it these days. He loaded the pistol with all six bullets and slid it into his waistband at the back, between pants and trousers as Russo had taught him. He went to say goodbye to his mother in her bedroom, brought her a glass of water and kissed her gently on the forehead. It was burning hot.

Tanino left the apartment and closed the door behind him. He left the umbrella with the rest of them, because he was bound to get wet anyway. He went out of the main door and there seemed to be few people on the streets, then he realised that Marano's citizens were all standing at their windows or sheltering under the shutters of the shops that were open for last-minute purchases before Sunday lunch. They were looking out at the pouring rain and the flooded road, a river in spate in the middle of the town, a river with no banks. Tanino had never even considered the possibility of not encountering D'Angelo, even in the middle of the deluge. He was driven by an invisible force, something that Tanino suspected moved all things and all persons, at the opportune moment. And indeed, just like the waters that flowed from the incessant rain, just like the eyes of the people at the windows, the footsteps of Tanino and Castrese were converging on the town centre. They had seen each other from a long way off and neither of them gave any sign of changing course. They forged their way through the flood as if crossing a ford, and it was high noon. There was no sun and Tanino imagined that it too was standing aside, watching, from behind thick clouds. On the pavements at the side of the road people greeted him, sheltering under balconies or inside shops waiting for the rain to stop. All the while, the *guappo* and il Mastrone were getting closer, Tanino was able to make out his features and his clothes, similar to his own. When they were about twenty metres apart Tanino thought he was already close enough to do it, in his head he saw the fragments of the bottle he had destroyed flying everywhere; one well-aimed shot from here and it would all be over. He imagined D'Angelo's body exploding as the lead hit him, he saw his crystallised entrails erupting with the sound of shattered glass. But D'Angelo did not stop, he carried on walking and Tanino too. Level with the baker's, they came face to face, soaking wet, and the baker paused in his serving of the customers, leaving a loaf half wrapped, the small change still on the counter. The man who was buying it turned round as well, and a woman in the queue stopped rocking the baby she was carrying in her arms, a tiny thing. Only the rain did not stop. Tanino planted his feet on the pavement and raised his head, with one hand on his hat; D'Angelo put his hands on his hips and waited for a remark or a comment that did not come, so he looked towards the baker's shop and said, 'What a good little kid, he's come to buy the bread for his mamma, if you don't mind I'll go first, I don't have time to waste.' He turned away, started to walk towards the baker's and Tanino followed him. Then D'Angelo stopped outside the shop and shouted loudly: 'A loaf of bread for me and one for my friend here, who has to take it back to his whore of a mamma.' The *guappo* span round just in time towards Tanino, who in that short second had slid his hand under his raincoat. Tanino released the safety catch as he raised his arm, he had no time to take a breath as he had been taught, he had no time to take aim or measure the shot but he fired anyway, with his eyes shut. D'Angelo flung himself to one side and finished up on his knees in the water, but before Tanino could fire again he splashed the filthy water at him and moved further away, took out his own pistol and fired a shot that flew harmlessly wide; Tanino squeezed the trigger again, blindly, squeezed it again and his enemy was on his feet, but D'Angelo had to retreat, he hadn't anticipated a shooting match, and so he ran towards the baker's shop and the people inside, as another bullet whistled past his ear and buried itself in the shop wall; D'Angelo took shelter behind the woman with a stick of bread and the baby in her arms and both of them yelled in terror, but the man realised he had run out of bullets and Tanino saw it, savouring already the splash his dead body would make falling in the water, so he took careful aim, the woman moved aside and D'Angelo stepped quickly to stay close to her, the baby girl was screaming, Tanino breathed one last time and fired again. There was silence.

Castrese D'Angelo fled from the spot, a rapidly receding figure in the watchers' eyes. Tanino stood motionless and dropped the pistol to the ground. The woman was on her knees in the street, her mouth gaping wide in a grimace, the most unspeakable agony captured in a single expression, a unique combination of facial muscles all moving at once. The newborn baby was gripped in her arms, limp, with a hole in its tiny back, the red ring contrasting with the white shawl. The blood began to mix with the water, which carried it away in an instant, along with everything else. Tanino removed his hat and held his head in his hands, his legs had gone weak. The crowd had gathered round him and even the people at their windows came down into the street, people were arriving from everywhere. The woman didn't make a sound, she just knelt there, eyes pointing heavenward and her mouth open, the bread still clutched under her left arm and holding the baby with her right. For a second Tanino thought of holy images, of baptism, the body and blood of Christ, of the sin which now entered his body forever and which he would never set aside, for certain things cannot be washed away even by the flood.

No one had ever said a word to me about the tragic event of that 15th of July. Everybody knew about it, in the family, they have always known. They came into the world as children of Tanino and understood what that meant from when they were very young. Of Tanino's sin they were informed when the time was right and accepted it, and they have carried it with them as a burden that has been measured in tired eyes, weak smiles, crops of black hair, rotten teeth, ill-treated bodies and poisoned organs. And now the meaning of it is beginning to colour the things that I know, the consequences I have seen and the persons with whom I share this blood. Right from the start there was something driving me on towards this abyss, this pit of mire, buried by Tanino and by Ada and by their children and siblings. The destiny of Tanino 'e Bastimento has rebounded on those he brought into the world, the Dirt and Filth that entered his mouth and body have not receded and have overflowed the confines of his own flesh, and if he has paid his debt and set those things right, the same cannot be said for the persons who have shared with him homes, name and blood. The children of Tanino have borne his sin with dignity, joining hands and sharing it between them to lighten the weight, but without ever escaping undamaged. They are not strong like their father, they have never been and have never sought to be. They have tried to put limits round it, the sin, to keep it amongst themselves, promising not to pass it on any further, across the generations now living and those to come. This is the thing they have always shielded me from, I understand it only now. But whether they have succeeded I cannot say. Ada was convinced they had, she was certain that I had been born healthy, unblemished, on the contrary more pure and bright by contrast, following the law that balances things out over time. I have grown up in Tanino 'e Bastimento's places, up at the farm, and in the houses he lived in, I have heard the stories about him, and I have heard about the love that was always reserved for him, but love alone it can't have been, and indeed it is not. Grandmother has always told me that the family is the most important thing, she said it again and again to Elena and Enza whenever they quarrelled with Bruno, to Angelo and Lello whenever they quarrelled with Tanino, to me when I quarrelled with my mother. But what she meant was not ignorant, unconsidered love, she has never asked anything of the sort from any of us. We had eyes to see, and a measure of judgement, and family does not mean shutting them to give space for love to thrive. For her it was something different, something ancient, a necessary suffering that we all must endure, with no need to mask it.

'Blood may be chewed but it can't be spat out,' that is what Ada has always said. And it is through blood that the children of Tanino have become what they are and we become what we must be. We are connected to the persons with whom we share it, and it is not a question of affection or compassion. We are connected because blood brings with it both contamination and cleansing, it runs in the fathers and the mothers as it does in the children, and its weight is transferred from vein to vein and some veins can deal with it and some veins cannot. And however much we may be disgusted by those who bear it besides ourselves, however much actions define people more than genetics, however much we would prefer to spill it on the ground rather than pass it on to some new-born life, we cannot spit it out; we look ahead, we march on, and with our teeth we grind away at the clots of this blood we have been chewing on.

The Apgar index is a clinical assessment based on checks carried out on a new-born baby, in its first minutes of life. Five parameters are taken into consideration: reaction to stimuli, colouration of skin, heartbeat, respiratory rhythm and muscle tone. Each parameter is scored from nought to two and added up. If it comes to more than seven, all is well.

On the morning of 28th February 1999, two of the Orlando siblings were married, the other five not. Of those five, two were at the Naples Medical Centre. Enza was waiting in the corridor outside a white door, she was twenty-two. On the other side of the door was Elena, who was a year older and that morning weighed two hundred kilos. She was lying on a bed that strained to support her and in truth the whole room was finding it difficult to contain her. Alongside her in the delivery room there were two other sisters, Ada and Angelina, the head midwife of the natal unit.

Also at the Naples Medical centre, in another corridor, Daniele was walking up and down and wondering how the hell the woman he loved could weigh two hundred kilos. Elena had been shut away inside that room since the previous day. Sixteen hours in labour and still the creature didn't want to appear. After all, only eight months had passed and the child did not seem to be in any hurry to come into the world. Nothing dramatic, what's a bit of waiting. It wasn't that Elena was getting bigger all the time and there was any risk of her dying by being stretched to such a size, if the normal timing of things was respected. When he was summoned, Daniele entered the crowded delivery room and looked at Elena, her legs apart, her face bathed in sweat and an expression of desperation and rage in her half-closed eyes. She yelled at Daniele, 'You shit, I hate you, it's your fault, if you hadn't made me pregnant none of this would be happening, scum.' Thanks for the shit, Daniele thought, holding his tongue, then he said, 'You can do it, you're strong, we're in this together.'

For the first five seconds after the baby's birth there was an unnatural silence, for such a crowded room. In those five seconds the doctor wondered why the baby was not crying. Elena must have understood something from the look in the doctor's eyes, because she suddenly thought, here we are, I've given birth to a retarded son. Then the baby cried and Daniele cried and Elena had already been crying for sixteen hours. The baby was given a score of five out of ten on the Apgar scale, Elena didn't want to hold him in her arms because he was all smeared in grease and blood, and he was taken away to the premature baby unit. When Daniele and Enza went to greet the new baby, he was very easy to spot. The room was full of incubators and the incubators were full of babies as thin as spiders. The incubator with their baby was in the middle of the room and I was sleeping inside it, my skin now clean, and a dark stain on my forehead. I quickly became notorious among the nurses as the nine-pound premature baby, and both Daniele and Enza thought I was the only one there who looked like a proper baby.

Elena was soon out of bed and as is customary, she fell in love with her child. She weighed two hundred kilos minus the weight of the baby, she had milk in abundance and for a while she even gave it to the other premature babies. Other tests were carried out, the baby was healthy but the lungs had not yet completely formed. It should really spend two months in another clinic, in Salerno. 'In Salerno,' Elena shouted, 'no way, my son is staying with me.'

Meanwhile, in Marano, Bruno was on the pavement outside a bar called XXIV May, a meeting place for the town's youth, which faced onto via Nova and via Edificio Scolastico. He was drinking Campari and gin and waiting for news from the Medical Centre, trusting in the law that says for every life that is taken from us another is given. A new life was what was wanted, someone to bring up, laughter and tears, nappies and first words. Lello popped up unexpectedly in the silence of the early afternoon. He was in a battered Fiat Punto, one hand on the steering wheel and one hand firmly holding the object he had on the roof. They had told him not to go to the hospital, there were already too many people there and then it was common knowledge that the Orlandos always caused an upheaval and that was the last thing Elena needed. He parked beneath the apartment block, Bruno left his glass half full on the pavement and ran towards his brother, laughing while the thing on the roof grew ever larger. 'He's come,' he said, and still couldn't believe it. 'He's come,' Lello replied, and the two brothers embraced and began to bounce up and down the way they did at the stadium, they hugged each other in a crushing embrace, their voices rousing the old people taking their post-lunch nap. Lello said to Bruno, 'Give me a hand, we've got to hang this thing out.' Twenty minutes later, from the Orlandos' balcony right down to the floor below hung a monstrous rosette in some blue material, three metres high and two metres wide. It would remain there for a month. A wind arose and blew its new breath on that Sunday, and on the ribbons of the rosette, which fluttered proudly over via Edificio Scolastico. Lucia, the friend of Elena and Enza, came out on to her terrace and saw above her the giant blue beast flapping. She brought China back to the floor above, to her own apartment, because she couldn't stay there by herself, still less go to the hospital with her sisters. Soon Ada and Enza returned, their eyes were still sunken with all that crying and the smiles had dug creases like streets in their hard faces, a broad, curving slash not seen on their features for a long time. After it had spent the necessary few weeks in the incubator, Daniele and Elena also returned, with the infant, which bore neither the special name of its mother's family, nor one of their classic forenames, nor their colouration. The mark on the forehead had disappeared but another one had formed, on the back, like a dark gash. They passed the baby from hand to hand all evening, like a rosary between the fingers of an old person in church, they wept and they laughed. Enza looked into the baby's face and asked the room, 'Who knows what characteristics his father might have given him?' Ada thought: he doesn't look like me a bit.

Carlo Gaetano Orlando became a fugitive in the May of 1949, following the involuntary homicide of an infant barely three months old. He escaped to Sicily, where the Mastroni had for some time had strong commercial connections with some market traders on the island. He spent the summer of his nineteenth year in hiding, he thought about his mother every day, her precarious condition became even worse thanks to the activities her first-born had become involved in. It seems that Elena constantly invoked her son's name, in her increasingly rare moments of lucidity. Tanino was arrested at Trapani in September of the same year. By telephone he made arrangements with the carabinieri at Marano, who in exchange for a confession promised to allow him to go and see Elena and spend one night with no bars at his window, before being escorted to the prison at Poggioreale. After a week Tanino was brought to Naples, in the belief that he had one evening before turning himself in, but that liberty was not granted him. He was arrested on October 1st by the forces of law and order of the Comune of Naples the minute he entered the hotel bedroom he was due to stay in, at the Hotel Vittoria.

Elena died on the 20th of December, aged thirty-eight, with the name of her son on her lips, while Tanino was locked up in the Firenze remand wing of the Naples district prison service. It was his lawyer who informed him of the loss; the young man was not granted permission to attend the funeral.

Castrese D'Angelo did in fact die, in another shoot-out, with Antonio Orlando, Tanino's uncle. The same uncle who would meet Pascalone in prison some years later, and following an altercation, receive a slap in the face from the big man, thus giving rise to the series of events that eventually resulted in Tanino 'e Bastimento being the man he was.

The first trial of Carlo Gaetano Orlando took place in June 1950. The only witness for the defence was in fact the very woman whose baby had been killed in the gunfight. The woman testified how it was D'Angelo who pushed her into the bullet's path, that Tanino was not to blame for the terrible outcome, that the ex-fascist was a tyrant, a dangerous man and a man without scruples, in contrast to the Orlando family and the values they promoted. In fact the woman was newly pregnant again, and when she gave birth to another daughter, the person chosen as godmother was Rosetta, a younger sister of Tanino.

In the end Tanino received only a two-year sentence, but he suffered the full life-time prohibitions of the law. Article 1 deprived him of the right to vote, to take out a driving licence, to serve the nation by doing military service; any political activity of any sort was forbidden. From that moment, Tanino lived a half-life, a life in which the things he wanted he had to take for himself and by force, hidden from the eyes of the law.

Nevertheless his spirit was not broken. As the saying goes, 'To cry over a death is a waste of tears.'

By the end of August the heat is still holding its grip on Marano, there hasn't been a breath of wind for months and there is a water shortage in the houses. The underground pipes have burst in several places around town and water trucks are making stops in the most heavily populated areas to allow families to collect and save some. In the old part of town, in the evenings, the street lighting rarely comes on any more and you have to tread carefully, minding your step, on streets that have seen no maintenance for years, picking your way round great cracks, over crumbling asphalt and lifted cobblestones. It seems that Marano is slowly wasting away, everything is dying and nothing is being born.

The farm is in a pitiful condition too: the big storm on

Assumption Day made the ground even more bumpy and uneven and the weeds have covered just about everything. The little house is full of spiders, on the floor is a layer of dust a finger thick and Enza has disconnected the electricity, because bills are what they are and if no one goes up to the farm then paying makes no sense.

I have been to Bruno's flat, he sat on the bed and I sat on a chair like the ones we have at the farm. I asked him to tell me about Angelo, Tanino's first-born child. I haven't seen much of him, less than all the others, because he married at eighteen and no longer lived near his parents. Bruno and his sisters have always seen him as a case apart from themselves, and as far as I know, he is the only one ever to have genuinely rebelled against his father. He says that as soon as he found the right woman he wasted no time getting away from the family home. He constructed for his own family a different morality, he found his own values and he passed them on to his children, five girls and a boy (who nevertheless was given the names Carlo Gaetano). In adulthood, he also found a faith, a faith different from that professed by the Mastroni, more ancient and tied to the words of the Holy Scriptures. He became a Jehovah's Witness and rejected the Trinity and the Madonna. He recognised God the Father as the one and only creator and Christ as no more than a son, who, yes, spread the word of eternal life amongst mortal men, but who in the end remained a son, whilst the Father remains the Father. And yet both Angelo and Tanino tried to remain close, they respected each other for being, both of them, self-made men, growing up in the shadows cast by generations of the town's heroes.

Angelo returned to the family a few years ago, when his

health was beginning to decline. He didn't go to via Roma, but when he invited us to lunch at his house, Ada was overjoyed, I would hover at his elbow and wait for something to happen, he had me sit next to him at table and would ask me what I wanted to be when I grew up. I remember him with hair already grey and with black eyes, with dark circles round them that made them seem enormous, bigger than his siblings', deeper; he kept his little fingernail long, compared to the others, as is the way in certain levels of society which see it as a mark of men who are important, noble by blood or through their values.

Bruno was the one who had the closest relationship with his elder brother, and in their own way they each considered themselves the first-born, one by right of birth and the other because he was the first that Tanino actually saw grow up. In his adolescence, Bruno sought out his elder brother's company on several occasions, because the seventeen-year age gap between them meant that Angelo had learned a few things. Angelo used to give him advice, taught him how to deal with Tanino as if he was any normal parent, gave him money for travel expenses when Bruno had to play away matches some distance off and couldn't tell his father, because football was a waste of time that would never get him anywhere.

When Angelo discovered he had cancer, a few years ago, he resumed full contact with his family and his mother. Ada remained in the dark about everything right until the end, when it was clear there was little to be done. Elena and Enza told me everything and they prayed every day for Angelo to get better, they were anxious their mother should not be forced to see a son of hers die for the second time, she would never have survived a blow of that nature, and yet time passed and Angelo grew steadily worse. In May 2016 he was taken to a hospital in Rome, where he underwent an operation on the diseased bowel. The operation seemed to be successful, but something went wrong. Septicaemia set in, an infection caused by the appearance of harmful pathogens in the blood. They had to intervene at once, and maybe a blood transfusion might have changed things, but Angelo never accepted the idea of mixing his own blood with someone else's, remaining faithful to the last breath to his own doctrine, which holds the practice to be unacceptable.

The house telephone started ringing one morning at the beginning of June, waking me up. With my head on the pillow, I heard my mother's footsteps going into the kitchen and answering, then I remember the 'What the hell are you saying, what the fuck are you telling me?' I remember mamma's voice, which lost all tension, then a 'No,' desperately repeated several times, 'No, no, no, my brother, my Angelo.' I remember Elena's despairing howls after she had hung up, while I buried my head deeper in the pillow, trying to sleep because it would have been better, it would have been easier if I had been asleep and instead, no, I had to feign it to spare myself that moment, to avoid going to my mother and hugging her and crying with her, to avoid feeling the pain and the responsibility of sharing it. Elena dressed, left the apartment, and when I heard the door slam I managed to open my eyes. I knew what was going on in via Roma, for Ada and Enza, and I knew that I ought to have gone as well. I stayed in bed for nearly half an hour, staring at the ceiling and finding the strength to get up.

When I arrived, grandmother's flat had already been invaded by hordes of visitors. People were shuttling between via Roma and Angelo's flat, where his children were, while the body of Tanino's first-born was still in Rome and would only be returned home the next day. I remember the desolate faces, the embrace with Elena and the despair of Ada, sitting helpless on the divan, her legs unable to carry her, her face in her hands, and Enza on her knees before her, confessing in a tormented wail, red-faced, to having prayed every day to the Lord that Ada might die first somehow or other, maybe that very night, to respect the laws of nature and spare her the greatest grief that any of us humans know.

I remember the funeral and Ada's lost look, the hole dug in the earth of the cemetery and the framed photograph of Angelo now standing next to Lello's, beside the TV set.

In the March of 1960, there began the great trial of Carlo Gaetano Orlando for the murder of Pascalone. Four years had passed since the duel on Corso Novara, which Tanino had spent in various cells from Naples to Viterbo. Four years without knowing anything. There had been talk of a life sentence, of thirty years in total for premeditated murder. Tanino hated the idea of being called a 'hired killer' and the facts of that July morning in 1955 spoke clearly enough. Pascalone had been shot in the wrist and had died from a haemorrhage, which happened the following night after undergoing an operation. Equally clear was the fact that Pascalone was the first to reach for his pistol, and that Tanino had simply been the quicker. In any case, the event made a big impact in the media and the whole of the country's press was in attendance. It was said that this was a trial of the *camorra* and Tanino couldn't believe it, they were calling a single pistol shot the *camorra*, a dispute about honour had turned into organised crime. The trial lasted forty-seven days and dozens of people were called to testify against Tanino, people who by strange chance were all residents of Castellammare or Palma Campania, the dead man's home district. Pupetta was present all the way through, sitting behind a host of lawyers who all looked the same. To Tanino they seemed nothing less than a pack of sharks, from the witnesses to the lawyers, from the magistrates to the newspapermen, they were all against him, or very nearly. Ada was always there, she never missed a session, she lived on the train between Naples and Rome and when she could she took Angelo with her as well, who was three years old and for the most part slept in his mother's arms. Every time he saw him, Tanino couldn't believe he had brought into the world a living creature, a creature who moved, spoke, breathed as he did himself, like all those others. He itched to be a husband and a father, but the longer the trial went on the more he could tell which way it was going, and soon his hopes began to fade, the hearings became more heavy to bear, Tanino's answers more confused, more weary. He seemed to be beating his head against a wall made of hundreds of people, to be speaking in a void and not to be listened to, on the contrary to be listened to only when he came out with something that could be misrepresented. As for Pupetta, she seemed to attract universal sympathy. She became the symbol of female strength, of redemption. A woman with a gun, who had lost her husband and had taken her revenge all by herself: it was impossible not to cheer for her. And since the presumed instigator of her husband's murder had paid with his blood, the moment had arrived for the assassin himself to undergo exemplary punishment. The sentence was delivered on the 15th of May by presiding magistrate Montefusco of the Court of Appeal, who confirmed the rumours that had been circulating for months: thirty years behind bars for Carlo Gaetano Orlando. In the courtroom Ada dropped to her knees, felled by the weight of the words pronounced by the judge. Tanino did not lose his composure, he continued to stand with his head held high, in the suit that was becoming increasingly too big for him, his feet firmly planted under his tired legs. It seems he confined himself to uttering just one remark: finally the farce is over. Tanino was taken under escort from the courtroom, he looked his wife and his son in the eye and in his gaze was all the determination of a man ready to face the consequences of a hostile destiny. He was taken back to the prison at Viterbo, where he remained for another three years. Sitting in the armoured police truck, the little scraps of springtime to be glimpsed through the small window reminded him of that day's date. He found the fact that it was May 15th funny, because on the same date, eleven years previously, he had genuinely attempted to murder a man for the first and only time in his life.

But there is another May 15th that Tanino remembered for the rest of his life: 1963. As it happened, after three years in the city gaol at Viterbo, the ruling of the Court of Appeal was being challenged and the Supreme Court was preparing to put the sentence on hold. Hope stirred anew in Tanino's limbs, and in conversation with his father, he learned that the date for any decision would not be later than May 15th. Angelo promised his son that if the miracle were to happen, he would send him, in the evening, a 'most urgent' telegram on red paper. In the event of losing, however, Tanino asked not to be informed at all, because if the original trial proceedings were confirmed the words 'matter concluded' would be spoken, and he really would spend the whole of the next twenty-two years in a cell.

That mid-May morning, Tanino informed the governor that a red telegram might arrive during the day, he asked him to send it to him immediately, because every minute without knowing was torture, and every tick of the clock like a crushing blow. Life or death, Tanino continued to think, death or life. He spent the whole afternoon walking up and down the gangway of the cell block, and at times, the slaps on the back from his fellow prisoners brought him back to reality, to a present he found dreadful and which he didn't think could truthfully be called 'life'. He wanted to be alone, he was irritated by every crude word spoken by the other inmates, their repeated advice, 'Don't think about it,' eventually made him feel nauseous, the resigned looks of the ones covertly encouraging him to be like themselves, there was so little he could do about it, so little worth believing in, and Tanino hated these dead-inside people, he didn't want to become like them, he didn't want to hand victory to the warders, to the magistrates, to Pascalone, to D'Angelo and to his most tenacious enemy, the foul face of destiny. And in spite of all that had happened over the years, in spite of the gaol sentences and the defeats, in spite of the obstacles and the spilled blood, in spite of the odds being always against him, perhaps for the first time on that 15th of May, Tanino was afraid. He was relieved when the lights went on and the warders ordered them back to their cells, because that way he could be alone and because after all that prowling up and down his legs could no longer carry him. He huddled under the thin sheets, his equally thin legs drawn up to his chest, shivering although it was springtime, because its warmth was reserved only for the world outside. He thought about what it would be like to wake up the next day if the telegram had not arrived, he thought about the idea of resignation, of acceptance, which he had so fiercely rejected and which, by dawn, might have been able to claim victory. He came to think that perhaps his life was over, it wasn't worth the pain of carrying on, that if he didn't win himself then it was better that no one else should either. Tanino was preparing to wave the white flag, to surrender for the first and last time, but he would not give satisfaction to the people here inside, who wanted him to. He got out of his narrow bed and knelt on the floor, assembled paper and pencil on the board he used as a writing desk and wrote three letters as the evening drew in. The first was addressed to the prison governor and set out the last wishes of Carlo Gaetano Orlando, explained that it was not his own hand but the hand of justice that had taken his life; that he cursed them all, with all his strength, from Montefusco to the last warder, while reserving for himself the mercy of Christ. He explained furthermore that there would be no need for a post-mortem, because he would kill himself by cutting his veins and swallowing forty Perequil tablets, the tranquillisers distributed to the inmates, which Tanino had never taken, keeping every single pill in the regrettable event that the day to put an end to it all might arrive. Meanwhile the sun had disappeared and of the red telegram there was no sign.

The second letter was addressed to his father. He thanked him for everything he had been to him as a father, for the sacrifices that had followed and for taking on his own shoulders all the legal expenses that had come his way. He urged him to take care of Angelo, who bore his grandfather's name and who was similarly destined to become someone, who needed a guide in the world and someone who would explain to him who Tanino had been in his life; he asked his father's forgiveness for the manner he had sometimes adopted, especially after Elena had fallen ill; then he told him not to be unhappy, because Tanino was freeing himself from the inhuman injustices of which he had always been the victim, that it was better to have a son dead by his own choice than a dead man living on into a shameful old age.

The most difficult letter to write was the last, because it was for Ada. This is what he wrote:

> Dear Ada,
>
> wife and life's companion, my greatest passion. My heart is torn because I have not been able to bring you the happiness you deserved and I wanted to give you. I want you to know, though, that you have brought happiness, to me. With you I have tasted in all its aspects a joy that I will take with me wherever I am. My love for you is infinite, I have loved you with every sinew of my young life.
>
> Now that I will cease from strife, my wish is that you will be able to do the same, because you have waited for me for too many years and I would not ask you to do so for another twenty-two. If I married you it was because I was convinced we would be apart for a short while, only a few years. And if I did not hesitate it is because I would never have suspected that justice could have made such an iniquitous error, otherwise I would never have joined our fates together. Forgive me. As for our son, the fruit

of our love, I have only a few things to ask of you. Love him always, and even more than before, because now your affection must stand in for mine as well. Remind him who his father was, do it often so that between you both you do not forget me. Speak of me as an honest man and an honourable one, and not the hired assassin they have wanted to condemn me as. You will make him understand that if I have taken my own life it is not out of cowardice, because his father has never been a coward, but in order not to give satisfaction to those who have contrived that my youth and my whole existence should be shut away behind these walls, which thank God you cannot see. Some will be pleased at my death, will perhaps celebrate it, but in the final balance I place my faith in the one person who has shown the purest of feelings for me. Adaré, remember me always with affection. I would have given my life for you, and you should know that my last thought is for you, and I take my leave remembering my great love.

Yours forever,

Gaetano Orlando, 15th May 1963

He folded the letters and piled them carefully one on top of the other, near the bars of the cell so that they would be found straightaway. The clock in their cell block showed it was now turned eight, Tanino took the rag, an old tea-towel he kept concealed behind his bed, and unrolled it. Inside were the forty Perequil tablets and a razor blade, which he turned over several times between his graphite-stained fingers. He rested it on his left wrist and began to apply a timid pressure, but he was shaking and could not force it down to make a cut, the clean cut that would have done the job and freed him from everything he could no longer bear. Then he heard a door clatter and footsteps in the distance, he felt a sudden lack of air and dropped the razor blade. He got up and ran to the bars and his breathing stopped until he realised that it was just a changing of the cell-block guard, that one man was leaving his post for another, that the world was continuing as normal for everyone and not for him. The warder came up to him and Tanino asked if a telegram had arrived, the other man said no and that he had already been notified about it. He reminded him however that even if it hadn't yet arrived he shouldn't get his hopes up, he shouldn't delude himself, because murderers get the punishment they deserve, only the innocent are pardoned. Tanino did not even look him in the face, he kept his eyes on the clock on the wall at the end of the cell block, which continued to tick indifferently, because his last act in life would definitely not be to give satisfaction to any warder. The warder repeated a couple of times, 'Do you understand me, do you understand that you're in here forever, but you know that if you do ever get out you'll be a useless old man no good for anything.' Then he went away smiling, satisfied, and only when Tanino was sure he was no longer within sight of the guard did he lower his head and slump against the bars. He lay on his bed again, the sheet pulled right over his head, with the evening wearing on and his surges of hope humiliated once again. Ten o'clock passed, and then eleven, the razor blade was still on the floor near the wall and the tablets in a pile like shiny berries. Tanino was fighting a battle different from any he had fought before, he shivered with non-existent cold and every minute that passed was like a knife in the back condemning him to founder ever more helplessly, to lose, with no right of reply. But at nearly midnight, when just about every inmate was asleep, he was disturbed from his own near-catatonic trance by the door to his section creaking on its hinges and regular paces coming towards his cell. The relieving of guards was over for the night and if anyone came in at this hour it meant something unusual had happened. The footsteps became more distinct and Tanino rolled down from his bunk, covered the razor blade and the tablets with the rag and crawled towards the bars on all fours because he didn't have the strength to get up and walk. He didn't want to raise his hopes again to no purpose but he pressed his face between two of the bars and his heart stopped beating, the warder was coming closer and now he could see him climbing the iron staircase that led to his gangway. The guard, a new one or maybe the same one as before, halted at his cell and Tanino used his legs to scrabble back and sit on the floor. The warder raised his left hand and between his index and middle fingers he was holding a rectangle of red paper, the telegram had arrived, that shitty telegram had actually arrived and Tanino reached his hands out to take it, to touch it and reassure himself he was not dreaming, because in his comatose state he had seen thousands of red pieces of paper but this one was real, he could already see the grain of the paper before he even touched it, he could smell for real the aftershave of the warder who must just have come on duty, and when he succeeded in taking the telegram in his own fingers his heart started beating again, the contours of the room became real and he felt the strength return to his body. The telegram read simply: “victory-sentence-overturned-butforyou-retrial-courtofappeal-Rome” and that was enough. Tanino looked at the warder, who was still standing there, curious, with no malice in his expression, and so he put his hand through the bars and the warder shook it, Tanino said, ‘You have brought me life, I am grateful to you,’ the man accepted his thanks and went away as he had arrived. When he was alone again, Tanino took the letters he had written and crumpled them up, then he picked up the old rag with the tablets as well and shoved the whole lot down the hole in the floor that served as his latrine, that revolting pit that now eased Tanino’s fear, the fear which no one should ever see because, at least for the moment, justice had been done and he would not die, not yet, not in that cell.

Seven months after the night of the letters Carlo Gaetano Orlando stood trial for the second time, with new lawyers and new strength inside him. In the meantime he had been sent to Forte Longone, on the island of Elba, where he met Montebello and La Marca, and where the ever-present sight of the sea heartened him despite his rage being even more powerful for being locked up in so beautiful a place. The day of the verdict was set for the 2nd of December and it was a smaller occasion than those that had gone before, without all the press and without the whole of Palma Campania there to gang up against him. The public prosecutor and Pupetta’s lawyers did not let up, they repeated the allegations against Tanino who couldn’t believe what he was seeing, an atmosphere that was so hostile again and the glacial eye of the presiding judge Tangari as it scrutinised him, without a glimpse of anything, beyond mistrust of a criminal like any other criminal. Almost nine years had gone by since the duel in Corso Novara and Tanino wondered what the hell he was doing here still, standing before a crowd of people who had not been there at the time and who only wanted to be participants in the issuing of an exemplary sentence. The hearing was full of claims and counter-claims in tones that pushed the margins of the professional. It was full of palpable tension because this was the last chance, the final act of a legal process that had lasted nearly a decade, a decade during which everyone in that courtroom had got on with their lives except Tanino, whose existence had come to an abrupt halt on the 16th of July 1955 and from the way things were going would remain that way for still longer. Since it was clear that Gaetano Orlando's one and only shot had been aimed at Pascalone's wrist, judge Tangari was obliged to exclude premeditation and also to exclude the notion that Tanino had been hired on someone else's behalf, as he found Tanino's motive that morning, a reaction, plausible. But the Court had to try to salvage what could be salvaged and Tanino's actions could not go unpunished, given the widespread interest in the case and the scale of the indictment, neither of which would have been any smaller even if he had been acquitted. Tangari confirmed the charge of homicide and Carlo Gaetano Orlando was finally condemned to twenty-one years imprisonment. Of these twenty-one, nine had already been spent and Tanino, even though he felt defeated once again and heard the sentence with death in his heart, realised that he could at least see, in the distance, the end of all this. And for the one child he would not see grow up there would be others, and for the nights Ada had slept alone in their bed there would be time enough to make them up.

After Forte Longone he was sent to the prison at Alessandria, where he spent the greater part of his remaining sentence. There, Tanino became a calmer man, more level-headed. He had learned the art of waiting, he had eventually been able to understand that he could not have everything and have it now, but if he could take a more long-term approach it could save him and might raise him to the status of a man wiser than others. He resigned himself to this forced withdrawal from the outside world and in Piedmont he devoted his time once more to educating himself. The prison allowed its inmates to work and study and Tanino pursued from his cell a certificate in surveying. He read hundreds of books and wrote most of his poems. He learnt the art of cooking for large gatherings and tried to muster a few garbled words of English. He forced himself to adopt an exemplary manner of behaviour as a prisoner, he never answered back and never raised his head. The years began to show in his physical appearance, premature lines had appeared on a face that had lost its youthfulness forever, and even the warders began to treat him better.

In the end, another four years were deducted for good behaviour and towards the end of 1971 Tanino won back his freedom. He returned to Marano and Ada and kissed her; he hugged his fifteen-year-old son in a tight embrace, told him you won't be without a father any more, I promise, and Angelo nodded. They all moved to the apartment in Edificio Scolastico and thus began Tanino's years as a father, the years of business ventures and famous singers, the years of gold and jewellery, the years without shootings and the years of 'the farm', which had been given to him by some Marano farmers as a token of thanks for services rendered and as a recompense for the summers spent locked away.

It is in these years that the myth of Tanino takes root in the collective memory of his district. After his father and his uncles had stepped down from public affairs in old age to live their private lives, Tanino 'e Bastimento became the point of reference for the Mastroni and assumed the leadership of Marano, as a free citizen. The town rode the building boom of those years and was transformed into a real city with its own identity, with fine apartment blocks and numerous businesses, and no wars or disorder. His children were born into a situation of domestic ease, in the shadow of a father who had made history, they were brought up with values that were hard to match up to and each of them was encouraged in a specific direction. Angelo was to follow him into business and be his natural heir in the running of Marano; Bruno was to study to become a deputy in parliament and guarantee the family a voice among the organs of the State; Lello was to become a father as soon as possible and produce a whole new generation of Orlandos; Elena would be the faithful wife of some respectable young Marano man; Valencia would grow old protected from all dangers and shielded from prying eyes; Enza would take care of China and be Ada's prop in her old age, and Ada would reign as queen over the decades to come.

Obviously, none of this happened. That Tanino could see further than the others was an established fact, a principle never debated, but with regard to the blood of his own blood his prophetic gifts failed him. Something went wrong, perhaps an error of calculation or an excess of confidence. Perhaps not, perhaps the root of the problem was to be sought in the past.

Perhaps the Sin of Tanino had burst the confines of his own body and insinuated itself into Ada's and into all who were born of her.

And looking back, this can be the only explanation, in this way everything falls into place. The subdued expressions on the faces of Tanino's offspring, their battered bodies and their weary features have always been in contrast with their words, which have portrayed Tanino 'e Bastimento to me as a hero, or more or less, despite the fact that everything he intended for them had backfired: children who failed in the pursuit of objectives imposed on them by the father. And for those errors, they don't know whether to lay the blame on themselves or on a parent unlike other parents, they continue to live in doubt, each with his own regrets, each with baggage full of 'ifs' and 'buts' that are no bloody good to anyone, anecdotes to be exhumed at family lunches and which leave a half-smile on the lips, unachieved desires that have deprived them of the ability to dream for themselves. I appreciate, however, that for me the luxury of such dreaming has always been granted. I have always had the right to choose, whether about my education and training, or about the places I want to see, or the people I want to be with. I have been given *carte blanche*, a gift I have always taken for granted, and whose value I now understand. At my age Tanino was already about to get married, he managed the work of several people and had already made decisions in various ways about his own life and even those of other people. I have done nothing. In the eyes of my family I am little more than a young lad; a young fellow with potential, perhaps, but with everything still to prove. The luxury of waiting is destructive, it makes me feel I am being treated in a different manner from all the others. My mother has not asked me to settle down to anything, to play my part in the world and to become significant, and so I have not done so. And if I have not done so it is because it suited me that way, which is not saying much.

September has arrived and I am beginning to think my time in Marano is coming to an end. Bruno's birthday is one of the last events of summer and this one was his fiftieth. Since his flat is too small, Enza suggested using her apartment in via Roma. There was only me, the two sisters and his children, who had come down from near Milan to see their father. There was also the Naples match on TV and Bruno couldn't have asked for more. His eldest daughter, Adelaide, brought the cake and Enza ordered the pizzas. The middle children, Arianna and Aurora, seemed a little unsure of themselves, because they had left the area when they were quite young and they only come to Naples once a year. Bruno takes them to Mergellina and to the streets of the historic centre that only he knows, because he has worked for years as a security guard at the University of Naples. He has always walked to work, and over the years he has learned all the shortcuts and uncrowded back ways that he can exploit when he is late. His only male child, Raffaele, is fifteen and has decided to remain here. He wants to live in Marano with his father and grow to manhood in his native district. He has felt the call of home too many times and has threatened his mother he will run away if she doesn't give her consent. For Bruno it has been an injection of new life. For years he could not act like a father and he had become cynical about it, he used to say my children are fine where they are, if they want me I'm here but they obviously don't want me, I'm only the person who brought them into the world and that's all. Yet now he has love in his eyes, a tenderness that seemed to have vanished years ago. He has begun to play with his children and tease them and when Napoli scored we all clutched each other and jumped up and down with our hands in the air.

After dinner, Bruno's daughters stayed on to sleep at their grandmothers' and Raffaele went back to his father's flat. He says he will apply for a place at school here in Marano and catch up on the lost years, because studying in Marano doesn't seem as much of a drag.

They went off arm in arm, the son taller than the father and still growing. It appears that Raffaele has inherited more things from his uncle Lello than you'd think. Often Bruno observes him closely, searching for unequivocal signs of kinship with the name he bears, he listens intently to his voice and finds echoes of his brother.

He told me that in hospital, when the leukaemia had by that time eaten up all Lello's energy, Bruno would sit on a chair at his bedside for hours. Then, taking turns, the sisters would come and spend the nights at the Cardarelli hospital, but someone always had to stay at home to look after China, who couldn't manage by herself and who had sniffed the fear and negativity in the air and so had become irascible and unapproachable herself, though not towards Enza and Ada, the only people she called 'mamma'.

Lello used to draw, he liked to paint and he used to dream of working in fashion, as a designer. This idea never went down very well with Tanino, and considering they already had daily arguments about Lello's physical shape, their relationship was always hanging by a thread. Bruno told him, 'Don't worry, I'll talk to papà about it, I'll see to it.' But Lello seemed to be fine even without his father's approval, he had created his own image, by himself, he was well-liked and respected for the sort of person he proved himself to be, and not because of the reflected glow of Tanino. He taught me to draw, when I was small. In the entrance hall of the via Roma apartment there is a little picture frame, and in it an outline drawing of his huge hand, and that outline was traced by me, and I filled it in with different colours. Then over the years I tried to become good at drawing too, I would take his pieces and copy them, sign the paper where he used to sign it, even trying to imitate his handwriting. I showed the drawings to my grandmother, on Saturday mornings when there was no school, she said very good but it upset her, because every time I got out Lello's drawings I was reminding her of his absence. I don't remember her reaction to her son's death, I was five and I didn't understand the consequences it would have for her. As far as I was concerned, the days before the event were very enjoyable ones. We were all together as a family, and even Daniele was almost always at Marano. The last memory I have of Lello is him taking a blood-red beef steak out of the fridge, holding it out to me and saying. 'This is dragon's meat, the dragon I killed earlier, only the strongest people can eat it.'

Then I remember that a few evenings later I was happy, because Elena and Daniele were at home with me. They were murmuring and whispering and kept looking round with worried glances, they were sitting near the telephone waiting for it to ring or not ring. Daniele had returned from

Milan, where for some years—four, to be exact—he had been working, that is since I was one. He had received a significant offer from a large hospital and had handed in his resignation from the medical centre where he had met Elena. They had tried to remain together, to keep the relationship going for the son's sake as well and to begin with Daniele used to come down every weekend. Then he started to appear every other weekend and then once a month. Elena was always more irritable when he was there, they often ended up arguing and raising their voices. But not that day, that day they formed a united front against something else, they were being especially nice to me and to each other, their sombre faces told me not to worry and I didn't understand what I ought to have been worrying about. The phone call came while I was bouncing on mamma's bed. I remember the phone ringing, then the silence, then the sound of Elena and Daniele weeping in the kitchen, and with the bedroom door closed I bounced, I bounced as hard as I could so as not to hear anything, only the springs of the mattress, only the energy that propelled me into the air each time I landed, and then the crack of splintering wood, a pair of slats that gave way under me and left me there without propelling me upwards again and my child's tears, the fear of having made mamma cross by breaking the bed, their footsteps coming towards me and the expectant pause before my imminent mortification. It was nothing like that at all, when they came through the doorway Elena's eyes registered only despair, she clasped me in her arms and Daniele was slumped against the doorpost, mamma said to me, 'Lello isn't with us any more, he's gone to heaven, he's an angel now.' I remember finding these phrases amusing, because in my imagination angels resembled delicate-looking babies, with blond locks and so on, not tall and fat with thick beards like Lello, and I wondered how he could fly with tiny wings like the ones cherubs had.

There was a funeral but I didn't go, swarms of people invaded via Edificio Scolastico but I was not there, I was at home with Daniele while Tanino's children faced up to the consequences of losing a brother.

From that day on, Ada hardly ever left the apartment, she took to wearing black every day and her legs lost their strength, they forced her to spend nearly all her time sitting beside China. After a few months, the Orlando family received notice to quit, because Lello's income was no longer there to support the household and the situation couldn't be helped. In a way Ada and Enza were pleased enough to be moving, because there were too many memories in via Edificio Scolastico and too many empty rooms. For a few months they came to stay at Elena's flat, we were packed in tight because the apartment was for two people and we were five, but in contrast to the others I remember it as a happy period because we were always together. For her part, Elena had grown accustomed to living without her sisters and her mother, she had gained the independence she always wanted, even though at the cost of major sacrifices and the separation from Daniele, but she liked being on her own, as she often reminded us. Enza, Ada and China soon found the flat in via Roma, we all helped with the move and the works on the new apartment, together we painted the walls of what would become my bedroom, a place all of my own, which I had never had, because at Elena's there was only one bedroom and we used to sleep in the same bed.

For a few years I lived in via Roma, mamma, left to her own devices, did ridiculous hours at work and at one point there was an infestation of cockroaches in her building. They came out of the lavatories and the cavities in the walls and Elena had to arm herself with a variety of poisons, embark on a battle that wore her down, she squashed cockroaches by the score and wouldn't let me come back home, she said there were too many toxins floating in the air, she said it was all right for her to breathe them but not me.

It was fumes that made Lello ill, fumes from the paint. Leukaemia attacks the bone marrow and produces diseased white cells, at the expense of the red cells and platelets. It is a cancer of the blood, blood which becomes poisoned for some reason and it kills you from within, even if you are the strongest of men, even if you slay dragons and eat their meat.

Bruno was his brother's best friend, and he told me he was in the operating room that day, at the hospital. He told me how Lello felt the cold and how he had brought socks for him and put them on, he revealed the last moments of his life, with Bruno stretched on the bed, lying across his brother and holding him in a final embrace, and Lello's grip becoming ever weaker, his arms slipping from Bruno's back and dangling in empty space, the tears of one brother choking on the lifeless chest of the other.

Now Bruno and Raffaele are returning home at night, together. It is another Raffaele, who like me can only imagine the person whose name he bears, but he bears it with pride, he knows its weight and implications even if he is fifteen years old, and so he takes from his father's tired hands the small bags filled with leftovers of the pizzas and cake from his fiftieth birthday. Tonight they will continue to celebrate together.

The Seventies and Eighties were fairly troubled years for the Orlando family, Tanino was in and out of prison for short periods, searches of the apartment in via Edificio Scolastico had become frequent and were now almost routine. The final arrest of Carlo Gaetano Orlando happened in mid-1982, when a Beretta 65 was found in his bedside table. During those years Russo had become the family's general factotum, he took the children to school and picked them up again, did the shopping and helped Ada with the cooking. He was never involved in Tanino's business affairs, among his peers he wasn't regarded very highly as a man, the figure he cut was strictly that of a family-oriented type. His own time he mostly spent in Tanino's blue Opel Kadett waiting to be called upon and meanwhile doing his crosswords.

Tanino began to withdraw more and more into private life, he only went out for social events and dinners, he received his business associates at home and Ada was present at all their meetings. He would call her '*la Megera*', the Fury, within the family and Adarella when with friends, her word was amongst the most influential in these meetings and over the years the presence of Tanino became optional, more decorative than decisive. Everybody had confidence in the wife of Tanino.

For the most part he stayed in his bedroom with China, got through whole packets of cigarettes every day and left the ends on the floor, without even stubbing them out properly or treading on them. He did not use drawers or clothes hangers and left his clothes on a nail he had hammered into the wall, because that was what he had been used to in his years in prison. He bought a professional-quality pair of binoculars, the sort used by hunters, which he used up at the farm to see over long distances and at home, when he was alone, to spy from his window on women in the buildings opposite, an old habit that recalled his years in prison on Elba, when it seemed always to be summer. Tanino felt an ever-growing distance between himself and the world he lived in, he couldn't find his bearings any more or rather he never had found them. But if he had felt himself, in earlier days, to be a hurricane about to overturn the laws of nature, now he began to doubt his own energies, he saw himself as old, weary, prematurely worn out. He began to dye his hair, which was turning grey, he rubbed a dark oily cream into his scalp and waited for it to take effect.

On the streets, synthetic drugs were beginning to circulate, dealing became a source of huge riches for anyone who did his business Tanino's way, and he immediately recognised that this was a battle he couldn't ever win. The system operated in a very specific manner, a process which didn't suit Tanino, and this contributed to the final cutting of ties with the *guappi* and the men of honour. He still had his role as a counsellor: his friendships and his persuasiveness often worked as peace-keepers, he tried to resolve the conflicts he could see coming by summoning those directly involved to his home. There would be long, secret, back-and-forth exchanges, on which his children used to try to eavesdrop, Elena hiding under the table or under the bed, Bruno behind a curtain or a doorway.

He spent the afternoons up at the farm, with the children, playing, and Russo in the car as ever, silent, doing his crosswords. Tanino took on all the jobs, keeping the trees and the vegetable plot tidy, cutting the grass and looking after dogs, cats and hens. His children teased him, calling him Saint Francis, they said he talked with the animals because he had a unique relationship with them, he could calm the most aggressive of strays and never had to chase after the hens. It was said that they would hatch their eggs in front of him, and that sometimes, when he had to kill one of them, he would hold out a hand to beckon it while holding an axe in the other, and it would scuttle over to him with no fuss, if somewhat sadly, surrender to death with no thought of running away, as if somehow aware of the way things were and resigned to it.

The dogs that lived at the farm had no masters, they were not shut up or brought into the house, but they all had a name and they were company for Tanino, waiting for their food and coming and going in packs.

When he organised grand dinners in the countryside, the guests commonly found the unusual setting beyond their previous experience, amongst ruins and chicken coops, flourishing trees and ripe fruits, in that commingling of rusticity and classiness that so marked out Tanino and his way of life. Politicians found themselves drinking alongside peasant farmers, singers with homeless orphans, models with Tanino's young children. The evenings passed in merrymaking but at night Tanino no longer slept, sleep wouldn't come and his eyes were so used to the dark that when the light faded he could see everything. He began to take large quantities of Tavor, swallowed a bottle of tranquilisers a week and was a martyr to the pain of ulcers that had never been cleared up. He discovered he had an aneurysm of the abdominal aorta, an 'AAA', in other words an anomalous swelling in the main artery running through his abdomen. The condition is not disabling in itself, apart from the strong pains that he was already used to, but if the aneurysm should rupture, then for a man of his age and in such perilous health, it would almost certainly be fatal.

Tanino's usual boldness and courage soon became a memory because, along with his ailments and the passing of the years, he began to lose faith in his own abilities. He was afraid of police in their uniforms, he started to shake every time he saw their colours, he feared being put back in a cell again because he didn't think he was still capable of dealing with it. He woke up at night prey to nightmares, convinced he could hear loud and clear the rattle of cell bars and smell the overwhelming stink of piss. Meanwhile his children were growing up, becoming adolescents one after the other and beginning to have lives of their own. They crept into his bedroom while he was asleep in the mornings, a deep, artificial sleep induced by the sedative effect of the tranquilisers, they rummaged in the pockets of his jacket and took money for clothes, ice creams and cigarettes.

Another thing Tanino now feared was oaths or blasphemies. In the Neapolitan, *jastèmme*, they refer to ill-omens, curses, whether applied to the divine or to anyone else. When he argued with Ada before going out and she spat an oath at him, Tanino broke into a cold sweat, he couldn't leave the house unless his wife took her words back, he would beg her on his knees with terror in his eyes. Hostile fate was no longer a stimulus to him, it had become an obsession. Only when, taking pity, Ada agreed to retract what she had said and send him on his way with her blessing (usually 'May Our Lady go with you'), was Tanino able to struggle back to his feet and return to the world of other people for a few hours.

In short, Tanino alternated moments of customary lucidity with periods of mental fog, for the most part he was sad and distrustful, but something within him had become softened, maybe as a result of ageing, maybe through the acquisition of wisdom, maybe through an awareness of having battled too hard, to the point of impairing his health. There were occasions when he was unrecognisable, like April 1st, a date he had begun to anticipate with eagerness all year for the chance to play tricks on anyone who came in range. He pretended to be lying dead on the floor when Ada came in, making her shriek with fear first thing in the morning, or he would go out into the square, call out my wife is ill, help, and when he saw that a small crowd of people had followed him in a panic up to the entrance door to the building, he burst out laughing like a young kid and would laugh until his ribs hurt, as he had done when he was a little boy, when he had first earned the special name Bastimento.

The middle of September is coming closer and with it my departure more definite. Soon I will have to return to Turin, I will have to leave Marano as at the start of every autumn, to come back here again for the Christmas holidays. When my departure is getting close, Elena begins to grow sad. She often cries, she weeps and says, 'How shall we manage, I'd got used to having you here.' I will have to leave her and Enza alone with the sisters, Valencia will have to get used to a new home and it will not be easy. Part of me would like to stay here to help, to give a hand when it's needed, to lend comfort. The more I stay here the less the idea of staying scares me, because here things never really change and perhaps they don't need to change, because there is something warm in the slowness of this city, which never moves forward and only deteriorates, like the people who live here and whom I return to see time after time, the same as before but a little more tired, as if no one slept for weeks, as if the air was thicker here, harder to draw down into one's lungs and expel. My mother is the person in whom I see this discomfort more than anyone. She was not made to stay here, she was not made to grow up here either, but to the choices imposed on her when she was small can be added those she made for herself once she had grown up, and it is probable that she regrets these latter choices. After Daniele, she has never been with anyone, she says that the father of her child was quite enough. When he went to Milan, Daniele tried to take Elena with him, he implored her, he knew that there was very little for her here in Marano. And then they had had a child, a child who was barely a year old and who would be brought up a long way from all this. Elena knew very well that Daniele was right, that it would be good for all three of them to start again from scratch, without all these family encumbrances, without the shadow of a name on one's back. And yet she couldn't. The roots that held Elena so deeply to the infertile soil of Marano bore the name Ada. She would not abandon her, even though Enza and China, and Lello and Bruno were always around, she knew her mother needed her children. The real centre of gravity of the Orlando family has always been Ada, she is the one who has always tilted the balance in family affairs, and it is for her that the whole family has fought, from her husband to her children, and indeed the grandchildren. Ada was always at home while Tanino was in prison, she was the point of reference for anyone who wanted to talk to him, she was Tanino's voice. For her sons and daughters she was the compass, a single mother for most of the time, a woman who made herself extra capable at everything out of love for the children she brought into the world, a person who, like all mothers, would lay down her life for each and every one of her seven children. If Tanino was the founder of the family, the face of a generation, an ideal to follow, Ada was the beating heart of via Edificio Scolastico, the voice to listen to, the person to whom, from Angelo to China, everyone swore their own personal loyalty. And I too have always moved within that orbit for as long as it remained alive. She brought me up, she told me her stories and those of Tanino, she set food before me at table every afternoon when I returned from school.

Following Angelo's death, Ada faded even more. She began to smile less, to lie in bed longer or just sit, she lost the energy to cook and to see to China. Then the same illness attacked her as well and everything deteriorated very fast. In the summer of 2019 she took to her bed and stayed there, she stopped eating and grew thin, haggard. The words she spoke started to make less and less sense, she smiled when there was no cause and wept without anyone knowing why. Her cancer metastasised at an incredible rate, it seemed to find no resistance at all in Ada's elderly body. That August Enza and I set off on our last trip together, we didn't acknowledge it was the last but we both knew it, we knew we were going away in a week that might change everything, that when we came back we would find her mother and my grandmother a step closer to the end. We sailed the northern seas on a gigantic cruise ship and whenever she had a moment Enza made a videocall home, saying hello to grandmother and China, who yelled and screamed because she wanted her sister back. When we stood on deck, fifteen levels up on the vessel's superstructure, Enza couldn't enjoy the panorama or the unique quality of the fiords, along which we slipped slowly and hesitantly, nor the waterfalls that plummeted down on to the dark rocks. We returned to Naples at the beginning of September and I went down with an attack of bronchitis, I stayed at home coughing and shivering with cold. Ada's condition had worsened even more and for the next two weeks Enza and Elena never left her alone. Bruno called by every afternoon, he put China's music on and laid his hand on his mother's forehead. He would say, 'What's this, am I going to have to wash my own underwear now, *Megè*?' partly to reduce the tension and partly as a new awareness dawned on him. There was a bustle of people coming and going and I understood that Ada's time was at an end, and she was ready for it. I spent little time in via Roma, and when I did I stayed in the kitchen, out of grandmother's way. When she did see me she laughed in a tone that wasn't like her at all, a child's laugh, not the laugh of a woman who knows everything, I was seeing a person I recognised less and less, I felt betrayed by her because she was playing tricks on me and it wasn't fair. I didn't want to speak because I was no longer talking to her but to her shadow, which spoke my name with wonderment and asked stupid things, who lay there with that air of resignation and faint irony, as if at this point she had already given in and was just waiting for the moment. The moment arrived on the 21st of September. I woke up in the morning and found a message from mamma on my phone, it said: "Come when you can, I think this is it". This is it. I was at home by myself and readied myself to face this thing with as much calmness as possible, relieving my feelings by crying my eyes out with no one to hear or see. I left the flat and walked along the street, passing in front of San Castrese church, which looked down on me as immovably as ever, the church that had stood in that spot for centuries, during which it had seen generations of Marano people and Mastroni rise and fall, had received the prayers of those who had borne my blood, but I do not know how to pray and I didn't even know at a time like this either. I did manage to smoke a cigarette outside the entrance, I looked at the blue cross and the steep slope flanked by walls and tall trees that led towards the farm. I stubbed out the cigarette and made my way over to via Roma and the only people in the apartment besides grandmother were her female children. Mamma had not slept, nor Enza, not even China and she, what's more, was kicking up a fuss because no one was paying her any attention and because the music had run out. Elena said to me, 'Come nearer, let her know you're here,' and I didn't want to, I rejected the idea, that was not grandmother, maybe it had been, it was very like her in every respect but she was already absent, sliding away from us day by day, with no goodbyes, no fine words or comforting phrases, without giving us at the end a great truth which, perhaps, we needed. She had some white garment on, and her hair had lost almost all its red colouring, it was more a faded copper, straw-like. She was lying on a small bed next to the double bed where Enza and China had been sleeping recently. I went up to her and the others in the room were watching me, waiting, as if something unexpected might happen, as if a lightning strike might hit the house at any moment, as if Lello and Angelo might have come through the door saying it's all a joke, we're all fine.

Nothing of the sort happened, I stood in front of her, her breathing slow, I took her porcelain hand, impossibly smooth, and our eyes met. She was not wearing her dentures and when she smiled she looked like a newborn baby, her blue eyes ringed with red, and her eyes only just staying open. The smile seemed to last an eternity, for me and for Enza and mamma it was a knife thrust, in a single movement of the lips was an entire life, a mass of priceless memories and of enduring beliefs, for there is no longer any time now for reconsideration. Then the smile changed to a grimace of pain, she began to cry and let go of my hand, I walked out because I was shaking and went to weep again, in the bathroom. Ada clung on for hours, evening came and she was still breathing, more slowly all the time but she was breathing. Other relatives arrived, her sisters and numerous nephews and nieces. There was nowhere left in the apartment to be alone, what had once been my bedroom was invaded by people talking about their own shitty affairs instead of leaving me a place to sleep. But no one was thinking of sleep, because every so often Ada began to cry out with pain, her whole body was aflame, failing flesh rejecting her and she refusing to go. Dawn came round, the 22nd of September and we were all exhausted, I was hoping it would be over soon, I couldn't take any more. At eight in the morning, a male colleague of Elena, a nurse, arrived to give her an injection of a powerful painkiller, because she had spent the last few hours in torment. After the injection she calmed down, her breathing began to slow and we all gathered for one last time round her bed. At nine in the morning the sun was high in the sky, it came in through the cracks in the shutters and then through the window panes, its warmth caressed our ruined faces. Mamma listened for her breathing and said in a whisper, 'This is it now,' and so we all stood in silence and the only sound was Ada's breathing, ever weaker, like a swing that no one is pushing any more, which continues to creak with an ever fainter sound until it stops altogether, only without the possibility of anyone coming back and making it swing again. I was hanging on tightly to someone's hand but I don't know whose, perhaps mamma's or grandmother's, perhaps Enza's or Bruno's, but I was holding on tightly and I was on my knees, almost everyone in the room was. Then the sound of her laboured breathing ceased, there was a cry of liberation and a clapping of hands, followed by trembling embraces and loud sobs. Bruno left without embracing anyone, his eyes dry, saying, 'I'll be back later.' Elena was stroking her mother's cooling cheek and trying to explain to China what had happened. Enza, at that moment, ceased believing in God, because the one thing she had asked the Father was that Ada might die without suffering.

Hordes of people began to gather in the apartment in via Roma, I met people I had never seen, sisters of Ada known to me only as names, and cousins and siblings of Tanino who came to offer their condolences. Elena received the visitors because all Enza wanted was for the whole lot of them to fuck off, China was frightened by all these people invading her rooms, and couldn't even get into her own bed because in it lay the body of Ada, now in a white dress, and one by one the visitors went to say their goodbyes, leaving a kiss on the icy forehead.

The following day there was the funeral. I remember that in church the family divided on either side of the coffin, the males on one side and the females on the other, all with their hands clasped or their arms folded. I tried to take my place on the women's side, I wanted to be with Mamma and Enza, I wanted to lean on them and I wanted them to lean on me, but when I approached, Elena told me to go back to my place, because Ada believed strongly in certain things and it would not do to anger her when she had only just died. One of the last things grandmother had said to me when she was completely lucid was that when the moment came, it would be for me to carry the coffin outside together with my friends, because she wanted to be transported to the other side by young people. I remember the weight of the casket on my shoulder, a weight divided between seven but enormous all the same, I remember the sun shining beyond the doors of the parish church and the cortège up to the cemetery, from which we returned for the first time without her.

Now, in the same wing of Marano's burial ground, are finally reunited husband and wife, and a little way off two of the Orlando sons. After the coffin had been laid in the ground and almost all the people had gone away, Elena came up to me and said: 'When I die, remember to have me cremated.'

The Nineties were the last decade Tanino was to see. Now he only appeared at special occasions, such as name-days and birthdays. He handed over the reins to his children, who began to lose their fear of him, because his character had also softened with the passing of the years, and he was increasingly dependent on young hands, on people who would help him willingly and without resentment. After having found work for Elena, Russo ceased to be the chauffeur and general factotum for Tanino, and Lello and Bruno began to divide up the tasks between them. He and Lello did not speak much, they chatted about this and that and practical matters, but the son accompanied him wherever he wanted to go. He had also found himself a girl, Patrizia, whom Tanino did not look on favourably because she was the daughter of a man who sold his broad beans straight off the cart. But she was a bright girl and quickly made herself useful to Tanino, and so it wasn't long before she entered his good books. Tanino was beginning to repeat himself, to say things that made no sense; Elena said that senile dementia was a family legacy, that sooner or later Orlanditis gets you and makes you lose your head, like Gaetano 'o Mastrone, Tanino's grandfather, who split his wife's head in two with an axe. But fieriness had played too big a role in Tanino's existence and his progressive loss of mental acuity did nothing worse than calm him down, made him pause for breath for the first time. Someone would drive him up to the farm and he would stay there on his own, sitting on a tree-stump smoking cigarettes, looking from his high point down on a world that no longer belonged to him, which had perhaps never really belonged to him, but for which he had fought, for which he had waited in a prison cell, for which he had killed.

Angelo, my uncle, had had his first and only male child and had called him after his father, not merely Gaetano but Carlo Gaetano, the name that had belonged solely to Tanino 'e Bastimento, a name which had signalled his double birth and his unusual status and which would now be carried on for at least another generation. Tanino spent a lot of time with his grandson, up at the farm. He showed him how to look after the hens and to slaughter them the right way, with a clean blow to the neck, he explained that it needed decisiveness, so that the creatures didn't suffer more than necessary. When Angelo arrived to collect his son, Tanino never had conversations with him, just good morning or good evening, because he found it impossible to accept the faith of his first-born child.

In any event, Tanino was becoming increasingly foggy-minded, he wandered round all day in his dressing gown and when anyone buzzed on the entry-phone he had Ada tell them he was asleep, he had flu and it was best he shouldn't be disturbed. Elena spent increasingly less time at home and Tanino began to wonder why. Despite his confused state of mind, the reason was not hard to find, he knew his daughter was in the flower of her youth, he saw her putting on make-up and arranging her hair, he watched her as she chose the right shoes to wear before going out. The excuse of Lello no longer held good, there was no sense in making yourself beautiful like that to go out with your brother on his motorbike. The thing that shocked Tanino was his own serene lack of reaction. He felt he had betrayed his own self. Only a few years ago he would have gone mad if he had got a whiff of anything of that sort, he still had shudders at the thought of Elena with a man, a man who touched her, undressed her, sullied her forever; but for the first time in his life, he sensed there was nothing he could do. This was the nub of the whole issue. Ever since Tanino became aware that he could change things, that he could reverse any situation he wanted, that he could fight as if a red mist had come down over his eyes, nothing frightened him. But his growing impotence in more and more different areas had caused him to retreat, had made him discover the sweetness of resignation, the comfort of standing aside, of watching things evolve without his forceful intervention. He understood that the world went on turning by itself, without him giving it a push, that his children would soon outlive him and they would set off happily along their own paths, that he would remain for them a memory, more or less pleasant according to the case, and not much else. He was not pleased about it, he never really managed that, but he understood that if he wanted to depart without further resentments on the part of his family, he had to change direction, adapt to old age. A virtually impossible proposition, because more than anything else Tanino would never betray himself or the ideals he had maintained for a whole lifetime. He did not know that he would be leaving his children a burden that amounted to much more than a special name, a *contranome*, and a few bittersweet memories: an inheritance of blood that no one had asked for, a blood that would run through the generations to come, marking them with an indelible stain, a blood thicker than most people could live with, which would poison the weaker bodies of sons and daughters who would never reject it, never spit it out, but would have to let it coil thickly in their veins, risking their very lives.

On the 18th of September 1998, the day before the Feast of San Gennaro, Tanino woke to find it was still summer outside. It was hot and he couldn't face anything for breakfast. Ada had put some fresh fruit and biscuits before him, but after taking a bite from an '*Oro Saiwa*' he was sick. He left everything on the table, drank the coffee and smoked two cigarettes one after the other, dropping them on the floor and Ada picked them up, cursing, 'What the hell are you doing, can't you see I'm getting old and I can't bend down, shame on you, you pig.' Tanino, said 'Sorry *Megè*,' kissed her on the cheek and went to knock on Elena and Enza's door. The older girl had already left for work, and when he went in he saw Enza lying untidily on the rumpled bed, her mouth open and her breathing noisy, making a sound both irritating and unseemly for a young lady. 'Wake up,' he said. In response Enza made a snorting sound and turned on her back. Tanino returned to the kitchen and filled a small cup with coffee, walked slowly back to her room, trying to avoid spilling the coffee, and placed it on the little table beside the bed. He shook his daughter by the shoulder and said again, 'Wake up, it's midday, are you going to wake up or not?' She snorted again and began to snore. So Tanino went into his own bedroom, where China was sitting on the bed with the Walkman plugged into her ear. On a side table stood a large Panasonic stereo player, the size of a microwave. The stereo was new, it had been given to China for her last birthday, and as well as cassettes it played mini-discs, those shiny new things, CDs, that were becoming more and more popular. He took a cassette out of the stereo, then lifted the machine in both hands, because it was heavier than one would think, and tugged at it, pulling the plug from the socket and causing it to dangle between Tanino's legs as he carried it to Enza's room. He set it down on the bedside table near his daughter's head and plugged it in, before noticing that the coffee cup didn't have coffee in it any more and the girl was having him on. He put the cassette in the player, turned the volume up to maximum and jabbed the play button. Renzo Arbore's '*A rumba de scugnizzi*' rang out filling the whole apartment, Enza opened her eyes with a start and clapped a hand to her chest, Tanino burst out laughing so hard he fell to his knees, Enza looked as if she was about to cry and then she too laughed, 'I'm awake,' she said. Arbore was singing "*Te ne scinne a sghizze a sghizze / Fin' a quanno nun scapizze / Chesta e 'a rumba de scugnizze!*" China arrived, with her little shuffling steps, a smile on her face, Tanino began to beat time with his hands and even China as well. Ada appeared from the corridor and cursed again. 'You'll give me a heart attack, it's impossible, what kind of place do I live in?' Then she turned back towards the kitchen swaying her hips in time to Arbore. Tanino told his daughter he wanted to go up to the farm, it was one of the last fine days of the season and he wanted to enjoy it in the fresh air. Enza replied that he could ask Lello or Bruno, given that she had already gone with him every day for the past week while her brothers were busy doing their own stuff. But Lello had slept at Patrizia's and Bruno had gone out shortly after Elena, early in the morning, and would probably remain out until evening. In the last few months he was always late back, at home he was always arguing with his father because he imposed set times, he told him either you get back before two or you sleep in the street, and so Bruno deliberately returned a half hour or an hour later, and while his father looked down at him from the balcony he lay down in the road, with a smile on his face, pretending the pavement was really comfortable, Tanino swore then turned back inside slamming the French windows behind him.

Enza had no choice but to accept the situation, and huffing and puffing, got out of bed. She got ready without ceremony, putting on the first pieces of clothing she found on the 'dead man', the dummy she used as a clothes hanger. Tanino told his daughter from the other side of the bathroom door to get China ready as well, because it would do her good to have some fresh air too. From the kitchen Ada heard and said, 'At last you're going out for a bit.' Enza calmly washed, did the same for China, dressed her and they were ready to go. Tanino put on his tracksuit bottoms and a loose, crumpled shirt, his sunglasses and the boots he wore for the farm. They left at lunchtime and Enza sat at the wheel of the Kadett with Tanino beside her and China in the back. The car climbed laboriously past the church and up the narrow road that led to the high ground, and when they arrived Tanino got down from the car, undid the padlock and opened the gates to the farm.

Tanino made for the kitchen garden and picked two bunches of fresh cherry-tomatoes, went into the little house, rinsed them under the tap and put them in the iron pan with plenty of olive oil. He boiled some water and dropped in the spaghetti, while Enza wiped the marble table clean of leaves and fallen fruit and China sat in a deckchair holding the Walkman in her hand. Tanino made two dishes of pasta and a plate of prosciutto cotto and cheese slices for China, brought it all out to the table along with a bottle of red country wine. They sat down and Tanino gave his usual "blessing": 'When you eat you're keeping death at bay,' Enza said 'Amen' and raised a forkful to her mouth. After tasting the spaghetti she spat it out again into her dish, said, 'But what have you done to this?' Tanino tasted it for himself and a sweet-and-sour flavour that was completely out of place made him screw up his mouth. 'I've put sugar in instead of salt,' he said, half to Enza, half to himself. He dropped his fork on the plate and sighed, he banged his fist on the table and cursed, 'What the hell's this, what was I thinking of?' Then Enza raised another forkful to her lips, swallowed it down and said, 'It's quite nice all the same, don't worry.' Tanino watched his daughter finish her plateful without saying anything, while his sweetened spaghetti cooled in front of him and a fly settled on it. 'Only flies can eat that,' he said, then he got up and went to empty his plate into the rubbish bin. He fed China her prosciutto and drank a glass of wine. When they had finished he carried the dishes back inside and put them in the sink, turned the tap on but only a few feeble drops fell on to the encrusted tomato sauce. He told his daughter to feed the hens and Enza went off towards the hen coop. Sugar in the pasta, he kept saying to himself, how could that have happened. He went outside and walked round the house, among the bushes were stacked several demijohns filled with water, he took hold of one and began to drag it out, but it was heavy, it had never been as heavy as this, Tanino's breathing became laboured and he had to sweat to carry it as far as the fig tree. On this tree was built a kind of pulley arrangement that enabled one to haul the demijohns of water up to the level of the roof. He tied a rope round the neck of the full bottle and began to haul the other end of the rope downwards, the demijohn began to rise, swaying, and continued on upwards as far as it could, some three and a half metres. He left it hanging there and went behind the house, put his hand on the rail of the wooden stairs by the wall and began to climb, dragging himself up with great effort, his wrists quivering as he mounted each step. When he was on the roof he stopped to look at the view. The position of the farm allowed him to have the greater part of Naples within his vision, spreading out downwards and towards the sea. At a certain point the architecture of the city, with *palazzi* and grand buildings all heaped together, perched one above the other in tiers, left space in the distance for a view of a rugged strip dividing the land from the deep blue, from the sea he had loved so much and hadn't been to for months, because the powerful sun hurt his eyes and head and because he could no longer stretch out on the sand, if he tried nowadays it just made his bones and muscles ache. He moved across the roof to the side where the tree stood and leant over the edge to catch the demijohn which was dangling in the void. He planted his feet firmly and pulled it towards him, let it rest on the roof and removed the rope from its neck. He dragged the bottle over to the cistern, from where a pipe ran down beside the chimneystack and fed the water to the taps. He rolled up his shirtsleeves and heaved the demijohn up again, his knees aching by this time and sweat beading his forehead. He tipped the water into the tank and it came out in a rush, spreading down the wall of the house and part of it trickling over the roof, because Tanino couldn't manage to hold it steady over the mouth of the tank. The water spilled all round him and splashed off the sloping roof, dripping on to the plants and the soil. Tanino sat down against the water tank to get his breath back, his head was spinning and he felt faint. China's Walkman was playing *Champagne* by Peppino di Capri and the sparrows were chirping in the trees, making a new kind of symphony, a wonderful mingling of sounds, so that Tanino stopped to listen, while the blue and cloudless sky gradually took on the firmer shades of afternoon. Down below he could see Enza, leaning into the hen house to clean out the hen shit while the birds raced round in circles. China was swinging back and forth as usual, immersed in her own world. Tanino thought about the sugar in the pasta again, something rose in his gullet and his lips started to tremble. It took him a while to realise he was crying, crying like a baby, with heavy sobs and his face screwed up and incapable of holding it all back, incapable of stemming this sudden despair that swept over him like a storm at sea. He pushed himself away from the water tank and crawled on all fours to the edge of the roof, opposite the fig tree, dragging behind him the empty demijohn, the glass scraping against the roof felt that covered the upper part of the little house. He lay on his side and leaned out to catch the rope, got it in his hand and very calmly began to tie a knot, still sobbing and shuddering, and it was hard to do with any precision because his fingers were shaking. He managed to get the knot tied nice and tight so that he could pay out the rope between his hands, carefully keeping it steady. The slipknot opened into a wide noose, which he could tighten or loosen as needed just by letting the knot run one way or the other. Tanino looked out once again over the city and over the farm, Enza was rounding up the hens and China was rocking in her chair, the world was turning and moving but not for Tanino, the sugar in the pasta and his frail bones, his foggy memories and Elena engaged, his eyes nearly blind and Bruno out until late, Lello wanting to paint and his breathing laboured, Angelo worshipping a different God and the world turning ever faster, the dizziness growing and that knot in his hands, the exact dimensions of his ever more skinny neck, the life he had fought for so hard and which could end at any moment, a possibility so longed-for and the water spreading across the roof and turning suddenly Tanino slipped, fell backwards over the edge of the roof with the slack rope still in his hand, knocked his head on the stone or perhaps on the ground and the grass and saw no more, heard only the cries of the horrified Enza and China, the squawk of a hen and then blackness closed in all round.

The doctors said he had taken a terrible blow, but the huge bruise on the back of his head would go down, all he needed was to rest and look after the wound; he would soon be as good as new. They said he could leave hospital and they brought him home, to his bed. But something had given way, that fall had removed with it a part of Tanino, that spark, enfeebled for some little while, which in the past would have flared brightly and provoked him to react, to return stronger. But when a puff of wind comes, some sparks, if they are too weak, might as easily blow out as blaze up. The days passed and his children took turns at his bedside, they kept him company, they tried to persuade him to eat something to build up his strength, they expected him at any moment to snap out of it and rise from his bed as if nothing had happened and ask someone to take a stroll with him to stretch their legs. It did not happen. Every day, Tanino seemed to sink more deeply into the embrace of his bed, his hair dye faded and for the first time in years his natural colour showed, a listless and alarming grey that made him look horribly like some old peasant farmer. And yet Tanino did not seem to care. His mind was foggy nearly all the time, with just a few periods of lucidity, when he would weep again, terrified, ask to die, and to die soon. Elena realised that if she wanted him to meet Daniele now was the moment, partly to take advantage of Tanino's unheeding detachment from the real world and partly because she knew in her heart that her father might not survive until winter. Tanino found that he liked him, a down-to-earth young man, with two clear blue eyes and a fund of jokes which he deployed to defuse the tension gripping via Edificio Scolastico. Elena couldn't believe what she was seeing, one part of her was convinced that the sight of Daniele would prompt an instant recovery, Tanino would leap from his bed and start shouting at his daughter and the stranger invading his home; and instead the two of them laughed together, like a normal encounter between son-in-law and father-in-law. Bruno started coming home in good time. He had been engaged to Carmela for a while, they saw each other often and even those two occasionally made joking references to the possibility of marriage. Even Lello's story was going well, he and Patrizia were an item, the very picture of togetherness, and the girl enjoyed the father's respect and esteem, things never to be taken for granted. Angelo, too, came almost every day, he brought his daughters to keep the aunts company and himself stayed in the kitchen with Ada, while the two Carlo Gaetano Orlandos were left alone in the bedroom to get to know each other, to imprint faces and voices in each other's mind, to create solid memories for both of them. The days slipped by and Tanino's condition visibly declined, contradicting the doctors' prognostications. The doctors continued to say there was no danger from the blow to his head, that Orlando should already have recovered by now, that he must be forced to eat and drink to regain his strength.

But Tanino didn't want to know, he limited himself to sipping a glass of water a day from the hands of Enza, when he couldn't stand any more of the constant coming and going and people poking their curious heads round the door of his room. From time to time he had China brought in to him, made her sit on the bed beside him and stroked her back, and she would shift closer and murmur 'papà'. The nights were long and sleepless for the inhabitants of via Edificio Scolastico, because Tanino was assailed by nightmares and pains, real or otherwise, which made him hunch his body into a ball and beg for the torment to end. He still thought in terms of his destiny, and of himself as someone defeated by it, he begged the saints for mercy and asked only that he should die. October arrived, and it was clear that Tanino had given up the struggle, shipped oars, that it was a matter of days. An air of tension hung over the whole of Marano, whoever passed along via Nova cast a glance up at the balcony of the Orlando home, where Ada and her children went to talk in private, asking each other what they should do and not finding any answers.

In the night of the 7th to 8th of October 1998 every member of the family gathered at the apartment. Tanino's siblings arrived, his uncles, aunts and cousins, all the Mastroni still living, ready to pay their final respects to the leader of their family, the standard-bearer of the name they bore, the man who had eaten life raw and in bold chunks. Doctor Moio visited him for the last time and apologised for the hope he had given, he was unable to explain what lay behind this decline, he could not understand how Tanino could have failed to recover. Everyone else however understood it well enough. They had known for some time, and they had not doubted Tanino's will-power, because in truth everything was again going according to plan. If he had wanted to fight he would have fought, there was little doubt of that, and they were still astonished at how he had managed to reverse the course of things, to suppress his vital signs by sheer force of mind and will his own departure from the land of the living. In the end, Tanino had refused to compromise with a life that had turned against him from the day he came into the world.

He called Enza and Bruno to him, he told them to be strong, not to do anything stupid, to take care of their brothers and sisters and of Ada. He asked Enza to promise him China would want for nothing, that this poor innocent creature of God needed love and patience. He called for Elena and his daughter sat on the edge of the bed, a little intimidated. He asked her forgiveness for the father he had been, for his failure to give her the affection she deserved and for having treated her harshly from the day when, still young, she had lost her virginity. Elena accepted her father's apologies, she felt they were sincere and that was good enough, but to claim she felt able to forgive him was a different matter. What she wanted was to be able to talk to him, she wanted to disclose her secret, she wanted to reveal that she was carrying a child in her womb, a male child who would be born in a few months' time. She couldn't do it, perhaps because she didn't want to give her already condemned father a fatal shock, perhaps because she wanted to keep Tanino in the dark, so that he could not cast a pall over the child's future with some prophecy or pronouncement, so that he could not bind him to the common destiny of those who bore the same blood. In her heart she hoped that if there was a curse, then her son must avoid it, she hoped she would not be bringing into the world a person under some sort of sentence, whatever the sentence was. Tanino also called for Lello, Angelo and last of all Ada, but they are no longer here and those truths have died with them, a father's last words now safely buried under six feet of earth, beneath marble slabs. To Valencia he said nothing, possibly because she had never understood him and he did not understand her, they spoke different languages, maybe because Tanino was ashamed of the decision he had made, or maybe because in the end he had nothing to say to her.

In the night Tanino died, an era ended in an instant and tears were shed while a moth flew in at the window and fluttered amongst the living, proclaiming their mourning in a silent beating of wings.

The doors of the Orlando home remained open for days, people arrived from everywhere to offer their condolences, they brought baking trays of pasta, they brought cold meats and cheeses, sugar and coffee, so much stuff that soon Ada and Enza had to ask for no more to be brought, all the space in the apartment was taken up. The funeral posters with the name Tanino were pasted up on all the electricity boxes in Marano, the newspapers were full of it and the local radio networks. The carabinieri appeared, patrolling via Nova two or three times a day, attracting whistles and fuck-offs from the young Maranesi of the district.

So died Carlo Gaetano Orlando, in his own bed, surrounded by people he had sworn to love. I never knew him, and he never knew of my imminent arrival. He left my family with a vast quantity of stories to tell, he inculcated in them that sense of mutual protection that has always been the bedrock of their lives, he gave them the responsibility of making their way in life by themselves, without private wealth and without the comfortable stations in life he had predicted for them. His most significant material legacy was undoubtedly the farm, a parcel of land divided into seven equal parts, a perfect symbol of the new life, of the life that continues to spring from the earth and grow, in the form of plants and fruits, which provides work and plenty, the means and the end. But the farm is now barren: like anything that receives no care it gets sick in the end and produces weeds and creepers that gradually engulf everything, parasites that devour new life as soon as it appears. And so I ask myself who is to blame for all this, whether it is incompetent children or an obsessional father, whether it is hostile destiny or an irremediable curse. And it is with you that I would like to speak of all this. I would like to meet you and ask you what you really thought, I would like to hear you say to me the things you said to them, without intermediaries, I would like to grow up under your shadow and see what it feels like. And yet I believe I already know. Your shadow has persisted without you, has liberated itself from your dead body and is everywhere, impregnating every spot I might place my feet, you have become immortal, but not in a fair way, because you can still speak to us, you remind me and the people I love, at every moment, that you have been, you are, and you will be. But I would like to confront you, do what the people I love are not in a position to do, and not because I am better or stronger than they are, but because nothing links us, no memory, no name or special name, only the blood in my veins, and whether that is healthy or unhealthy I can't tell, perhaps it is too soon or perhaps I really am free, and in that case I can confront you.

I know I am being cowardly, because you are dead and I am not and so it's easy that way, but your voice is perhaps still stronger than mine. And yet, like me you too have nothing to lose, and so I can step forward with no fear any more.

Summer ended a few days ago and signs of rain and cloud have begun to appear at points in the clear sky. The arrival of autumn, apart from its natural consequences, also announces my departure from Marano. The 24th of September is Enza's birthday, midnight ushers in China's and every year we turn it into an occasion to celebrate them both at the same time. Tomorrow I shall go away. I will leave with the knowledge of the things I have discovered over these last few months and leaving home now seems a bigger deal. Part of me would like to tie myself to this place, I would like to live here without dreaming about better prospects, though admittedly such things depend on where you are. In the afternoon, Biagio, Peppe and Gennaro collect me for a trip round Naples, we drink a beer in piazza Bellini and then slowly stroll along the length of via Toledo as far as Mergellina. The seafront unfolds before us in all its sweeping grandeur, a parapet several kilometres long separates us from that untameable water which eddies and swirls as it sees fit along the jagged coastline. One after the other we climb over the railings and go and find ourselves a convenient rock. This is where Tanino met Milena, where the life that we know came close to taking a different turn, and who knows where it might have led. Biagio makes up the mixture and I press the filters in the ends, we light our last 'torch' together and puff our smoke out over the ripples of the waves. Gennaro asks when I'll be coming back and I automatically reply Christmas. Months will have gone by but I know that nothing will have changed, I will find everything exactly as I left it and maybe that is not a bad thing, because to pause for a break every so often you need somewhere dependable, a place that always welcomes you in the same way and where time seems to move, not forwards, but in circles. Peppe asks if I have finished my investigations and I say I think I have, at least for the moment I have answers that will do, but I don't rule out returning to the stories about Tanino one day, or maybe further back, to the legends of the old Mastroni. 'Yes, but don't forget you need to get laid every now and then,' says Biagio and we all laugh. The sky takes on a pink and orange tinge and the sun is beginning to sink before us, beyond the waves we can see. I say I have to go back home, I have to pack my bags and I have Enza's birthday and I can't miss that. In turn we all stand up and climb back over the parapet, retrace our steps up the hill and the city rushes to meet us. After fifteen minutes in the car we are back in Marano, I ask the boys to drop me off at Enza's, in via Roma, and that's what they do. One by one we embrace each other, we promise to keep in touch, they say they must definitely get tickets whatever the cost to come and visit me in Turin. I say whenever you like, there's room at my place, I get out of the car and it sets off again only once I have pressed the entry-phone button marked G. Orlando—A. Manna. When I enter the apartment, Valencia is standing in the doorway waiting for me, she smiles at me and asks if I have brought her Coca-Cola, I say yes and she replies 'eh.' I give Elena and China a hug and Enza a kiss, I wish them happy birthday and out on the balcony are Bruno and the two children who have chosen to return to Marano, Adelaide and

Raffaele. This is all that remains of us. This is the remaining garrison defending the last outpost of the family, the flat in via Roma. After a while the pizzas arrive and we all sit crammed together round the small table in the kitchen, designed for four people and no more. Bruno says he is going to speak to the peasant who used to look after the farm, and that if he doesn't want to come back has other friends who would be interested. He says they will cut back all the weeds and next summer we'll return and ensure it's all kept down. Enza informs us she means to initiate some works on the little house, knock down a couple of walls and add some new ones, to make it bigger and more comfortable. She wonders how well Valencia will get on there, she's only been once or twice; Elena replies the first thing to do is for her to feel comfortable with her surroundings here, a new home and a new family are a serious adjustment for anyone, let alone someone like her. When she has eaten, Elena goes off and shuts herself in the small bedroom, the one that used to be mine and is now Valencia's. I knock softly on the door and she opens it, her eyes are red, she is sniffling, she says, 'What about me, what am I going to do now you're going?' She hugs me and cries on my shoulder. I feel like crying too, I can feel the pressure in my temples, but I don't shed a tear. 'What you've always done,' I reply. 'Think how good it will be to have the flat to yourself, with no crap going on around you.' I add that if she feels lonely she can always come and sleep here with her sisters, she laughs at the idea and says that will never happen, it's a madhouse. At midnight Adelaide brings the cake to the table, lights the little candle and Enza and China stand side by side over the tiny flame, we turn out the lights and sing happy birthday to you, Enza makes China blow out the candle because it's the bit she likes best, I am convinced she understands very little but birthdays are one of the things she does understand, the celebration of a moment at which a person has grown by one clear measure with regard to the last time, the accumulated and unpredicted experiences of one more turn around the sun. I don't believe she sees it in quite those terms, but certainly she gets a sense of some of the underlying significance. And so we shall continue, year after year, summer after summer, in the hope of remaining united. Life happens, it rolls ever onwards for the bearers of this blood, different from other people's, they know that all manner of things can happen and while they are angry with the Eternal Father for what he has taken away from them they still manage to be grateful to him for the things he has nevertheless left them with. In the silence of mouths filled with cake I propose switching on Lello's old siren, to make it ring out on this night of peace and togetherness. Enza runs to fetch it from the sitting room, hidden away under various boxes. In the coldest room of the apartment it has survived intact, unchanged. The photographs of Lello and Angelo and Tanino and Ada and their forerunners who are no longer here look down on us from their frames, we like to think they have our lives in safekeeping, that in the most ancient of beliefs they protect us from up in heaven, from a place we cannot see and which has gathered them for reasons we don't know, but which we can only imagine as joining the dots back into the past.

We return to the kitchen and go out on to the balcony, nearly all the windows around us are closed and the lights are going out one by one in the apartments. Enza places the siren in my hands, it is heavy and the metal dome is gleaming even though no one has dusted it. Elena pushes the plug into the socket and the song of the siren rips the night apart, it vibrates in my hands, I have to hold it firmly. Bruno gives one of his great theatrical laughs, flinging his arms wide and so on, while his children cluster round him. From the divan China and Valencia are staring at us in amazement, they are wondering where that noise is coming from and what it is for. The truth is, we're not very sure ourselves, but we make it ring out as loud as we can, hoping that this piercing howl may set the taut strings of the world vibrating, a message of life for those who are still here and those who are not; the wounded song of a proud animal who does not wish to die.

THE THIRD DUEL

If there was, in the folds of time, an unlikely knot, a point at which timelines intersect and flow together and the present were the only timeframe available, our meeting could actually happen. I know that nothing of the sort exists, this is nothing but science-fiction talk, but perhaps there is another way. Let us suppose that on this new September morning I woke up and it was the year 1985. I know, I could have chosen one that put us at about the same age, to face each other when we were both at our strongest, but to confront you I need a place I am familiar with, and out of respect it will be a place familiar to both of us. As I was saying, a day in September 1985, just another day like the hundreds there have been before and after. I would wake up in my own home, the one I've been living in with my mother, but she would not be there. I would calmly make my breakfast, I would have milk and coffee. I would put on trousers and a shirt for the occasion, because I know how much appearance matters to you. I would comb my hair carefully, trying to conceal its length, which you would no doubt consider excessive. I would leave the house in the morning sunshine and walk through the streets of Marano, which would look as I have never seen them, both older and newer. I would go to stand outside the apartment in via Roma and I would find an empty space, a building that does not yet exist. Then I would walk along the street until I came to via Nova, I would see the old faces that I know at the age I am now, I would absorb the vitality and energy I have been told about. I would arrive outside the block in via Edificio Scolastico and looking up towards the second-floor balcony I would find the blinds drawn nearly completely down and the shutters half open. Perhaps I would see Ada hanging out clothes, at home by herself, but she would not recognise me, she would only notice a curious young fellow observing her from below, she would not be able to make out any familiar features on my distant face, or eyes similar to hers. So then I would pass on and continue my walk. At a certain point I would find myself standing before the church of San Castrese, which would be practically the same as I remember it except for its colours, less bright, out of respect for a certain sense of the sacred which perhaps no longer exists. I would turn into the narrow street and its long, steep slope, at that time still covered in asphalt. To scrunch up the gravelly surface would be more difficult, and there would be many more plants than I remember spreading across it. I would toil with difficulty up the hill while the sun strained towards its highest point and at noon precisely I would find myself at the gates of the farm, tired and sweating.

I would enter your domain and make my way past the kitchen garden, in the full flush of its splendour, with mature fruit trees growing as far as the eye can see and all around a greenness of a brilliance I can only imagine. In the distance I would see the hen-run, the ruined barn, the little house, and outside it children running and playing. So I would hide behind the bushes, I would creep closer, concealing myself behind the tall trees, bigger and more numerous than I recall. I would gradually see the children from closer up and at that point I would be able to recognise their features. Bruno I would recognise by his golden locks, by the battered old football between his feet and by his constant chatter, the elder brother trying to bring order where there already is order. Lello would have the same hair, but a bigger head and body, more solidly planted, he would be telling his brother, stammering, not to bloody well break anything with his football, or else he'll flatten him. Elena would be a little further on, playing hopscotch by herself, on a pattern of squares marked out on the ground, a precise and restricting set of tramlines, only seven possible steps and then back again, on one leg, the illusion of going wherever she wants and being mistress within an already determined framework but still with all the demands of chance. Loitering by the doorway of the little house I would be able to look inside, I would see China sitting on the divan, just as I know her now but in a smaller version, she would know the same two words but nothing more. Next to her would be Enza, she would be speaking to her sister, convinced she could understand, and perhaps she would be right because no one knows her better, no one can say with more knowledge of the case than her what there is in China's eyes. And if I leant too far in, perhaps Enza would see me, a girl of nine looking up to stare at the sight of a stranger in her house. Then I would put my finger to my lips in a sign to stay silent, I would tell her, quietly, 'I am here to speak with your papà, don't be afraid,' but she obviously wouldn't be, having grown accustomed to worse surprises, to facing potentially dangerous situations calmly, any danger I might represent being nothing to a daughter of Tanino 'e Bastimento. Then Enza would take her sister by the hand and lead her outside, would leave me here, alone, to prepare myself, to collect myself one last time before going back outside and confronting my destiny. I would begin to open the drawers, look under the furniture and behind the divan. I would find the raised tile in the floor, the one you trip over, which I have never attempted to lift in my time because there was no reason to, but now there is. Now I would go up to it and put my fingernails into the crack, lift it and slide it to one side, revealing a small square hole in the floor, and in that hole the thing I was looking for, that I knew I would find here somewhere but have never needed to look for before. I would take the pistol in my hands, that black and gleaming object, heavier than I could ever have expected, and then I would experience a certain sense of power, a sense of safety that I have seen only in you and which I would now understand, because I would have in my hands the death of anyone who stood before me. I would tuck it into my trousers and walk out of the little house again, this time the children would see me and would all stop at once: Bruno's football would fall to the ground, no longer bouncing up off his instep; Elena poised on one leg in a white-chalked square; the devastating fist of Lello's Big Jim would not deliver a knock-out blow to the other Big Jim, lying on the ground and begging for mercy; the finger of Enza would stop tracing circles on the incredulous China's open palm while the nursery rhyme—'*This is the little fountain where butterflies come to drink*'—would be left hanging uncertainly in the air around us. We would all cease to feel the breeze on our skins, then as if nothing had happened they would go back to doing what they had to do, maybe they would cease to see me, maybe they would do so purposely, removing themselves from an action that is not theirs, retreating into whatever fate has in mind for them. My steps would take me further into the farm, over the damp and luxuriant grass, I would pass by the long marble-topped table, not yet set for lunch, and I would go straight towards the old ruin, as much a wreck as in my own day now, forever a ruin in the eyes of anyone who has passed this way in the last fifty years, and who knows, before that. I would make my way past the creepers and the nettles, getting my ankles seriously scratched as I look for an opening in the dilapidated wall, I would find my way through the thicket of bushes and branches that conceals the entrance to the building, and by edging patiently along the wall I would finally succeed in spotting the empty archway, the entrance to the empty and floorless ruin. It is there that I would find you, standing squarely on the floor of the barren room, waiting for me. The flagstone floor would be visible still, not strewn with those hidden but never thrown away copies of the book you have not yet written, but which is taking shape in some part of your mind, you are still joining up some dots, you are still seeking a finale worthy of you. Maybe at that moment you would recognise who I am, your weak eyes would manage to make out the curves of my face, you would find its contours identical to your daughter's, the same shaped nose, you would see eyes no different from those of the woman you loved and married, and finally, your gaze would dwell on my body, you would be surprised to find it just the same height as yours and you would touch your breastbone, because you would note in me the same hollow chest, identical structures enclosing two very different hearts. But they are hearts that pump the same blood, and send it through a network of veins that allows me to move my arm just enough to take hold of the pistol and drag it from my trousers; you would have plenty of time to laugh at my idiotic action, to get your hand to your belt a fraction before me and in a flash raise the other Beretta, the one you always keep on you, point it straight at my heart without a thought, completely naturally. You would tell me to drop it and stop acting the fool, you would have me at your mercy and you could choose whether I lived or died, you could end it with a single shot, the easiest shot of all since I would be standing right in front of you, a kid with no special reflexes, no noteworthy abilities and without the nerve that you would still have, that desire to seize and devour life, as opposed to my scant hunger. But you would not fire, because your blood would recognise mine and because in spite of everything it is, at least for you, the strongest bond there is, and so I would let the gun fall to the ground and you would put yours away, you would slowly approach me, a step at a time, and lay a hand on my shoulder, you would say, 'It's cramped in this old ruin, there's sunshine outside, it does you good,' we would step out under the archway and you would wade through the barrier of undergrowth, leaving an opening for me to follow without further damaging myself. You would lead me round the back of the little house so that the children wouldn't see us, to allow them to carry on playing happily while you get answers to your questions with your usual discretion. You would direct me towards the outside stairs behind the house and one at a time we would climb up to the small, red-covered roof. We would sit with our backs to the water tank, under a midday sun that leaves us without shadows, and then you would finally tell me to talk. I would tell you that from my earliest childhood I was taught to respect you, to be surprised and impressed at the things you achieved. They spoke of you as a hero, your career an arc that spanned your whole life, not an instant wasted. I would tell you that you genuinely convinced them all, all except me. Because if your children's words and feelings remain faithful to you, their situations say otherwise, they tell the story of lives sacrificed, of existences led with heads always looking to the rear, towards a past whose image is imprinted in their eyes and stops them from seeing the rest, the life they might have had and didn't. I would tell you that you have been a massively selfish man, that you have always put yourself before anyone else and that the plans you sketched out for your offsprings' futures were impractical, especially given the heavy burden you loaded on their backs. For yourself you made your decision, yes, and it does you honour, but you committed the error of subjecting the people around you to your own particular vision. Each of your children has outlived you with at least one big regret, and each of them, convinced they could never match your distinction, has lowered his sights, has begun to construct his own story out of ifs and buts. And what remains of all this? Memories, happy or less happy; the titles you earned; anecdotes to repeat over and over again all in the same words, the same story retold thousands of times to the point where I am sick of them; an all-consuming form of education which has rendered your children fearful and bigoted without ever intending to be, you have taught by dogma and trauma and this is the result.

You would let me speak, perhaps you really would be curious about what I am telling you, you would light a cigarette and smoke it calmly, you would let it drop in front of you and it would roll across the imperceptible slope and fall off the roof still burning, and your eyes hidden behind the sunglasses would be inscrutable, shielded once more from confrontation. You would tell me that I'm not talking complete rubbish, that I'm an intelligent lad and moreover how could I not be given that I am your descendant, but I am young and inexperienced, basically I know shit all and I'm talking about things I never saw and don't know about, trusting other people's reports. You would tell me that everything you have done, you did for your wife and for your bloodline, me included, and that if you hadn't behaved as you famously did, things would have turned out even worse, maybe your children wouldn't have achieved even the little they managed to do for themselves, perhaps I wouldn't even have been born. You would add that I have no right to speak to you like this, that I have taken on my shoulders a load which is not mine to carry and that thanks to you I have lived a comfortable life, I have experienced neither hunger nor cruelty, I have not had to fight for what was due to me and I have had the luxury of studying and of being able to dream of one day becoming a respectable man, that this was no mean thing and not to be taken as guaranteed or owed. Then I would yet again repeat that this is not about me, the real issue here is the generation between us, the one that comes after you and before me. That I hardly come into this story, I forced my way in, even in these pages I have said masses about you and very little about me, because I too was afraid to cut a poor figure, to have nothing to say and only to be able to shine in your reflected light, like the light of this noonday sun beating down on us, this sun which stands motionless in the sky even though I have been here for ages, as if the star we revolve round had halted in its tracks to witness this confrontation inside the folds of time. I would tell you that two of your children are no longer alive, that Ada has gone, leaving a family in disarray, and that she was, in every way, the focal point of everything and not you, and that each of them would have sworn their loyalty not to you but to her. With tears in my eyes, I would reveal that I have always suffered from being measured against you, because they have always believed in me, but with significant reservations, so that if I wanted to be someone one day I would have to deal with the problem that is you, with your judgement of me and the character I cut in comparison. Then you would laugh, you would say that now I too am acting out of ambition, that this whole crusade in defence of your children is in fact for my own profit, that these seven are as much victims of your exploits as they are of my words. You would say that the difference between us lies exactly there: that I am good with words and you with deeds, that the effects of a strict education and of a rhetorical narrative are pretty much the same, that maybe I should come back here when my ideas are clearer and I have a genuine issue to bring to light. You would say that I am as self-centred as you, except that unlike you I don't have the balls. And those, the balls, I have had to seek in your past, because I haven't managed to find them in my own present. The courage to gobble up life that has always marked you out and of which I am envious. You would say this is the reason I have come here. That I have been talking about you in order to justify my own lack of success, to lay the blame for my own cowardice on some greater design, on destiny. Isn't that perhaps your game as well? You would point to your children playing below us, you would ask me if I didn't think they looked like happy and carefree children, running about in the open air and looking after each other, children who know the right sorts of values and respect limits. So I would answer you with another question: Valencia, where is she? Why is she not here playing with them? Because your fine declarations don't apply to her. At that point you would remove your sunglasses, you would let me look into your eyes, a luxury granted to very few of the people who have met you; they would seem very small, as you screwed them up under the stationary sun of midday, and finally you would tell me that when I have a family and am the one who has to make decisions, then I can speak; you would say that Elena's twin is having a better life growing up in a place where someone loves her, you would admit love was exactly the thing you did not feel when you first set eyes on her, and that in this instance as well you made the right choice, because you removed her from your presence and your cynicism, the cynicism induced in you not by a person but by life, the things you have seen and the injustices you have suffered, and if you suffered, imagine what it would have been like for a schizophrenic and vulnerable young girl. I would be unable to reply, because I would realise you really mean what you say, that you aren't trying to convince me of anything you're not fully convinced of yourself. I would be unable to reply not least because I wouldn't have the right, because as you have said I am a coward, someone who can't make choices, and better someone who makes bad choices than someone who never chooses at all. I would realise that I have been silent for a while, that the things I had to say to you no longer have all that importance under this hot sun. I would look at your children again and I would feel similar to them, united by the same destiny. Your words would come to mind again, 'when you're eating you're keeping death at bay', you need to stop talking; and I would realise that in the end what I am doing, I too, is nothing more than eating, chewing, over and over, this blood that we carry inside us, without speaking ill of it; without spitting it out any longer.

You would tell me that it has been an honour to meet me and that my time here is finished, that this present belongs to you and not to me. I would tell you I have other things to say to you and you would say there will be other opportunities. I would want to respond to that, tell you it's not true, there won't be, tell you that you will die before I am born, but as I'm getting ready to say this I stop, because your dark eyes are saying everything. It is clear that you know already. I would ask you if you want to come down with me and you would answer no, you want to stay up here by yourself for a bit, you like being high up. As I go down the stairs I would see you for one last time over my shoulder and without looking at me you would remind me to shut the gate when I left. The sun would begin to move again along with all the stars, it would begin its long descent towards night and I would return home, taking, with firm steps, the only road there is.

TRANSLATOR'S NOTES

Francesco Aloia's original title, *Questo sangue masticato* means *This Chewed Blood*, hence the dedication to Ada 'who taught me how to chew'.

Two references that may need further explanation:

Page 159 *The Veiled Christ*, *Il Cristo velato*, an eighteenth-century effigy by Giuseppe Sanmartino of the dead Jesus covered in a veil, all carved from a single block of marble. It may be seen in the Sansevero Chapel at Naples.

Pages 251-2 *Big Jim* was one of a popular line of toys made from 1971 to 1986 by Mattel. He was an 'action-man' figure about ten inches high. A key in his back made his arm perform a karate chop.

The songs referred to in the book can all be found and listened to on YouTube.

Octavio Mesa's *La Pelea con el Diabolo*,
in the preliminary pages, is a Spanish folk song.

Page 60 *Aummo aummo—Secretly, secretly*,
sung by Renzo Arbore

Page 95 *Don Raffaè*,
sung by Fabrizio De André, the version with Roberto Murolo

Page 104 *Night moth—Palomme 'e notte*
sung by Sergio Bruni and Roberto Murolo

Page 117 *Carmela*,
sung by Sergio Bruni

Page 132 *Moth, this is a lamp—Palumme chist' 'e nu lume*
is the same song as *Night Moth* above.

Page 233 *A rumba de scugnizzi*, sung by Renzo Arbore. The lines mean:

The rumba of the street urchins
You splash in the puddles and go all wobbly
Until you fall down
This is the rumba of the street urchins.

Page 236 *Champagne*,
sung by Peppino di Capri

Finally, many thanks to Elion Angjelo and Caterina Varriale for their help with a number of Neapolitan dialect terms and expressions.

Italian Literature from Dedalus

Italian Language Literature in translation is an important part of the Dedalus list. It includes classic and contemporary fiction titles:

Bloodlines (*Questo sangue masticato*) — Francesco Aloia
Senso — Camillo Boito
La Madre — Grazia Deledda
Marianna Sirca — Grazia Deledda
The Christmas Present — Grazia Deledda
The Queen of Darkness — Grazia Deledda
Naples Noir — Giuseppe Miale di Mauro
Cleopatra goes to Prison — Claudia Durastanti
*Portrait of a Family with a Fat Daughte*r — Margherita Giacobino
The Price of Dreams — Margherita Giacobino
The Ridiculous Age — Margherita Giacobino
God's Dog — Diego Marani
New Finnish Grammar — Diego Marani
The Celestial City — Diego Marani
The Interpreter — Diego Marani
The Last of the Vostyachs — Diego Marani
Venice Noir — Isabella Panfido
The Mussolini Canal — Antonio Pennacchi
The Late Mattia Pascal — Luigi Pirandello
The Notebooks of Serafino Gubbio — Luig Pirandello
I Malavoglia (*The House by the Medlar Tree*) — Giovanni Verga
Mastro Don Gesualdo — Giovanni Verga
Short Sicilian Novels — Giovanni Verga
Sparrow, Temptation & Cavalleria Rusticana — Giovanni Verga

Ebook only:

L'Innocente (*The Victim)* — Gabriele D'Annunzio

Portrait of a Family with a Fat Daughter — Margherita Giacobino

'This memoir of four generations of a family provides a vivid and eloquent picture of Italian life stretching from the late 19th century, when the peasant lifestyle had changed little from medieval times, up to the consumer culture of the 1950s. In writing about her female-dominated family, some of whom she is old enough to remember—most notably the matriarchal grandmother Ninin—Giacobino imbues her account with a real sense of intimacy. She has a powerful feel for traditional Italian culture, her early chapters conjuring up a time when the hierarchy of the family was the only true reality, fairness was unknown and "a moment's tenderness must last a week".'

Alastair Mabbutt in *The Herald*

'It's like a rural version of Elena Ferrante's Neapolitan saga. A powerful and atmospheric record of largely unexplored terrain.' Margaret Drabble in *The Times Literary Supplement*

'This sweeping narrative explores what it means to be Italian across oceans and historical epochs. Its vivid descriptions and deep cultural understanding leave a lasting mark.'

Italian Prose Award 2019 shortlist

£12.99 ISBN 978 1 910213 48 3 304p B. Format

The Mussolini Canal — Antonio Pennacchi

'Antonio Pennacchi's boldly engaging novel could be read as a graphic social history. It is this to some extent but it is also lively and funny. *The Mussolini Canal* is an earthy story of underlining seriousness told with a gruff bluster of a narrator possessed of an astonishing grasp of his family's story – which also happens to be that of his country... There are obvious echoes of *One Hundred Years of Solitude* and *The Grapes of Wrath* and even slight hints of *The Tin Drum*, but most of all Pennacchi's large-hearted narrative balances the domestic with the international. As the narrator announces: "Heed me I have a story to tell." And he certainly does.'

Eileen Battersby in *The Irish Times*

'...the story itself is utterly compelling... *The Mussolini Canal*, the winner of the Strega Prize, Italy's most prestigious literary award, in 2010, is surely Pennacchi's masterwork, written with a rare feel for the present-day idiom across memory, nostalgic but sardonically so. Judith Landry's translation hits the mark every time... It's a big, generous read, a historical giro with stamina and heart.'

Brian Morton's Novel of The Week in *The Tablet*

'My favourite novel of the year, it is a sweeping, giddying tale of those impoverished northern Italians who were relocated in the 1930s to farm the area of former swampland south of Rome, many of whom became ardent fascists. An exquisitely composed work of political and social insight, it is as humorous as it is haunting.'

Rosemary Goring in *The Herald's Books of the Year*

'*The Mussolini Canal* by Antonio Pennacchi is an epic account of the rise of Fascism. It's the story of the (fictitious) Peruzzi clan of sharecroppers, moved from their native north to the malaria-ridden Pontine Marshes for the building of the canal and the New Town of Littoria. It mingles family legend and up-to-date political commentary with personal appearances from Edmondo Rossoni and Mussolini, and takes us through Italy's Imperium and the campaign in Ethiopia to the Anzio landings. The complex chronology and the demotic and combative narrative voice (of a young Peruzzi descendant) are imaginatively handled by the translator, Judith Landry, and the novel presents us with a whole new landscape, complete with the kiwi fruits and eucalyptus that thrived in the reclaimed land. Better than any guidebook, it explains how and at what cost Mussolini succeeded where Romans, popes and emperors failed. A challenging but very illuminating read.'

Margaret Drabble's Books of the Year in
The Times Literary Supplement

'...his glorious mishmash of a peasant's eye view of the first half of 20th century Italy deservedly won the Strega Prize. A book of many layers, beneath the history, political commentary, and humour, it is a novel about the strength of the family. right or wrong, they stick together and that is how they survive. Credit must go to the translator Judith Landry, for capturing the spirit of the work. A spectacular work of earthy humour.'

Scarlet McGuire in *Tribune*

£12.99 ISBN 978 1 909232 24 2 536p B. Format

Naples Noir: La Strada degli Americani
— Giuseppe Miale di Mauro

'*Naples Noir* is a brutal, fast-paced Italian thriller, full of bad language and very bad people. When Carmine Scognamiglio is laid off from his wood-working factory job, he runs into an old acquaintance who rejoices in the name of Ciro Incoronato. Ciro is now a cokehead hoodlum, and soon Carmine finds himself enmeshed in a violent world. Ciro does odd jobs for a criminal gang he wants desperately to be part of, and to make his mark agrees to murder a woman who is about to testify against the head of the gang. He also torches the factory where Carmine worked, as an act of retribution. It's clear that Ciro has more than one screw loose. Haunted by the death of his wife and son in a car accident, the deluded, drug-addled man is convinced that his son is still alive, and directs much of his conversation to the phantom boy as he careers round Naples's ring road terrorising women drivers. Accompanying him on a succession of violent chases, Carmine is a helpless witness to the fevered action. Many crime thrillers have an implicit promise of redemption in their pages, but there is none of that in *Naples Noir*. Only Carmine, the one innocent in the drama, shows penitence, and it seems that only he will pay a price. Grim and darkly ironic, this is a terrific read.'

Andrew Rosenheim in *The Spectator*

'A powerful novel with strong characters which permeate your senses with their intensity. It is so alive you want to turn it into a film.' Marco D'Amore (Ciro di Marzo in *Gomorra*)

'A fast-paced powerful novel with the characters so well delineated you feel that you hear them talking.'

Maurizio de Giovanni, author of the Inspector Ricciardi novels.

£9.99 ISBN 978 1 912868 97 1 208p B. Format

Cleopatria goes to Prison — Claudia Durastanti

'Like Cleopatra—the Egyptian one—Caterina is adept at juggling lovers. But whereas Cleopatra's affairs were all wrapped up in the upper political echelons, Caterina's are distinctly low rent. Every Thursday she visits her boyfriend Aurelio in Rebibbia prison in Rome. He is in custody following a raid on his nightclub and being held under suspicion of pimping out the strippers who worked there. After visiting Aurelio, Caterina hooks up with the policeman who arrested him. Awkward—or so you would think, but Caterina has an endearing blitheness that carries all before her. Claudia Durastanti is one of the rising new voices in Italian fiction and it's easy to see why.

In this novella, which explores Rome's underclass, she deftly draws the relationships between the protagonists—often in a single, usually pointed phrase—and her spare prose skilfully evokes a demi-monde of cheap hotels and run-down apartment blocks. It's also packing plenty of mordant wit and Dedalus should be applauded for making it the first work of Durastanti's to be translated into English.'

Book of the Month in *The Crack Magazine*

£8.00 ISBN 978 1 910213 96 4 144p B. Format

The Celestial City — Diego Marani

'It's all quite charming and amusing, though of course in its arc and many of its elements all quite familiar. Marani has a sure enough hand that he easily shapes this into an engaging read, making for a nice little melancholy—and nostalgia-tinged read.' M.A.Orthofer in *The Complete Review*

'This book is a joy to read. It is lively, colourful, full of stories, with a rich cast of characters, a good introduction to the fine city of Trieste and its Yugoslav border area, lots of humour, a good deal of irresponsibility and a good account of growing up and not always getting it right.' *The Modern Novel*

'…in Diego Marani's *The Celestial City* Trieste provides the setting for a coming-of-age novel from the author of the highly acclaimed *New Finnish Grammar*. The nameless hero, who elects to study translation and interpreting at the University of Trieste, must leave his Emilia Romagna home and the punitive asceticism of his bookish and pedantic father. The intimate description of this Oedipal tussle is the best part of the work as the son struggles to meet the father's maddeningly imprecise expectations and resents the calculated tyranny of his emotional distance. As was the case with Finnish in the earlier novel, so is the situation with Slovene in the latest; language and love for Marani are ever-troublesome playmates.

Michael Cronin in *The Irish Times*

£9.99 ISBN 978 1 915568 22 9 207p B. Format

Marianna Sirca — Grazia Deledda

Brought up as a servant in the austere household of an uncle, Marianna is now a woman of property. But at thirty, she knows little of life. For others in the town of Nuoro and its surrounding hill farms, Sardinia is a harsh and unforgiving place. When she meets a former companion in service, now forced into banditry to support his family, her calm existence is turned upside down. The defining moment of her life has come. Does Marianna love for Simone Sole triumph over her common sense, social convention and what is expected of her by her family?

Grazia Deledda explores the layers of temptation and doubt in a novel of Sardinian life coloured with her own intimate knowledge of its beauties and dangers.

'Richly imagined and uncompromising in its powerful descriptions, *Marianna Sirca* is an engrossing novel that vividly evokes a time and place far removed from the modern world. It left me curious to read more of Deledda's extensive body of work.'

Aneesa Abbas Higgins in *The Riveter*

£9.99 ISBN 978 1 915568 34 2 236p B. Format